The Murder of Major Pennington

K.T. McGivens

The Murder of Major Pennington

Cover design by Regina Madlem

Copyright © 2020 Lillian Finn

All rights reserved.

ISBN: 979-8-6482-7075-6

DEDICATION

To Clare Hollingworth, Elizabeth "Lee" Miller, and all the female war correspondents who covered the fighting in the European Theater during World War II.

CONTENTS

1	The Little Miss Daisy Beauty Pageant	1
2	The Arrest	11
3	Mr. Bradford Sinclair	20
4	A Story of Courage	28
5	Deathbed Letter	37
6	The Chemist	48
7	Pictures of the Garage	60
8	The Only Boy	72
9	The Trial	84
10	Mr. Chishelm	105
11	Family History	115
12	The Radio Broadcast	132
13	The Autopsy Report	143
14	Katie Figures It Out	155
15	The Final Witness	167

ACKNOWLEDGMENTS

This is book five of the series and it's about time acknowledgment was given to the wonderful team that helps get the Katie Porter Mysteries ready for publication. Ms. Kelley Finn and Dr. Carla Reid have been the proofreaders for every one of the manuscripts. They have the unique ability to make the necessary corrections and suggestions without changing the author's voice or crushing her spirit. This has been an amazing gift for the author and her characters.

Ms. Finn also served as the technical advisor for *The Plot at the Pearson Playhouse*.

Ms. Regina Madlem designed the amazing covers for books two through five. They say that you can't judge a book by its cover but in the world of literature, books *are* judged by their covers and Ms. Madlem's designs are creative, beautiful, and eye catching.

The Katie Porter Mysteries could not be published without the help of these three gifted women and this author is extremely grateful for their continued support.

CHAPTER 1
THE LITTLE MISS DAISY BEAUTY PAGEANT

"Be honest, E.M.," teased Katie Porter, brushing a lock of light brown hair from her face. "You had a wonderful time at the charity gala. You're just upset because I had the winning bid for those opera tickets during the auction."

"Which is unfair because it's impossible to outbid you," E.M. pouted. "You're richer than the Roosevelts and the rest of us don't stand a chance."

"That's a bit of an exaggeration," Katie chuckled. "But I get your point."

Coffee cups in hand, the two friends and newspaper colleagues had just entered the lobby of the *Fairfield Gazette* and turned towards the newsroom.

"You have to admit that the band was wonderful," Katie continued. "I can't remember a time when I danced so much."

"You're lucky that Jim loves to dance," nodded E.M., following Katie to her desk. "The only time you got a break was when the orchestra begged him to sing. Man, what a marvelous voice he has!"

"Yes, doesn't he though?" Katie agreed. She blushed at the memory of Jim's performance the night before. He had been persuaded to sing the 1944 hit, "Till Then" and, although it was meant for the entire ballroom audience, Jim's eyes seldom left hers as she sat at their table across the room. He had such a beautiful voice and Katie remembered being greatly moved by it when she had first heard him sing at her dinner party at Rosegate when they had first become acquainted.

"I'm sure you two will enjoy the opera," remarked E.M. with a sigh. "It should be wonderful as the company performing it is first class."

"It's a shame that the tickets are not for us, then," replied Katie, smiling. "Jim has just left for an assignment in London and will be gone for an entire month. And I'm not really a fan of Wagner."

"Katie Porter!" exclaimed E.M., miffed and placing his hands on his hips. "If you didn't want the tickets, why on earth did you outbid me for them when you know that I love the opera!"

"Oh, stop fussing," chuckled his friend as she reached inside her handbag and brought out a small box. It was nicely wrapped with a small bow on top. "Happy Birthday, dear E.M.! I got the tickets for you, silly goose." She handed the box to him and leaned over and gave him a quick kiss on the cheek.

"Why, er, I don't know what to say," muttered E.M., shocked. He stared down at the box in his hand. "My birthday isn't until Saturday."

"I know that. But I can't bear to see you pouting for a week so I'm giving you your gift a little early," smiled Katie. "Open it! I've added a little something to go along with the tickets."

Returning her smile, E.M. set his cup of coffee down on the corner of her desk and carefully unwrapped the present. Inside lay the two opera tickets and, on top of them, he saw a small black velvet jewelry box. He glanced up at Katie with a puzzled look before gently lifting the lid to reveal a beautiful pair of gold cufflinks.

"Oh Katie!" he exclaimed, taking them out to examine them more closely. "They're wonderful! And you've had my initials engraved on them. You're spoiling me! Thank you! I will treasure them always!" And he reached over and hugged her.

"I'm delighted you like them," Katie replied as they separated. She draped her coat over the back of her chair and sat down. "Now all you have to do is pick someone suitable to go with you. And no one stuffy, please. You know how those opera types can be and I want you to have a good time."

"I always have a good time, Katie dear, but I do get your point," chuckled E.M. "I'll ask Midge. She likes opera and we always have a great time together."

"Midge Pennington?" replied Katie, somewhat startled.

"Yes," responded E.M. "Why the surprised look?"

"Oh, I don't know," shrugged Katie. "Midge seems to me more the type to enjoy a softball game than an opera."

"Midge enjoys many things," E.M. replied with a shake of his head. "In fact, the two of you have quite a lot in common. You should get to know her better." He picked up his coffee cup and turned in the direction of his desk which was located across the newsroom. "Thanks again, Katie!" he added over his shoulder. "You're a peach!"

Katie smiled at the retreating back of her good friend as he walked away and then reached into her bag to retrieve a beautiful silver picture frame. She had bought it when she had purchased E.M.'s cufflinks and it now held a picture of Jim Fielding. She gazed down at his handsome face for a moment before placing the framed photograph on the corner of her desk.

"You sure are one handsome devil, Mr. Fielding," she murmured to herself. "And I miss you already."

She had taken Jim to the train station early that morning so that he could travel up to New York to board the RMS Queen Elizabeth to Southampton, England. He would be sailing tomorrow morning and be gone for nearly four long weeks. They had discussed having her travel to New York with him and seeing him off there, giving them one more day together. But that would have only delayed the inevitable. Besides, they had only been dating for two months and the relationship was very quickly becoming rather serious. A brief period of separation might slow things down a bit, giving them time to keep things in perspective although the goodbye kiss that Jim had given her at the train station pretty much crumbled all resolve.

"Porter?" said a male voice behind her. "If you could pull yourself together for a moment and stop gazing at that picture, I'd like to see you in my office. I've got an assignment for you."

Katie turned around quickly to see her editor, Mr. Connor, looming over her.

"Yes, of course," she replied, dropping her head so that he couldn't see her blushing. "Just let me grab my notepad and I'll be right behind you."

Seconds later she was sitting across from Mr. Connor in his office.

"The Little Miss Daisy Beauty Pageant?" Katie groaned. "You don't mean it, Mr. Conner?"

"Yes," nodded the editor. "Unfortunately for you, Katie, our publisher demanded that I assign the story to one of my best reporters and that happens to be you."

"But why?" Katie asked in exasperation.

"Why the story?" smiled Mr. Connor. "Or why are you one of my best reporters?"

Katie glared at him in silence.

"Alright, I'll tell you," chuckled the editor. "Our publisher's kid is in the pageant and he thinks that makes for a frontpage story."

"For heaven's sake!" exclaimed Katie, slouching back in her chair. "Really Mr. Connor, can't you get someone else to do the story? E.M. perhaps? He loves that kind of pageantry and I just despise it!"

"E.M. is already covering the Van Hollen wedding and the Isabella Humphrey debutante party. He won't have the time to cover two weeks of pageant events. Besides, you just finished covering that tough bank heist story. I figured you might enjoy an easier assignment this time."

"I hardly think the Little Miss Daisy Beauty Pageant in which our publisher's daughter is a contestant is going to be an easier story," replied Katie, frowning.

"Another reason why you should be the one doing it," grinned Tom Connor. "Mr. Chishelm won't dare attempt to have me fire you. Your family is far too important to the *Gazette*."

"Small comfort," winced Katie, standing and turning towards the office door.

"Thank you, Katie," Mr. Connor remarked sincerely as he opened his door for her. "I know this isn't your kind of assignment but consider it taking one for the team. Besides, you might get lucky and discover some sinister plot by one of the competitors to bribe the judges or some such nonsense."

"Highly unlikely," smiled Katie, gazing over at her boss. "Considering the young ladies are between the ages of eight and ten."

"Ah," replied the smiling editor. "But sometimes they can be the most ruthless!"

* * *

"It could be worse, darling," said Jim over the telephone that evening from his hotel room in New York. "You could be covering a dog show."

"Frankly, that would be easier," Katie replied. "I have an affinity for dogs. Children, however, completely baffle me."

"That's only because you don't have any," chuckled Jim. "Yet."

"What's worse," she continued, ignoring his comment. "Mr. Connor told me that our publisher's daughter is one of the contestants. I believe I was only given the assignment because I'm a Porter."

"Well, being Katie Porter doesn't hurt," Jim agreed. "But your editor knows that you are an excellent reporter who can handle a delicate story although, honestly, I don't envy you the challenge."

"Thanks," Katie teased. "It's obvious that your editor thought the same of you which is why you're on your way to London. What's the big deal about a missing duke anyway?"

"He's not just a duke, Katie," replied Jim. "He's also a member of Parliament and a very influential one at that. I spent quite a bit of time in London during the war so I know my way around the city. That's why I was given the assignment. Ironically, only a few years ago I would have given my eye teeth for the job but now I'm dreading it."

"Really? Why?" she responded. "London's a wonderful town."

"But I'll be away from you for weeks," he replied sadly. "Five days on the ship going over, two weeks to do the story, and another five days on the ship coming home. I left you only this morning and I already miss you terribly."

"I miss you too, Jim," said Katie softly. "Promise me that you'll write to me every day."

"I promise," he assured her. "As long as you do the same."

"Well, I will be awfully busy covering the Little Miss Daisy Beauty Pageant," she joked. "But I think I'll be able to squeeze in a letter or two."

"Fair enough," he replied with a chuckle.

They continued talking well into the night, reluctant to hang up the telephone although both were very tired. It would be weeks before Katie would hear his wonderful voice again, but she finally glanced at the small alarm clock next to her bed and saw that it was 3:00 am.

"It's nearly morning, Jim, and we'll both be exhausted if we don't hang up soon," she remarked. "Will you send me a telegram from the ship once you're on your way and another when you've arrived in

London? It sounds silly, I know, but I need to know you're safe."

"Yes, of course darling," he replied. "I understand."

"OK, then," she sighed. "I suppose we should say goodbye now."

"I'm never going to say goodbye to you, Katie Porter," Jim replied firmly.

She was silent for a moment and then said, "Until later, then, darling Jim."

"Until later," he whispered and quickly hung up the phone.

* * *

"Please allow me to introduce our contestants, Miss Porter," shouted Mrs. Webster, the excited pageant director. "We're delighted that the *Fairfield Gazette* is covering the pageant this year. Apparently, yours is the only newspaper that sent a reporter! You'd think the others would want to cover such an important event as this!"

"Yes, well..." Katie began before she was shoved aside by a group of giggling youngsters as they hurried up onto the stage. A gaggle of older women, presumably their mothers, noisily entered behind them and settled in chairs around the auditorium.

"Girls, girls!" Mrs. Webster shrilled, clapping her hands. "Careful now! Line up shoulder to shoulder and let Miss Porter have a good look at you. She's from the press and we need to make a good impression!"

"That's really not..." was all Katie got out before being interrupted by the pounding of piano keys.

"No, no, Rachel," scolded the director, looking over and shaking her head at the young woman seated at the instrument. "We don't need that now." She turned back to the girls on the stage and announced, "young ladies! When I call your name, you are to step forward and greet Miss Porter just as we've practiced. Are we ready?"

"Yes, Mrs. Webster," said 20 girls in unison.

"Wonderful! Patricia!" commanded Mrs. Webster.

A tall blond-haired girl with ringlet curls stepped forward and curtsied. "Hello Miss Porter," she yelled and then stepped back in line.

"Hello Patricia," replied Katie, nodding.

"Emma!" shouted Mrs. Webster.

A short brunette with ringlet curls stepped forward and, grabbing the hem of her flowery party dress in each hand, curtsied and gave the proper salutation. "Hello Miss Porter," she shouted before she rejoined the line.

Good grief said Katie to herself as she mentally counted 18 more girls in the line. *This is going to be an awfully long afternoon. And why are all these poor little things wearing ringlets? Is the Shirley Temple look of the 1930's making a comeback?* Somewhere midway through the introductions, Amelia Chisholm stepped forward and tried to give her greeting. She got through the curtsy all right but seemed to struggle to speak any words.

"Poor Amelia is afflicted with a stammer," Mrs. Webster informed Katie in a loud disapproving voice which was heard throughout the small auditorium. Amelia blushed and stepped back in line. As Katie smiled reassuringly at the embarrassed girl, she recalled that Chisholm was the last name of the *Gazette's* publisher. Amelia must be the gentleman's daughter. Along with the stammer, the child had a sweet but rather plain face and was slightly plumper than the other girls.

"Why on earth would her father put her through such a terrible ordeal as the Little Miss Daisy Beauty Pageant?" Katie muttered under her breath as the next girl went through her paces.

"My husband believes that competition will toughen her up," said a pleasant looking woman coming up alongside her.

Startled, Katie realized that the woman must have overheard her. "I'm terribly sorry," Katie began. "I didn't mean to imply…"

"No need to apologize," replied the woman with a warm smile. "I agree with you. The pageant is no place to test a young girl's affliction. Especially Amelia's. I'm Lillian Chisholm, Miss Porter. How do you do?" she added, extending her hand.

"Mrs. Chisholm," replied Katie, shaking the woman's hand. "It's an honor to meet you and please call me Katie."

"And please call me Lillian," responded Mrs. Chisholm, nodding. "Mrs. Chisholm is my mother-in-law and an awful woman. Well, perhaps awful is too strong a word but I'm sure you understand."

"Yes, of course," smiled Katie. She found that she liked her publisher's wife already.

"I'm sorry you've been forced into covering the pageant, Katie. Quite a step down after you've done such remarkable work writing about former spies, forged artwork, and bank robberies," remarked Lillian, tilting her head to one side. "Doesn't your editor like you? Or perhaps you prefer covering this type of assignment."

Katie had to laugh at the woman's blunt honesty. "I have to admit, Mrs., er, Lillian, that this isn't my usual beat but I'm happy to do it. I got myself in some dangerous situations covering the other stories so this will be a welcome diversion."

"You'd be surprised," replied Mrs. Chishelm, her eyes twinkling. "You haven't endured pageant mothers yet. They are a frightful bunch. But, then again, with your pretty face, perhaps you've competed in pageants yourself and have experienced all this before?"

"Oh no," Katie quickly replied, shaking her head. "My grandmother would never permit such a thing and, frankly, I've never been comfortable performing for others."

"No, of course not," agreed Mrs. Chishelm, nodding her head.

"Does your daughter enjoy pageants?"

"No, indeed!" exclaimed Amelia's mother, shaking her head emphatically. "She is terrified of them and dreads participating but my husband insists. This is her third."

"Rosemary!" shouted Mrs. Webster, pointing to the last girl in line. "It's your turn."

Little Rosemary was not paying attention at all and was, instead, poking the girl next to her with one hand as she picked her nose with the other.

"Rosemary!" shouted Mrs. Webster, clapping her hands twice. "Pay attention! It's your turn to greet our visitor."

Rosemary gazed over in Katie's direction and yawned.

"Rosemary, honey," came a loud female voice from somewhere behind them. "Now do as you're told. Remember what mommy showed you. Give the nice lady your best curtsy."

The young contestant shuffled forward and, looking directly at her mother who curtsied along with her from the center of the room, gave a slow curtsy and lisped, "hi lady," before turning on her heels and skipping back to her place in line.

Katie and Mrs. Chishelm chuckled. "Thank you for such a wonderful greeting," Katie said, stepping forward and addressing the group on stage. "And you all did very well."

"Just wait until you see them on talent day!" exclaimed Mrs. Webster gleefully. "Now girls," she continued, turning quickly to the young contestants. "It's time to rehearse the processional. Please exit the stage and go to the back of the auditorium."

Katie was prepared this time for the stampede that rushed past her and she put out a hand and grabbed the back of one of the chairs, bracing herself from being knocked over.

Lillian Chishelm gave her a wink and a wave as she fell in behind her daughter and proceeded to the back of the room. For the next two hours, Katie sat in misery as 20 young girls, with loud direction from Mrs. Webster and simultaneous and often contradictory direction from their mothers, solemnly marched up and down the center aisle of the auditorium trying their best to keep in step while not trouncing on the girl in front of them. The entire scene was a study in the oddities of human behavior and Katie made a promise to herself that she would never subject her own daughter to such a catastrophe. If she ever had a daughter, that is.

She had a splitting headache by the time she arrived at Rosegate but, thankfully, realized that she was just in time for cocktails with Gran. Upon entering the hallway, she saw that a telegram was waiting for her on the small silver tray by the telephone. Tearing it open quickly, she was relieved to see that it was from Jim. "*Safely onboard QE somewhere in middle of Atlantic,*" it read. *"Miss you terribly. Remember apple tree is just for you and me. I love you. Jim."*

"He's such a nut," she chuckled as she took off her hat and gloves and placed them on the table. "But a romantic nut. I'm not sure how I'm going to get through four weeks without seeing him," she added with a sigh as she slid the telegram into her pocket.

She found her grandmother sitting in her overstuffed chair in the library working a crossword puzzle.

"Hello dear," said Gran, gazing upward as her granddaughter entered the room. "You're just in time for cocktails. Will you take wine or something stronger?" she asked, noting the exasperated expression on Katie's face. She set her puzzle aside and started to get up out of her chair.

"Stronger," smiled Katie, giving her grandmother a kiss and waving her back down before walking over to the liquor cart herself. "I just spent the day with 20 screaming Little Miss Daisy Beauty Pageant contestants and I have a terrible headache. I think a sherry will work wonders. What shall I get you, Gran?"

"I'll join you in a sherry," replied Gran, smiling. "That way I'll be well fortified as you tell me all about it."

Andrews, the Porter's butler, entered the library just as Katie was handing Gran her glass.

"Excuse me, Miss Katie," he said. "Mr. Butler is on the phone. He says it's an emergency."

Katie took a quick sip of her sherry before setting the glass down on the coffee table and quickly returning to the hallway to pick up the phone.

"E.M! What's the matter?" she asked into the receiver.

"Katie! Thank goodness you're there," came E.M.'s anxious voice. "I need to borrow some money for bail."

"Bail? Are you in jail?" she asked, glancing around for her purse. "Are you all right?"

"Yes, I'm fine. It's not for me," he replied. "It's for Midge. She's been arrested for the murder of her husband."

CHAPTER 2
THE ARREST

"Goodness!" exclaimed Katie, arriving at the police station 20 minutes later and meeting E.M. in the lobby. "I didn't know that Midge was...well, I wasn't sure...she's never spoken of a...oh for heaven's sake, just tell me what happened!"

"For starters," replied E.M., sliding his arm through hers. "Midge didn't do it. She's as innocent as the day is long!"

"Yes, of course," responded Katie as they walked down the hall toward the clerk's window. "But why do the police suspect her? When and where did they find the body?"

"Five years ago in his garage."

"What?"

"I just received the call from Midge myself about half an hour ago," replied E.M., somewhat flustered. "I don't have any answers yet. All I know from my friendship with her is that it happened five years ago. The major was home on leave and Midge found him in their garage laying in a pool of blood beside his sedan. He had a large cut on his forehead and at the time the authorities figured that he had fallen against the car and knocked himself out. He then bled to death. Midge was cooking dinner and went to tell him that it was nearly ready when she discovered him. She called the cops."

"Then why has she been arrested now?" asked Katie. "After all these years? New evidence possibly?"

"It's possible although I can't imagine what it might be," shrugged E.M. "It was a pretty open and shut case at the time."

"She'll need a good lawyer," advised Katie. "Perhaps Poppy will be willing to represent her."

"No go, my dear," countered E.M., shaking his head. "As the senior district judge in Fairfield, he'll be presiding over the case."

They had arrived at the clerk's window by now and requested information on Midge Pennington's bail.

"Sorry, no bail," replied the clerk, yawning while he looked at a document in front of him. "The lady's been charged with a capital crime."

"That's ridiculous!" exclaimed Katie, leaning forward and resting her hands on the counter. "She's obviously innocent and should be released until her trial."

"Funny, they all say that," muttered the clerk, chewing on his toothpick. "But Judge White has set no bail. Mrs. Pennington is to remain in jail."

"Well, we'll just see about that," replied Katie empathically. She took E.M. by the arm and they turned and walked back down the hallway toward the lobby. "I could speak to Poppy myself but I'm afraid my interference could jeopardize Midge's case. It's bad enough that she's a colleague of ours but, in a town the size of Fairfield, I don't think that's reason enough for him to have to recuse himself from being the judge hearing the case."

"Agreed" responded E.M. "In fact, I think it's imperative that he be the judge on this case. Midge needs a fair trial!"

"Now all we need is a good lawyer," Katie said thoughtfully.

"I wonder if my cousin would take it. He doesn't like me very much, but he is one of the best criminal lawyers in the business," E.M. said, mulling over the idea.

"You never told me that you had a cousin who's a lawyer," said Katie, glancing over at him. "Have I heard of him? Does he practice here in Fairfield?"

"No, he's in Chicago but you may have heard of him," replied E.M. "He's taken on some fairly high profile cases. His name is Bradford Sinclair."

"Good gracious!" exclaimed Katie, stopping to look at her friend. "Of course I've heard of him! *Everybody's* heard of him! Why haven't you ever told me that Bradford Sinclair is your cousin?"

"And break that aura of mystique that surrounds me?" responded E.M. smiling. "Surely you jest, my dear. Besides," he continued in a more serious tone. "As I told you, he doesn't like me, so we don't associate much. However, I'll call him if it means saving Midge."

"Let's make the call from Rosegate," said Katie. "Afterwards we can have dinner while you tell me all you know about Major Pennington."

* * *

"He'll do it! He'll take the case," proclaimed E.M., returning to the library to join Katie and Mrs. Porter after placing the call. "Luckily, he's licensed to practice law in this state. He'll catch the train tomorrow morning and arrive in Fairfield at noon."

"Wonderful!" exclaimed Katie, handing E.M. a glass of scotch. "That's a relief. Did you tell him that the first thing he'll need to do is convince Poppy to allow Midge out on bail."

"He already asked me about that," replied E.M. plopping down on the couch beside Katie. "And I'm afraid I volunteered you to act as surety for the bail."

"That's fine, E.M." smiled Katie, taking a sip of her sherry.

"It could be an outrageous amount," E.M. admitted somewhat timidly.

"How outrageous?" asked Gran, her eyebrows rising.

"Could be as much as $50,000," replied E.M. "Cousin Bradford says that would not be unusual for murder suspects."

"But that would only have to be paid to the court if Midge failed to show for trial," added Katie quickly. "Isn't that right?"

"Yes, that's right," replied E.M. nodding his head. "And I can assure you that she'll show. Even if I have to handcuff us together and drag her in myself."

"No need for that," chuckled Katie. "I'm sure Midge will want to clear her name. I can act as surety for that amount." She cast a glance at her grandmother who nodded back at her.

At that moment Andrews entered the library to announce that dinner was ready and Katie continued the conversation as they entered the dining room and slid into their chairs around the table.

"Did you know Major Pennington?" she asked E.M. as she reached for her wine glass.

"Only slightly," he replied, draping his napkin across his lap. "I met him briefly when he was home on leave and I came by to pick up Midge for an assignment. He was several years older than Midge and rather attractive. He was a banker, I believe, before the war broke out. Honestly, I have to admit that I didn't find him very pleasant."

"Really? What do you mean?" asked Katie.

"Well, to start with, I found him somewhat arrogant," reflected E.M. "He didn't say much but you know the type. It's not what they say, it's what they don't say."

"Or do," nodded Katie. She did indeed know the type. She had grown up among them. They were often the very wealthy, leading them to believe that they were better than everyone else and treating others accordingly. She and Gran stayed away from them as much as possible.

"Midge once told me that she and Bill had almost nothing in common except for a love of old cars. They used to tinker with them and attend car shows together whenever they could. In fact, I believe they met at a car show. Of course, that all changed with the war. Major Pennington was stationed in Los Angeles and only made it home on leave once. And Midge was a war correspondent and overseas most of the time. She still enjoys the car hobby, though. She's rebuilding an old Buick right now."

"Do you find Mrs. Pennington arrogant as well?" asked Gran.

"No indeed!" exclaimed E.M. "Just the opposite. Oh, I know that Midge can come off as aloof at times but she's really a dear."

"You are a good friend to say so," said Katie, smiling at E.M.'s loyalty. She remembered when she first met Midge. The woman had definitely seemed aloof although less so as Katie got to know her better. "Perhaps the Major wasn't as bad as all that. After all, Midge must have loved him if she agreed to marry him."

"As much as I would like to believe that, Katie dear," replied E.M., cutting into the slice of ham on his plate. "I'm not sure she ever did. People get married for all kinds of reasons."

"Yes, that's true," responded Katie, nodding.

"You mean to say that it could have been an arranged marriage?" asked Gran. "Does such a thing exist nowadays?"

"Not in the formal sense, ma'am," replied E.M. "Let's just say that at times it can be more advantageous to be married than to remain single."

Mrs. Porter glanced discreetly at Katie. She wasn't looking forward to losing her only grandchild to marriage but she did, more than anything else in the world, want Katie to be happy and if that meant being married to someone she truly loved, then so be it. In a fleeting thought she wondered if Jim Fielding could ever be persuaded to live at Rosegate.

"Midge is a very independent woman," continued E.M. "Being married to a man who gave her the means and freedom to do whatever she wished seemed to work out best for both of them."

"I see," said Katie softly. "Very practical although I believe that it is usually better to marry for love if at all possible."

"I agree," replied E.M. nodding as he picked up his wine glass. "And you are lucky to have your own means and not be reliant on anyone else. You, Katie Porter, can marry for love if you wish. Or not at all, for that matter."

"If the marriage was working for both parties," remarked Gran. "Why would Mrs. Pennington murder her husband?"

"Good point, Gran" replied Katie, nodding. "One would think that Midge would want the man to stay around for a long time. Unless one of them had fallen in love with someone else."

"I don't think so," said E.M., shaking his head. "And even if that were true, I don't think it would have necessarily ended the marriage. Either one was free to carry on affairs without going through the trouble of divorcing.

"Are you sure about that?" asked Katie, her fork and knife pausing in midair as she raised her eyebrows.

"Yes, absolutely," replied E.M., giving her a look that signaled that he knew more then he could share.

They ate silently for several minutes enjoying the dessert that Andrews had just brought them until Katie finally spoke once again.

"Well, there could be another reason," she began thoughtfully. "One that meant that Major Pennington was worth more dead than alive."

"Oh dear," exclaimed E.M., looking over at her. "You mean…"

"Life insurance," she responded. "Did Midge have a policy on her husband?"

"I don't know," replied E.M., somewhat alarmed. "But even if she did, that wouldn't necessarily prove that she killed him."

"That's true," nodded Katie. "But it certainly doesn't look good either."

"You seem convinced that she did it, Katie," exclaimed E.M., looking at her forlornly.

"No, not at all," she assured him, reaching over and placing her hand on his. "It's just that I've always found it useful to weigh all the possibilities. That way, we can eliminate those that don't fit and find a way to handle those that do."

"Shall we retire to the library to continue this discussion?" asked Gran, pushing away from the table and standing. "We'll have coffee, or, if you prefer, a brandy."

"Coffee for me, please, Mrs. Porter," smiled E.M., dropping his napkin next to his plate and standing. "I will need a clear head tomorrow when I pick up my cousin at the station. Bradford can be challenging."

"Would you like me to come with you?" Katie asked. "I have to be at the Little Miss Daisy Pageant in the morning, but I think I can break away just before noon in time for the arrival of your cousin's train."

"Would you?" exclaimed E.M., his face brightening. "That would be wonderful! I'll swing by the auditorium and pick you up. That way we can discuss Midge's case together after we pick up Cousin Bradford."

"Sounds perfect, E.M." Katie replied. "I'll be waiting outside."

Her friend didn't stay long after finishing his cup of coffee, leaving Katie time to ponder Midge's predicament. She wanted to believe that their *Gazette* colleague was innocent, but the entire situation seemed very strange. For instance, why did the police wait five years before deciding to make the arrest? It didn't make sense. Some new evidence must have just come to light but how and why? Hopefully obtaining the services of a crackerjack attorney like Bradford Sinclair would quickly clear things up and bring the entire nightmare to a close.

"Katie?" asked Gran, her voice breaking through Katie's thoughts.

"Yes, Gran?"

"What does Jim Fielding think of Rosegate?" Gran asked casually. "Has he ever expressed any opinion about it?"

Katie glanced over at her grandmother and paused for a moment before answering. "He's never said much about it other than to comment on the vastness of the estate. But I do believe he likes it very much, Gran," she answered, smiling. "Especially your rose garden. Why do you ask?"

"Oh no reason in particular," replied Gran with a shrug but there was a twinkle in her eyes.

Katie knew that her grandmother never asked any question without a reason and she raised her eyebrows. "Don't you think you're putting the cart before the horse?" she asked, guessing at the real reason behind the question.

"Let's just say that I've always found it useful to weigh all the possibilities," replied Mrs. Porter with a grin. "That way, I can eliminate those that don't fit and find a way to handle those that do."

Katie blushed and then chuckled. "I don't think we need to worry about that yet, Gran," she replied softly. "But if you will excuse me, I do need to send "the horse" a telegram before he thinks I've forgotten all about him."

She went to her bedroom to make the call to the telegraph office and, as she picked up the receiver, suddenly realized that she would be dictating a rather romantic message to a complete stranger. "Oh for heaven's sake," she said out loud, hanging up the phone. "I'm being silly. The telegraph office doesn't care what people say!" Still, she decided to write out the message on a piece of paper, giving her the opportunity to choose just the right words that would convey feelings that she hoped Jim would understand without having to reveal her heart to some telegraph clerk over the telephone. Worse yet, it would likely be someone she knew.

After working for several minutes, she finally picked up the telephone and recited the message. Thankfully, the young man on the other end appeared not to know who she was. Or at least pretended not to know.

Jim. The apple tree is reserved. Wish you were here. Things have really picked up. Will write and tell all when I hear which hotel. Katie.

"That's to go to the RMS Queen Elizabeth, is that correct Miss Porter?" asked the clerk.

"Yes, and please charge it to our account."

"Certainly," replied the young man. "And thank you for using Western Union. Goodbye."

"Goodbye," said Katie, hanging up the phone. She gazed out her window and thought of Jim. She missed him more than she could say, and she felt guilty for sending him such a vague message. "I will make it up to you, darling Jim, I promise," she whispered to the moon. "Please stay safe and come home to me soon."

* * *

Katie was never so glad to see E.M. as she was the next day standing outside in front of the auditorium. She had spent a stressful morning making notes on each Little Daisy's costume, some so elaborate and expensive that she wondered how their families could possibly afford them. Obviously, it took a lot to be able to enter your child in pageants like this one and Katie secretly wondered if it was all worth it. Still there was something to be said for the value of hard work these young ladies were learning through competing.

"How's it going?" asked E.M. as Katie hopped in beside him. "Are you enjoying covering the pageant?"

"Let's just say it's convinced me never to have children," she replied with a groan.

"Really?" responded her friend, chuckling. "That's too bad because you and Jim would have gorgeous ones!"

Katie glared at him and then gave him a poke in the ribs as he pulled away from the curb and out of the parking lot.

They arrived at the Fairfield train station ten minutes later. Katie only knew of Bradford Sinclair by his legal reputation and, having never seen a picture of him, was somewhat surprised when E.M. pointed to the extremely handsome man stepping from the train. Mr. Sinclair was tall and broad shouldered, with jet black hair that was starting to gray at the temples. As he approached them, he removed his hat and Katie noticed his large brown eyes and dimples when he smiled. He wasn't Jim Fielding gorgeous, but he did come in a close second.

"Hello, Dapper," Bradford greeted his cousin, shaking E.M.'s hand. "And this must be the delectable Miss Porter! My cousin has told me a lot about you," he declared, sweeping Katie tightly into his arms and giving her a kiss on the cheek.

Katie, not expecting the embrace, blushed and found that she was at an unfortunate loss for words.

"For goodness sake, Bradford, let go of her!" exclaimed E.M. tugging Katie out of his cousin's arms. "She's already taken!"

"Not by you, surely," retorted Bradford Sinclair, sliding Katie's arm through his own as they proceeded down the platform. "And not engaged," he added with a wide grin as he ran his hand over the ring finger of Katie's gloved left hand. "So one can still hope."

"You're rather a rude man, aren't you Mr. Sinclair?" said Katie, finally finding her voice as she removed her arm from his grasp and stepped back to walk beside E.M. "I do hope your behavior is more civil inside the court room."

Bradford placed his hat back on his head and chuckled loudly. "Don't worry, Miss Porter. I've never failed to impress, nor have I ever lost a case."

"Yet," Katie heard E.M. mutter under his breath.

"Well, let's not have this one be your first, OK?" she countered firmly. "The case is tricky and jurors in Fairfield are not the same as those in Chicago."

"Point taken, honey," nodded Bradford as they reached E.M.'s car. He opened the door for her, taking the opportunity to leer at her legs as Katie slipped into the back seat. "But you wait and see. I'll get your friend off all right."

"You'd better," threatened E.M., tightening his hands on the steering wheel as his cousin slid into the passenger seat beside him. "You'd better."

CHAPTER 3
MR. BRADFORD SINCLAIR

"So Madge. Did you do it?"

"No, of course not, you fool," replied Midge evenly. "And my name is Midge, not Madge. You should probably remember that if you're going to be my attorney."

"Hey, OK," replied Bradford Sinclair, putting up his hands in surrender. "I get it. But look here, I'm on your side. I got you out on bail, didn't I?"

"Yes, about that," interjected Katie. "How did you manage that, Mr. Sinclair?"

"Call me Bradford, honey," said Sinclair, giving Katie a wink. "I just pointed out to Judge White that according to the Judiciary Act of 1789, a district judge, such as himself, has the discretion to set bail for a suspect of a capital crime. Midge, here, has no prior criminal record nor does she pose a flight risk since she could have left the state at any time during the years it took your local constabulary to arrest her."

"And it doesn't hurt that Katie is acting as surety for the bail money," murmured E.M. thoughtfully as he looked down at his hands.

Midge looked over at Katie. "Thank you," she whispered gratefully. Katie nodded and smiled back at her.

"Yes, that's true, Dapper," replied Bradford, giving Katie an appreciative look. "Nice to have rich friends, isn't it? $50,000 is nothing to sneeze at. Great looking legs and money to match. I can't wait to get to know you better, honey."

"I recommend you concentrate all your efforts on proving our friend's innocence, Bradford," responded Katie coolly. "I can promise you that there won't be time for anything else."

"Hm, well, we'll see," replied the attorney.

They were sitting in Midge's comfortable living room enjoying cups of hot tea and a variety of pastries that Katie and E.M. had picked up on their way over. They had dropped Bradford at his hotel shortly after picking him up from the train station and, after discarding his bags in his room, the attorney had immediately taken a cab over to the Fairfield courthouse to try and convince Judge White to allow his client to be released on bail. Bradford Sinclair wouldn't admit it, of course, but it was Katie's willingness to guarantee Midge's return for trial that moved Poppy White to agree. Midge was released late that same afternoon and her friends were relieved to find her in good spirits despite looking tired and a bit disheveled.

"As you can imagine, I didn't get much sleep last night," Midge explained shaking her head. "They dumped me in a cell with two other women. One was a working girl who snored and the other was a young runaway who cried all night. I didn't sleep a wink."

"We have a few days before we go to trial," said Bradford, showing some humanity for the first time since his arrival. "We can put off talking about your case until tomorrow if you like."

"No, let's talk about it now," replied Midge, putting her cup down on the coffee table. "There really isn't much to say so I'd rather get on with it."

"OK, then," responded Bradford, taking out a large pad of paper from his briefcase. "When was your husband accidently killed?"

"6:00 pm on Sunday, November 8th, 1942," replied Midge. "Or at least that's the time I found him."

"You seem very certain about that," challenged Bradford, tilting his head to one side.

"Yes. I'm trained to be certain about facts," countered Midge. "I'm a newspaper reporter."

"Of course," replied Bradford. "That's a good thing. Should work in our favor."

"How do you figure that?" asked E.M.

"It means that Madge, er, I mean Midge here probably won't get rattled on the witness stand," explained his cousin.

"So you do plan on putting Midge on the witness stand?" asked

Katie.

"It's possible but let's not get ahead of ourselves," replied Bradford, and turning back to Midge, asked, "I've been told by my cousin that you were the one who found the major."

"Yes," replied Midge. "I was just about to put dinner on the table and went to our garage to tell him. I had planned to just pop my head around the door but when I didn't see him, I stepped in and walked to the other side of the car. That's where I found him. He was lying on the floor. There was blood everywhere."

"Did you touch him?" asked Bradford.

"Yes, of course," replied Midge indignantly. "I bent down beside him to assess his condition before calling for an ambulance."

"That might be a problem," countered her attorney. "You see, the prosecution will say that you deliberately delayed making the call to make sure he was dead before help could arrive."

"They would be wrong," Midge replied firmly, looking intently into Bradford's eyes. "When I saw that he was unresponsive, I checked for a pulse."

"Was there one?" asked Katie, leaning forward.

"No," replied Midge, slowly shaking her head. "Bill was dead."

"What did you do then?" Bradford asked, jotting down some notes.

"I went back into the house and ate my dinner before it got cold," replied Midge sarcastically. "What on earth do you think I did? I got to my feet and hurried into the house to call the police."

"Not an ambulance?" asked Bradford, unaffected by Midge's irritation.

"No, I called the police. In my judgement, an ambulance would not have done my husband any good. I believed the situation called for an investigation by the authorities."

Midge paused as E.M. poured her another cup of tea and handed it to her.

"Did the police come right away?" asked Katie after a few moments.

"Yes," replied Midge, nodding. "In about five minutes."

"The whole thing must have been awful, Midge," said E.M., looking at her with concern. "Was anyone there with you when they arrived? A neighbor perhaps?"

"No, I don't get on very well with my neighbors," answered

Midge. "They're all nosy busy bodies. And you were out of town covering the Thompson story if you recall."

"Oh yes, that's right," replied E.M. regretfully. "I'd forgotten about that."

"So, what happened when the police arrived?" continued Bradford.

"They asked a lot of questions, took a lot of pictures, and called the coroner," replied Midge. "He came and did a quick examination of Bill's body. Apparently, my husband had been dead for about 15 minutes, having bled to death from the cut on his head. The police detective figured that Bill had fallen against the car, knocking himself out and cutting his head when he hit the concrete floor of our garage."

"I've only just arrived this afternoon and spent most of the time at the courthouse seeing Judge White. I haven't had time to go over to the station and get a copy of the police report," Bradford explained. "Did they do an autopsy?"

"No," replied Midge. "They didn't think it necessary. It was pretty obvious that it was an accident." She got up and walked over to a desk in the corner of the room. Pulling out a drawer, she flipped through several files before lifting one out and returning to her chair. "Here's an article written by one of our reporters at the *Gazette*," she explained, opening it and handing a newspaper clipping to the attorney. "The paper ran the story on the front page."

Katie stood and looked over Bradford Sinclair's shoulder to read the article. In large letters was the headline, *"Gazette reporter loses husband in tragic accidental fall"* and there, above the fold, was a picture of Midge standing with the police, her eyebrows knitted together, and a frown spread across her face. Her dress was covered in blood. Katie shuddered. Only a few months ago she had been covered in Jim's blood as she had held his prone body in her lap trying to stop the bleeding from a knife wound in his back. Katie would never forget the sheer panic she had felt at the thought that he might die. In fact, it had been that incident that had helped bring them together. Fortunately, Jim had survived. Midge's husband had not. How awful. Katie looked over at her colleague with a renewed sense of compassion.

"Hm. Says here that the police believe Major Pennington slipped on a grease spot near his vehicle and fell to the ground, hitting his head either on the car or the floor," said Bradford, reading aloud from the clipping. "Based on the amount of blood, it looks like he bled to death in a matter of minutes."

"Could you have heard him fall, Midge?" asked Katie. "And not been aware of what was happening?"

"No," Midge responded, shaking her head. "I was listening to John Daly on the radio while fixing dinner and didn't hear a thing. The police asked me the same question."

"John Daly?" Bradford asked.

"CBS World News Today," replied E.M.

"Oh, right," nodded Bradford and then turned back to Midge. "That's too bad. If you had heard him, that would have given us an exact time of the accident."

"Can't we just subtract 15 minutes," E.M. interjected. "Since, according to the coroner, that's how long Bill had been dead. Sorry Midge."

"That's OK," replied Midge wistfully. "But you're assuming Bill died instantly. For all we know he could have been lying there for half an hour before finally dying. If only I had heard him, I might have been able to save him."

"You can't assume that," said Katie, shaking her head. "If he truly bled to death, that would have only taken minutes. Or, he could have fallen to the ground due to some other cause, such as a heart attack, and died because of that. The head injury could have just been the consequence of hitting the floor but not the actual cause of death. It certainly would have been helpful if the coroner had done an autopsy."

"Yes, I suppose that's true," sighed Midge. "But who would have guessed that I'd be suspected of murder five years later?"

* * *

Katie was finishing her dinner that evening when a letter arrived for her. She glanced at it and, seeing that it was from Jim, looked over at her grandmother seated at the head of the table.

"Go ahead, granddaughter," smiled Gran, waving a hand at her. "I know you're dying to read it."

"Thank you, Gran," said Katie, returning her smile. She jumped up from her chair and, giving her grandmother a quick kiss on the cheek, bounded out of the dining room and up the stairs to her bedroom.

My darling Katie, Jim started the letter. *"I'm writing this from the ship because a telegram just wouldn't do though this will have to be shorter than I would like. I need to get it to the mailroom shortly so that it can be picked up this evening by the mail plane. I love you. I miss you. I can't wait to get back home to you.*

Life aboard the Queen Elizabeth is quite nice. My cabin is small but more than adequate for a mere newspaper reporter like me. Each morning I wake up early and take a run around the deck before sitting down to go through the newspapers. News of the Duke is slim. He's still missing. There's been no body found. No ransom note sent. Nothing. It's as though he vanished in thin air. I hope there will be a story to write once I arrive. Until then, I'm at loose ends.

Fortunately, everyone I've met so far has been very nice and there are plenty of things to do. The first night onboard I played poker with a group of men. Didn't do too badly and broke even. For meals, I often dine with a young married couple. George and Sarah Miller are their names and they're on their way home to England. George served in the Royal Navy during the war. He's my age and an excellent billiards player. He's beaten me so many times that I try and avoid playing against him although it does help to past the time. He and Sarah have been married a little over a year and, although they are very subdued in public, one just has to look at them to see that they are very much in love.

Last night the ship hosted a concert on the top deck and those of us in second class were invited to join first class in attendance. It was wonderful although I was seated next to Mrs. Meadow's daughter who worked awfully hard all evening to get my attention. I believe Elmira was put there on purpose. She engaged me in conversation between numbers and, although I tried my best to politely ignore her, more than once she slid her arm through mine as if we were attending the concert together.

Katie paused to look out her window. She felt an immediate pang of jealousy although she had to smile at the thought of Jim trying to ward off the young lady. Of course women would flirt with Jim Fielding. He was extremely handsome, educated, and well mannered. And he was hers, she reminded herself. She took a deep breath and, turning back to the letter, continued reading.

When I was invited to join them for drinks afterward, I was forced to use my old standby fib and tell the young lady and her mother that I had to return to my cabin to finish writing to my wife. That produced the desired effect.

Which reminds me, I wonder if I might have a picture of you for my wallet? I hope my asking doesn't bring back painful memories of Ruddy because he carried your picture during the war. I know that he'll always be your first love and I just count myself lucky that your heart is big enough, Katie Porter, to have room in it for me. I will understand completely if you simply can't bring yourself to repeat history, but I sure would like to be able to look at your beautiful face when we are apart. Looking at your picture is how I fell in love with you in the first place, you'll recall. I loved you then and I love you now.

There are a thousand things I want to write but if I don't stop now this letter will never get out to you in this evening's pickup. Please write as soon as you can. I just reserved a room at the Charing Cross Hotel, London. We should be docking in Southampton in two days.

I hope everything is all right. Although I believe that I could read between the lines, your telegram sounded a little formal. I imagine it can be hard being a Porter in Fairfield sometimes. Or perhaps I'm reading too much into this because I'm missing you so much.

Yours only and always, Jim.

Katie once again gazed out the window as she folded the letter and held it against her heart. It was uncanny how Jim could almost read her mind. His understanding of her position was remarkable. Somehow, he had sensed the difficulty she had experienced in sending the telegram even though she had admonished herself for being silly.

Well there was a way to rectify that now. She pulled out some stationary from her desk drawer along with a wallet size photo of herself. The picture had been taken about three years earlier, during the war, when she hadn't heard from Ruddy in several weeks. She had felt no interest in posing, but Gran had insisted, wanting to send an updated picture of their daughter to Katie's parents who were stranded in Russia. Looking at it now, Katie thought it still fairly good. It would have to do until she could get to the photographer's studio and have new ones taken. Perhaps she and Jim could sit for one together.

Darling Jim, she began. *How smart of you to see behind the awkwardness of my telegram. In all honesty, I wanted to start and end it by telling you how much I love and miss you. I panicked though, once I picked up the phone and realized that I would be pouring my heart out to someone other than you (as if the telegraph clerk would care!) It was very silly of me and I felt badly about it right after I sent it. So I will say it now in this letter. I love you. I miss you. I can't wait until someone finds that darn old duke and you can write your article and come home.*

By the time you get this, you will be off the *Queen Elizabeth* and in your hotel. I'm glad that your trip across the Atlantic was pleasant although I must confess to a prick of jealousy when you wrote about your encounter with Miss Elmira at the concert. I don't blame her, of course, for making advances, but you belong to me, Mr. Fielding, and don't you forget it!

Along with missing you terribly, I've been spending time working on the Little Miss Daisy Beauty Pageant which has been fascinating in a disturbing sort of way. But I will fill you in on that in a later letter. Right now the big news is that Midge Pennington has been arrested for murder. Her husband was killed accidently, or so everyone believed at the time, about five years ago but now the police have changed their minds and believe that Midge killed him. It's outrageous and E.M. and I are determined to get her off. Poppy is the presiding judge, which is good except that I will have to be careful and keep my distance should the prosecutor feel my involvement disqualifies Poppy from hearing the case. And, believe it or not, E.M.'s cousin is the famous criminal lawyer, Bradford Sinclair! He has agreed to defend Midge, so we feel she's got a good chance of being found innocent.

I suppose I should tell you that you haven't been the only one fighting off advances as Mr. Sinclair is quite a scoundrel. He's made several passes at me already and insists on calling me 'honey.' But don't worry. I belong to you, dear Jim, and have no hesitation in giving him a good whack across the face if he gets out of hand.

Midge's case is quite interesting, and I wonder if Mr. Connor will let me cover the story while I'm writing the pageant article. That ends in about a week, but Midge's trial could go on for some time.

Gosh, I wish you were here so that I could get your thoughts. I guess letters will have to do for now. Here are the facts: It was November and Midge's husband was home on leave. Midge was about to put dinner on the table and went out into the garage to tell her husband, Bill, to come inside. When she didn't see him at first, she stepped around their car and found him lying on the floor in a pool of blood. He had hit his head and cut it, causing him to bleed to death. Midge bent down to examine him before running back into the house to call the police. They arrived in minutes and figured that he slipped on some grease and fell. The coroner determined that the major had been dead for about 15 minutes. All pretty cut-and-dried until now, all these years later, when the police think she killed him. I suppose new evidence has been uncovered but it's all pretty fishy.

It's late and I need to sign off. As you can see, I've enclosed a photo for your wallet. Of course you can have my picture! I'm delighted you asked for it. This one *was taken several years ago but it's all I have for now. I will go down to the photographer's studio when you get home and have another one taken for you. And I was hoping that perhaps we could have one taken of us together. How sweet of you to consider my feelings and perhaps my reluctance to give you my photo because of Ruddy. Your thoughtfulness and respect for me is perhaps what I love most about you. Well, that and the fact that you're awfully cute.*

I love you.

Yours always, Katie.

She folded the letter and slid it into its corresponding envelope, addressing it to Mr. James Fielding, Charing Cross Hotel, London, England. Then, placing a stamp on it, she walked down the staircase to the telephone table and placed it on the silver tray for Andrews to mail. It had been an incredibly stressful day but now she could end it with pleasant dreams of Jim.

CHAPTER 4
A STORY OF COURAGE

The young pianist was adjusting the piano stool when Katie arrived at the auditorium. It was the third day of the Little Miss Daisy Beauty Pageant and the stress and excitement in the air was almost palpable. Dropping her bag in the nearest chair, Katie approached the young woman who ducked her head as soon as she saw Katie coming towards her.

"Hello," said Katie, extending her hand out to the pianist. "My name is Katie and I'm here to cover the pageant for the *Fairfield Gazette*."

"I know who you are, Miss Porter," replied the woman shyly. She did not reach out to return Katie's handshake. "I'm Rachel Webster."

"Ah," nodded Katie. "Webster? Are you the pageant director's daughter?"

"Yes," murmured Rachel, resting her hands on the piano keys. "I am," and she began warming up her fingers by playing the scales.

Taking the hint that the young woman did not wish to be bothered, Katie backed away and glanced around the room. In front, near the stage, she noticed a man and two women sitting at a table intently studying some papers.

"The judges," a voice said just behind her.

Katie turned and saw Lillian Chishelm coming up behind her with daughter Amelia in hand. Mrs. Chishelm was dragging the young girl along and if her mother hadn't been clutching her hand tightly, Amelia looked as though she may bolt out the door.

"The woman on the right is Miss Pamela Owens, a former Miss

Junior Orange Blossom winner," explained Mrs. Chishelm, nodding at the woman at the table. "The other woman, the one with the large intimidating hat, is Mrs. Loretta Bonifay. She's from South Carolina and judges all of the Little Miss Daisy Beauty Pageants across the region."

"An interesting occupation," Katie replied smiling. "And the gentleman in the middle? He looks like a fish out of water."

"I imagine he feels it too," chuckled Lillian. "His name is Matthew Radcliff and he's from the famous Julliard School in New York. He's here as a scout and could award a scholarship to one of our contestants should he see someone with exceptional talent."

"Surely these girls are too young to attend Julliard," replied Katie, peering more closely at the judge.

"Yes, *now*," explained Lillian. "The scholarship is to be used when the young lady reaches the age of 16. This is the first time Julliard is offering it and it has caused quite a bit of excitement. It's nearly as big a prize as winning the pageant itself."

"I can imagine," replied Katie, taking out her reporter's pad and jotting down a few notes. "So, what's on the agenda?

"Talent rehearsals today. Interview Day tomorrow," said Mrs. Chishelm.

"I beg your pardon?" queried Katie. "Interview Day?"

Lillian Chishelm let out a chuckle. "It's when each girl gets asked a lot of silly questions by Mrs. Webster and hopes that their answers impress the judges. You see, it's the first time the judges will be introduced to each competitor and each girl will try to stand out from the others."

"Oh, I see," nodded Katie.

Mrs. Chishelm sighed. "If it's like last year, Mrs. Webster will ask them what they want to be when they grow up, and each little girl will say that she wants to grow up to be just like her mother. She'll want to get married and have two children."

"Surely they're way too young to be thinking of such things right now," repeated Katie, slightly aghast.

"Yes, I agree," replied Amelia's mother, nodding, but then she added. "The fun part is that there is always one little girl who will say that she wants to grow up to be a doctor or lawyer or something like that. Mrs. Webster will quickly corral her back to reality, or at least Mrs. Webster's sense of reality."

"You don't think much of Mrs. Webster, do you Lillian?" Katie asked.

Mrs. Chishelm looked grim and sighed. "It's not Mrs. Webster per say. It's the way she treats Rachel that I object to. She's very unkind to the poor girl."

"Rachel?" asked Katie. "Oh, yes, our piano player. She seemed a little shy when I spoke to her earlier."

"Yes, I believe she is," replied Lillian Chishelm. "Poor girl has never been considered a beauty although I think she's quite pleasant looking. Rumor has it that Mrs. Webster has always resented not having won a pageant herself when she was a young competitor and her hope was to have a daughter beautiful enough to compete and win."

"Sounds as though Mrs. Webster wanted to live vicariously through her child and is taking it out on Rachel," remarked Katie, dropping down in a nearby chair.

"Exactly. Living vicariously is probably what many of these mothers do," agreed Lillian, taking the seat beside her. She pointed to a side door just beside the stage. "Amelia, honey, I believe it's time for you to go backstage. Remember to speak loudly and clearly when it's your turn."

"Yes, mother," stammered Amelia, and she skipped away to join several of the other girls making their way towards the door.

"So, Katie," continued Mrs. Chishelm, turning to face her. "Do you have a beau or have you decided not to tie yourself down for now? You're still young and women don't need to snag a husband like they used to do before the war. Especially if they are employed."

Once again, Katie had to smile at Lillian Chishelm's directness. She was a bit like Katie's grandmother. Direct and modern in her thinking.

"I have a beau, Lillian," Katie replied with a slight blush.

"I see," said Mrs. Chishelm, smiling warmly at her. "How wonderful! He must be very special to have captured your heart, Katie."

"He is," Katie replied softly as the sounds of the piano filled the air, announcing the beginning of the morning's program.

* * *

"It's almost too painful to watch," Katie lamented to E.M. when they met for lunch that afternoon. "Most of those poor young things would rather be outside playing with friends or riding their bicycles."

"Katie, dear," replied E.M. "You're assuming that the girls aren't enjoying themselves. I bet they're having a great time! Why else would they compete?"

"Because their mothers insist that they do so," countered Katie. "Or, in the case of our publisher, Amelia's father. E.M., it's awful! The poor little thing has a terrible stammer and it's all she can do to get a single word out!"

"OK, I agree that in her case competing in the pageant is probably sheer torture," nodded E.M., "but the other girls are getting some benefit from their participation."

"Such as?" Katie asked scornfully.

"Such as learning how to handle a stressful situation with grace and poise," answered E.M. "Then there's how to apply make-up and fix one's hair," he continued, counting on his fingers. "And walk gracefully. They must be able to think fast when asked questions by the judges. And, during the talent portion, they must do their best to impress the audience."

"Humph!" responded Katie, putting her chin in her hands.

"But the most important lesson to be learned by competing in the Little Miss Daisy Beauty Pageant, or any competitive event for that matter, is how to handle losing," E.M. added, nodding to the waitress as she placed their orders on the table. "A valuable lesson indeed. And if you're going to be such a sourpuss any time Jim Fielding goes away on assignment, then you'll be having your lunches alone, dear friend."

"I am not a sourpuss!" exclaimed Katie, glaring at him. E.M. stared back at her and raised his eyebrows. She sat gloomily for a few minutes and looked down at her hands. "I am sorry, E.M," she said, finally pulling herself. "You're absolutely right, of course. I *am* out of sorts and I don't mean to take it out on you. This pageant thing is making me a little crazy, I guess. I'm having a difficult time finding an angle to write about. Then there's Midge's arrest, which is a much better story to cover although I'm very afraid for her sake. And I find your cousin Bradford rather repulsive. Sorry, E.M."

"No need to apologize, Katie," replied E.M., biting into his sandwich. "I find him rather repulsive myself."

"And I must confess that I am missing Jim," continued Katie, gazing wistfully out of the window. "Funny, we've only been dating a few months but I feel as though I'm missing a limb or something with him away. I know it sounds crazy."

"Not at all," replied E.M. softly. "I understand completely. Jim is the Yin to your Yang, or vice versa. I'm not quite sure."

"What?" Katie asked, tilting her head to one side and looking over at him.

"It doesn't matter," he replied with a wave. "I just mean that sometimes two people fit together so well that, although they're fine on their own, they are even better together. You and Jim just naturally seem to complement one another."

Katie studied him for a moment. "Have you ever met a Yin to your Yang, E.M.?"

He paused and then looked up at her. There was sadness in his eyes. "Yes, Katie, I did once," he said finally. "But that was a very long time ago." And then, taking another bite of his sandwich, he said no more.

Katie decided that it was best to change the subject. "Why does Bradford refer to you as Dapper?"

"Oh, he's just trying to get my goat," replied E.M. "It's a name I acquired during childhood. You see, my brothers are a scruffy lot but I've always liked to be clean and keep my clothes tidy. I was that way even as a youngster. It drove my father crazy because he thought it made me look like a sissy. He often told my mother that I would grow up to be a Dapper Dan and I guess the name just stuck."

"But being called dapper is a compliment," remarked Katie. "Isn't it?"

"Yes, usually, and especially coming from someone such as you," he replied. "But not in my family," he added with a shrug. "If Bradford can get Midge acquitted of murder, I really don't care what he calls me."

"I agree," smiled Katie. "But I must tell you that if he doesn't start keeping his hands to himself when he's around me, I may have to do something about it."

"And no jury will ever convict you, my friend," replied E.M., chuckling.

"Speaking of Bradford, how's the case coming?" Katie asked, finally picking up her sandwich and taking a bite.

"Well, he was finally able to get the report from the Fairfield Police," said E.M. "But it didn't reveal anything we didn't already know. Body discovered on the floor of the garage, blood everywhere, cut on forehead, Midge was the one who found him and called the police. Most likely victim slipped and fell. One thing unusual, though, is that no pictures of the crime scene were included. That's rather strange."

"Yes, indeed," replied Katie, raising her eyebrows. "Midge told us that the police took some. They would be following standard procedure."

"I agree," nodded E.M. "The department acknowledges that they probably did but that the photographs must have gotten mislaid. They're searching around for them now."

"Hm," was Katie's only reply.

"You don't sound convinced," noted E.M., gazing over at her thoughtfully.

"It's not that," replied Katie. "It's just that pictures can tell us so much, especially police photos."

"Worth a thousand words," muttered E.M. taking a sip of his tea.

"Midge showed us the article from the *Gazette*," continued Katie. "But it included only one photograph. Do you know if our photographer took any inside shots?"

"I don't think so," replied E.M. "Bob Bannister wrote the story and, according to Midge, arrived late and nearly missed the whole thing. He only had time to take the outside shot before the police cordoned off the crime scene. He also managed to get a few words from the detective in charge but even that was slim."

"Maybe we can talk to this Bob Bannister and get some more information," remarked Katie.

"Not a chance," replied E.M.

"Why not?"

"Because Bannister died about two years ago from cirrhosis of the liver," said E.M. "Too much drinking over too many years."

"Oh dear," sighed Katie.

They ate in silence for several minutes, each contemplating Midge's fate.

"I wonder why the case has been reopened after all this time?" Katie pondered, beginning again. "Most likely new evidence has come to light. I wonder what on earth it could be?"

"That's the million-dollar question, isn't it?" responded E.M. "The answer of which we all would like to know, especially Midge."

"How long have you known Midge Pennington, E.M.?" Katie asked, glancing over at him.

"Oh gosh," he answered, gazing up at the ceiling in thought. "It's been about five years now. We met during the war. Early 1942, I believe. About six months before her husband died."

"In the States or overseas?"

"London," replied E.M. looking at her intently. "Why?"

"Oh, no reason really," responded Katie as casually as she could.

"She didn't kill her husband, Katie," remarked E.M. softly.

"No, of course not," Katie replied, shaking her head. "But tell me about her, E.M. You know her very well and I hardly do at all. She's proved that she can handle an emergency. I remember how she took charge when Ruth fell and broke her leg at the Pearson. And she worked miracles on the theatre's old lighting, so she's got some ingenuity. But she's such a private person that it's hard to make her out."

E.M. sat back in his chair and looked off into space. "Midge Pennington is one of the most courageous women I know," he began. "After you, of course."

Katie smiled fondly at him but remained silent.

"We met in a jeep on a country road on the outskirts of London," he continued, his thoughts going back to wartime. "I got a hot tip and had wrangled a jeep so that I could drive out of town to investigate a farmhouse rumored to be sheltering some Italian spies.

"Wasn't that dangerous?" Katie asked, raising her eyebrows.

"I suppose so but, if it was true, what a great scoop it would have been!" he exclaimed, chuckling and rubbing his hands together. "I was about halfway there when one of my tires blew and I pulled over to the side of the road to change it. That's when Midge and Lee Miller stepped from behind some bushes and nearly scared me half to death."

"The well-known female war correspondent from Vogue?" Katie asked.

"Yes. She and Midge were dressed in Army fatigues although they were both civilians. The military outfitted them during the war, you know," he explained. "They told me that they were members of the press and asked if they could hitch a ride. I tried to get rid of them by saying that I was a driver on my way back to the post to pick up some brass but Midge said that was nonsense because she had seen me often enough around the Quonset hut press room and knew that I was a correspondent for *Stars and Stripes*. Then Lee said that they were chasing the same tip and had beaten me off the post. However, their Jeep had broken down about a half mile down the road and they decided it might be a good cover to continue walking toward the farmhouse to ask for help and end up with the story as well."

Katie rested her chin in her hands and looked at E.M. intently. "So, Midge is just as crazy as you are!" she teased him.

"Apparently so. All of us being Americans far from home, and fellow reporters, we decided to join forces. We hopped in my Jeep and proceeded on our way. The farmhouse was just coming into view when suddenly there was an explosion directly in front of us. To this day I don't know if the spies had boobytrapped the road or if we had accidently driven over a bomb left over from the blitz, but it sent our Jeep flying off the shoulder of the road and into a field. Lee and I were in the front seats and were knocked out and Midge, who had been in the back seat, caught a piece of metal in her leg and forehead."

Katie straightened up in her chair and leaned forward.

"She was bleeding pretty badly but she got out and managed to drag Lee from the passenger seat and put her in the back," continued E.M., "then she pulled me over into the passenger seat and slid behind the steering wheel. She told us later that she was slowly maneuvering the jeep out of the ruts in the field when several men came rushing out of the farmhouse and began shooting at us. That's when she realized we had fallen into a trap and were in danger. Keeping her head down to avoid getting hit, she managed to drive us out of the field and back onto the road. I remember coming to just as we were nearing the post. I didn't believe it at first when Midge told me what had happened but afterward I counted over 25 bullet holes in the sides of the jeep.

"Gosh, if Midge had been knocked out also, the three of you would have been captured," said Katie, shaking her head.

"And killed," replied E.M. "We were lucky, indeed. It was Midge's courage and quick thinking that got us safely out of there. Those men meant business and if Midge had decided to surrender instead of trying to get away, we most certainly would have been shot. You see, those spies couldn't afford anyone discovering them. We learned later that they quickly fled back to Italy after out little visit. Tough break."

"So, despite her own injuries, Midge saved your life," whispered Katie.

"Mine and Lee's," nodded E.M. "The two of us had concussions and had to stay in the hospital for several days but once we recovered, I took both ladies out for celebratory drinks at a nice pub in downtown London. I must confess, we got rip-roaring drunk and didn't make it back to the post until the wee hours of the morning. Shortly after that, I got reassigned but Midge and I remained in contact through letters. We found out that we were from neighboring towns. Hers being Fairfield and mine Cumberland and that she was covering the war for both the *Gazette and AP*."

"Wow," Katie replied. "Is she the one who got you the job at the *Gazette*?"

"Yes," he nodded. "She introduced me to the temporary editor when we both happened to be home on leave at the same time. Well, not on complete leave. Our papers managed to give us both assignments while we were here. I forget the name of the fellow running the *Gazette* at the time. Mr. Connor had enlisted and was overseas. But he said that I would have a job with the paper if I made it back and Mr. Connor honored the offer when the war ended."

"And it was when you and Midge were here on leave that her husband was killed?"

"Yes," replied E.M. "A tragic thing to happen but it was an accident. I owe Midge Pennington my life and I'm not going to have her found guilty of something she didn't do."

"Of course not," responded Katie softly. "And neither am I."

CHAPTER 5
DEATHBED LETTER

Darling, Jim's letter began. *"The Duke has been found! And you are not going to believe this, but I swear this is true. He had run off and joined a band of travelling gypsies. At first, they didn't recognize him. But as soon as they discovered who he really was, they bundled him up in a sack and dropped him off on the doorsteps of the nearest police station on their way to the next town.*

Katie shook her head and chuckled under her breath as she read through the letter. It had arrived just after dinner and she was curled up on the couch in the library reading it. Gran was seated in her comfortable chair nearby reading the newspaper, sighing now and then when an article stated something she didn't like.

The official report is that he has been undertaking secret negotiations with another nation's government and the stories about him missing were done to help him remain incognito. It was supposed to be very hush, hush. The truth is that the poor fellow has suffered a nervous breakdown and is now in the hospital. His service during the war as a British Marine, along with the current pressures of rebuilding England, finally took their toll on him and, although it was because of him that I've been dragged away from you, one does have to sympathize. He thought that he could escape the depression growing deep inside him by disappearing for a while. He happened to stumble upon the gypsies while driving from his country estate into the city one morning and told them that he was the Duke's driver. Not quite sure why they allowed him to come along but there it is.

Katie quietly cursed the Duke under her breath although she understood his condition. She wondered if Jim experienced any lasting effects from the war. She knew that E.M. still shook at times, especially after a stressful event, but she hadn't noticed anything from

Jim. Perhaps he had nightmares like many soldiers still did only two years after the end of the war.

The English papers have blocked the real story and are going with the "official" secret mission version. Jim's letter continued. *They have asked all foreign newspapers to do the same. I got my orders from my editor and wrote my article accordingly. We don't want to upset our British friends, do we? No use reminding them of old wounds when this country has already been through so much. But now I'm at loose ends. The Queen Elizabeth doesn't sail again for a week so I must wait to come home to you. Thank you for the picture, by the way. It's a perfect likeness and I will carry it with me always! You are so incredibly beautiful. I miss you terribly! Please write soon. I love you, Jim.*

Katie folded the letter and returned it to the envelope all the while calculating the feasibility of purchasing a plane ticket and flying to England for a few days. She could surprise Jim and they could spend the weekend touring the city. They could be together.

"No, that wouldn't work, would it?" she muttered out loud.

"What's that, dear?" asked her grandmother, looking up from her newspaper to glance at her.

"Oh, nothing Gran," replied Katie. "I was just trying to fight the urge to buy a plane ticket and join Jim in London."

Mrs. Porter smile sweetly. "I understand the temptation, Katie. But you have the pageant article to write and the competition has just begun."

"Yes, that's true," responded Katie wistfully. "And then there's Midge's difficulty. I suppose I was just being silly."

"Not at all, granddaughter," replied Gran. "Gertie and I miss him, as well. So does Nugget."

Katie chuckled and turned to her Yorkshire Terrier sleeping beside her on the couch. Nugget did not raise his head but, instead, twitched his ears as if to say, "yes, I miss him, too."

"Well, perhaps I'll send him a telegram tonight," she said, standing up and turning toward the hallway. "Before I write him a letter tomorrow. That might help curb my impatience."

She picked up the hallway telephone and called the telegraph office, dictating the brief message to the clerk.

Darling. Glad to hear about duke. Can't wait to see you. Will write soon but wanted to tell you I miss you. I love you. Katie.

"Charge it to my account, please," Katie instructed the clerk on the other end of the line and then hung up the phone, realizing that she hadn't cared who had taken down the message and what they might be thinking. "You're definitely getting better at this, Porter," she chuckled to herself. "Yes indeed."

* * *

On the following day, the Little Miss Daisy Beauty Pageant wasn't scheduled to start until noon, giving Katie and E.M. time to meet with Bradford to go over Midge's case. They really had no business being involved but the attorney told them that since he was not from Fairfield nor did he know his client very well, it would be helpful to have them be a part of Midge's defense team as advisors.

"I now know why the case has been reopened," Bradford explained to his visitors seated on a couch across from him in his hotel room. "One of Midge's nosy neighbors sent a letter to Major Pennington's sister telling her that she witnessed the murder." He ruffled through the file until he found the letter. "Here, I'll read it to you."

Dear Pam,

I'm dying. I wanted to send this to you so that something can be done. Midge killed your brother. I saw her through the window. She was holding his head in her lap and there was a bloody hammer lying next to her. She must have hit him in the head and then watched him die. Doc says I've only got a few days so I'm having my daughter write this down for me as I dictate it. You've got to go to the police. She can't get away with this!

Mildred Willow

"How convenient," muttered E.M., chagrined. "An accuser who can't be called as a witness to testify."

"True," agreed Katie. "Even more, she claims she saw Midge kill her husband without actually seeing it. All she saw was Midge holding her husband's head in her lap with a hammer nearby. She doesn't say she actually saw Midge hit him."

"Yes," nodded Bradford. "But her letter has gotten Midge's sister-in-law all excited. It was enough to cause her to go to the state attorney's office and insist that they open the case."

"But I don't understand," Katie remarked. "Why would the state attorney think this letter was enough evidence to have Midge arrested. It's hardly proof."

"For starters, Midge's sister-in-law personally knows the state attorney," replied Bradford, shrugging his shoulders. "I think they dated once or something. And I suppose the fact that Midge and the Major had a terrible argument on the day of his death didn't help. According to the new police investigation, several people remembered hearing it."

"People remembered an argument that occurred five years ago?" said E.M., looking at his cousin in disbelief.

"Yes," said Bradford. "It took place in the supermarket and caused quite a scene."

"Oh dear," sighed Katie. "I guess we'll have to ask Midge about it. Hopefully, she'll remember."

At that very moment there was a knock at the door and E.M. jumped up to answer it, revealing Midge Pennington herself, standing outside.

"Can you believe it?" she declared as she stepped through the door and threw her coat across a nearby chair. "Our local police department has a cop tailing me. He's followed me all over town!"

"I suppose that's to be expected," replied Katie, smiling. "They want to make sure you don't skip town."

"Which is ridiculous, of course," responded Midge, placing her hands on her hips. "If I wanted to, I could ditch this guy in a heartbeat but that would hardly prove constructive. After all, I have nothing to hide."

"Except an argument you had in the supermarket," countered Bradford, looking at her intently.

"Well, Marvin puts his thumb on the scale!" replied Midge, curling her hand into a tight fist. "I just haven't been able to catch him at it yet, but I will!"

"Marvin?" asked her attorney, looking at Katie and then E.M.

"The butcher," explained E.M., shaking his head. He turned to Midge. "No, dear. Bradford means the fight you had with your husband in the supermarket on the day he died."

"How on earth am I supposed to remember that?" declared Midge, flopping down in a chair near Katie. "It was five years ago! Besides, we argued all the time. I can't remember every single fight we ever had!"

"I certainly wouldn't mention that while I was on the witness stand," cautioned Katie, clasping her hands around her knee. She noticed Bradford looking at her legs and quickly unclasped and tugged the hem of her skirt down a bit. He gave her a wolfish grin before glancing back at Midge.

"It says here that you threw a tomato at Major Pennington in aisle 3, but that you missed and hit a Mrs. Haverson instead," Bradford stated, citing the police records.

"That would be Mrs. Sarah Haverson of Haverson Meadows," explained Katie thoughtfully. "She and her husband own an estate about five miles down the road from Rosegate."

"How nice for them," Bradford responded rather sarcastically.

"I didn't miss," Midge objected. "Bill ducked just in time or else I would have nailed him."

"And then you yelled 'I'll kill you, Bill Pennington, if I ever catch you doing that again.' Isn't that right?" continued Bradford, cocking his head to one side.

"Yes, I remember now," replied Midge nodding. "I did say that to him. I often said things like that because he never listened. He just kept doing it."

"Doing what exactly?" asked Bradford. "Cheating on you? Stealing money? Beat you?"

"Don't be daft," huffed Midge curtly. "Lending my tools out. He would let the neighbors borrow my auto mechanic tools and then I would have to search the neighborhood to get them back! He never lent them his own tools, just mine!"

"And that's why you told him that you were going to kill him?" asked Katie incredulously.

"It was just an expression," Midge replied. "I was never really going to kill him. But, you see, one's own tools are very special. You get used to their size and shape in your hand. They have a certain feel and balance to them that is developed over time and use. On that particular day, we had just finished adjusting the tappets in an OHV engine and I needed to check the clearance between the camshaft. I went to get my feeler gauge and couldn't find it. At first Bill denied seeing it and accused me of losing it. But later that day, when we were in the produce section of the supermarket, he remembered loaning it to the kid next door. That's when I blew a gasket and threw the tomato at him, hitting Mrs. Haverson instead."

Bradford, Katie, and E.M. sat silently and stared at her, their eyebrows raised and their mouths hanging open.

"It's marvelous, really. Like she's speaking an ancient foreign language," E.M. said finally, looking over at Katie. "Like a strange version of French."

"I speak French, but I didn't understand a single word she just said," Katie added, shaking her head.

"Yeah, this isn't good," remarked Bradford. "She sounds like she could easily kill someone and not think twice about it."

"Just because she's knowledgeable about automobiles?" Katie challenged, turning swiftly towards him.

"I get what you're saying, honey," Bradford replied, holding up his hand. "Most women worked on machinery in factories during the war, but juries are mostly filled with men and they don't want to be reminded that you gals took their jobs while they were overseas fighting for America."

"I was overseas right alongside them," remarked Midge softly. "As a war correspondent for the *Fairfield Gazette* and the *Associated Press*."

"England," added E.M., glaring at Bradford. "And the front lines in France."

"Really?" replied Bradford, his expression brightening. "Good to know. That bit of information might come in handy." Then turning to Midge, he added, "but in the meantime, if you're asked, you had a fight with your husband over his misplacing things like tools. That way you won't be lying under oath, but the jury will interpret that to mean that the major didn't keep a very tidy shop. Wives worry about keeping things clean and orderly. It will also help stipulate that he slipped and fell."

"You really are a despicable man, aren't you?" remarked Midge evenly.

"Yes, absolutely," replied Bradford, nodding. "But fortunately I'm your despicable man."

* * *

Half an hour later, Katie was on her way to the auditorium and the Little Miss Daisy Beauty Pageant. She had just enough time to grab a sandwich from the deli and drop by the *Gazette* to check for any messages.

"Hello Katie. These just came for you," said the *Gazette's* receptionist, Nancy Applegate, from behind a large counter in the front lobby of the newspaper. She pointed to a large bouquet of flowers set in an ornate glass vase. They were a mixture of carnations, daisies, and tulips.

"How lovely!" Katie exclaimed, looking around the arrangement for the card. "Jim's over in London for the next several weeks. I wonder why he didn't send his usual selection of roses. But no matter, this arrangement is simply beautiful!"

She found the card and opened it, her expression suddenly turning grim. The card was signed "Bradford." She stood for a moment before looking up at the receptionist. "My mistake. These are not from Jim and I simply can't accept them. Would you ask our delivery service to pick this up and deliver the arrangement to Midge Pennington? Here, if I might borrow your pen for a moment, I'll make a correction to the card." Writing around Bradford's name, she rewrote the card to read, "To Midge, from Bradford and your defense team." She then returned it to the flower arrangement and walked away leaving a puzzled Miss Applegate gazing after her.

Katie arrived at the Fairfield auditorium ten minutes later and nearly collided with Lillian Chishelm in the lobby coming out of the Ladies Room.

"Ah, I see we haven't frightened you off yet," chuckled Lillian, reaching over to take Katie's arm and turning with her in the direction of the main hall. "You're just in time. The dreaded interviews are just about to start."

True to Mrs. Chishelm's expectation, Anna Culvert and Emma Morgan, the first two contestants, both told the judges that they wanted to grow up to be just like their mothers. Emma added that she wanted to have eight children, four boys and four girls, which elicited chuckles from the audience and smiles from the judges.

"Oh, here comes Elizabeth Whitting!" declared Lillian, leaning over to whisper in Katie's ear. "This should be good!"

"Oh yes?" asked Katie, glancing up at the little girl on the stage. "Why?"

"You'll see," chuckled Mrs. Chishelm, folding her hands across her lap.

"Our next contestant is Elizabeth Whitting, age nine," announced Mrs. Webster, reading from the script in front of her as an attractive looking brown-haired girl stepped forward. The director held the microphone down so that Elizabeth could speak into it but there was little need as the youngster's natural voice was exceptionally loud and could have been heard from across the street.

"I want to be a chemist!" announced Elizabeth in a booming voice.

"But Elizabeth, dear," Mrs. Webster responded, sneaking a quick glance at the judges. "I thought you told me once that you wanted to grow up to be just like your mother."

"I do!" declared the youngster, nodding up at her.

Katie could guess what was coming next and she smiled to herself.

"I don't understand," continued Mrs. Webster, perplexed. "I thought…"

"My mother *is* a chemist," interrupted Elizabeth, rocking back and forth. She threw back her shoulders proudly. "She works for Held-her-top company and turns stuff into useful things like 'monia and alcohol!"

Laughter could be heard throughout the auditorium. "Her mother sounds more like a bootlegger than a chemist," Katie heard one mother say to another.

"But what about children?" Mrs. Webster stammered. "Don't you want to get married and have children?"

Elizabeth Whitting looked up at Mrs. Webster with an expression of disbelief. "Sure, Mrs. Webster. I can be a chemist and be married and have children. That's what my mother did. I'm here, aren't I!"

The room exploded into more laughter and then applause. Mrs. Webster blushed deeply but Elizabeth Whitting, completely undaunted, smiled sweetly as she gave the judges a quick curtsy and started to leave the stage.

"One moment, please!" shouted Mr. Radcliff, the judge from Julliard. "I'd like to ask this contestant one or two questions if I may."

Elizabeth froze in place and then looked over at Mrs. Webster. "Are you sure?" Mrs. Webster asked, shaking her head as if to warn the judge off.

"Yes, certainly," replied Mr. Radcliff. "Elizabeth, you do not need to return to the microphone, but I would like to ask how your mother became a chemist?"

"She went to school for a very long time," explained the little girl, moving to the edge of the stage and looking down at the judge's table. "She learned all about chemical stuff and how to mix things to make other things."

"Very interesting," nodded Mr. Radcliff, giving the girl an encouraging smile. "And then she went to work for a chemical company?"

"Yes," Elizabeth answered. "When my daddy went to fight in the war, my mother got a job so she could help."

"And when your daddy came back from the war, did your mother continue working as a chemist for the chemical company?" Mrs. Loretta Bonifay cut in, looking somewhat surprised.

"Yes," replied Elizabeth, placing her hands on her hips. "My mother is a genius!"

"Thank you, Elizabeth," interjected Mrs. Webster, motioning the little girl off the stage. "That will be all. Now our next contestant is Frances…"

Katie leaned over to Lillian Chishelm. "Held-her-top?" she asked, with raised eyebrows.

"I think she means Haldor Topsoe," replied Lillian, smiling. "You know. That laboratory over on the west end of Meadowbrook Lane."

"Oh yes, of course," responded Katie, nodding. "Isn't that a branch location for a Danish company? I seemed to recall reading about them during the war."

"Yes, I believe you are correct," replied Lillian. "Are you interested in chemistry, Katie?"

"No. I have no particular interest, really," said Katie, shaking her head. "Other than Elizabeth might provide at least one good angle for my article."

"Well in that case," remarked Lillian Chishelm. "Dr. Whitting will be here this afternoon to pick up her daughter. Elizabeth's father is sitting over there. He works in a factory south of town. He and his wife work in shifts so that one of them can be home with Elizabeth and her siblings. They'll switch off just as today's pageant activities end."

"How very modern," replied Katie, making a note in her reporter's pad. "Wonderful for the children but I can't imagine that they see each other very much. It must be terribly hard on a marriage."

"I suppose it is," responded Lillian wistfully. "But we all make sacrifices in our marriages at one time or another."

Katie looked at her publisher's wife closely but Lillian did not meet her eye, instead opting to keep her attention on the stage.

"Next we have Amelia Chishelm, age ten," Mrs. Webster announced lowering the microphone. "Amelia, please tell the judges a little bit about yourself and what you want to be when you grow up."

Amelia smiled sweetly at the judges and opened her mouth. Nothing came out. She tried again, a look of panic spreading across her face. This time she managed a strange "ca... ca... ca" sound but no words.

"That's all right, honey," said judge Pamela Owens, the former Miss Junior Orange Blossom. "Take your time. There's no rush."

"Except that we don't have all day," whispered Mrs. Webster under her breath. Her voice, however, was picked up by the microphone and heard by everyone in the auditorium.

Lillian Chishelm, her mouth in a tight straight line, leaned forward. She looked intently at her daughter as if willing the child to speak but poor Amelia could not produce a single word.

"That's fine, Amelia," said Mrs. Webster. "You can go now, dear." And she placed her hand on Amelia's shoulders and started to guide her off the stage.

"Just one moment," shouted Mr. Radcliff. "If you don't mind, I'd like to try something." And he jumped from behind the judge's table and onto the stage. He stooped down in front of the little girl and smiled at her. "Miss Amelia, I would like to try a little experiment with you. Is that all right?"

Amelia nodded shyly and then looked out into the audience at her mother. Lillian Chishelm nodded back.

"Wonderful!" said Mr. Radcliff gently. "Now I want you to say your name but instead of speaking it, I would like you to sing it."

Amelia looked puzzled.

"Like this," explained the judge, and he started singing the song *Twinkle, Twinkle, Little Star*. But instead of using the real lyrics, he substituted the words with, "Amelia Chishelm is my name. I can sing it just the same."

Amelia giggled as did several of the other girls who were watching close by. "Go on," Mr. Radcliff encouraged. "You can do it. It's fun!"

Amelia paused for a moment and then, taking a deep breath, started to sing. "Amelia Chishelm is my name..." her words flowing from her easily. Everyone gasped.

"Oh my," whispered Mrs. Chishelm, tears coming to her eyes.

Even Amelia herself seemed surprised.

"That's wonderful, Amelia," remarked Mr. Radcliff, patting her shoulder. "You see? You can use that trick whenever you can't quite get the words out. It used to help me a lot when I was your age." And, with that, the judge returned to his seat behind the judge's table and made a quick note on the pad in front of him.

"Er, yes," murmured a stunned Mrs. Webster. "Thank you, Amelia. That was quite nice."

"Amazing," whispered Katie, making a note in her own pad.

"Yes," replied Lillian, watching her daughter leave the stage. "Quite amazing."

CHAPTER 6
THE CHEMIST

Dr. Patricia Whitting was a stunningly beautiful woman with dark auburn hair and deep green eyes. Katie found her standing just outside the auditorium waving goodbye to her husband with one hand and grasping the wiggling hand of a small child with the other.

"Dr. Whitting?" Katie called out as she approached her. "My name is Katie Porter and I'm a reporter with the *Fairfield Gazette*. May I speak with you for a moment?"

"Yes, certainly," replied the chemist. She turned to her daughter, who was just coming up behind her, and said, "Elizabeth, please go back inside and see if you can locate your brother. He's probably trying to set fire to the stage or something." Then turning back to Katie she asked, "can we go over and sit on the bench? I've been on my feet all day."

"Of course," responded Katie, turning with Dr. Whitting towards a bench situated a few feet from the building.

"This is my youngest, Todd," said Patricia Whitting, pulling the child onto her lap as they sat down. "He's just turned 18 months and he'll make a run for it if I don't keep hold of him."

"It appears you have your hands full," remarked Katie, smiling down at the baby.

"Yes, indeed," replied Elizabeth's mother. "So, what can I do for you, Miss Porter?"

"I'm covering the pageant and was completely taken by your daughter's interview with the judges today," Katie said. "She told them that she wanted to be a chemist just like her mother. That might work as a possible angle for my story."

"Well, that's what she says she wants to be today," replied Dr. Whitting, smiling. "She most likely will change her mind tomorrow and want to be a teacher, circus performer, or even a reporter just like you, Miss Porter."

"Surely not a reporter, Dr. Whitting!" Katie joked, retrieving her reporter's pad from her bag. "Can I assume, then, that you would be supportive of whatever occupation Elizabeth chose to pursue?"

"Yes, of course," nodded Patricia. "As long as she could support herself and was happy. And if her plans included marriage and children, then we would support that as well."

"That's quite a wonderful attitude to have towards one's child," remarked Katie. "Especially with a daughter."

"You have a career," Patricia Whitting countered. "Your parents must have endorsed your choice, surely?"

"My parents?" replied Katie, somewhat disconcerted. "Well, my parents travel quite a bit and…"

"What a minute," interrupted Dr. Whitting, suddenly looking at Katie intently as little Todd squirmed in her lap. "Porter. You're not related to Mrs. Agatha Main Porter of Rosegate are you?"

"Yes," nodded Katie, not sure whether she should admit it or sidestep the question. "I'm her granddaughter."

"Good gracious! Of course!" exclaimed Elizabeth's mother. "How silly of me. You're *that* Katie Porter! I should have realized! My apologies!"

"There's really no need…" Katie began.

"You see, I know your family quite well," Dr. Whitting continued. "Well, Sara mostly. Let's see, you must be her brother's child so that would make you her niece. Imagine that! Sara and I met at school. She was several years ahead of me, of course, but we shared a love of chemistry. She used to tutor me in the subject and was a real whiz at it! I don't suppose she continued in the field?"

"No," replied Katie. "She helped my grandmother run the estate for a few years before she got married. She's Sara Timmons now."

"How wonderful. And your father?" Patricia Whitting asked. "Is he still travelling? He used to send me soil samples from various regions around the world. The samples were extremely valuable for my experiments and I did not have the means, myself, in which to collect them. I owe him a debt of gratitude."

"I'm sure he didn't mind helping since he was already there," murmured Katie, not quite sure what to say. "What type of experiments would you have been conducting that needed soil samples?" she asked, quickly changing the subject. She was not prepared to talk about her world travelling parents who had been continuously absent throughout her life.

"I work in natural gas," replied the chemist, lowering her toddler down on the ground in front of her, all the while keeping a firm grip on the waist band of his trousers. "At Haldor Topsoe, we've developed a process of turning natural gas into chemical compounds such as Ammonia, Hydrogen, and Methanol that can be used to make useful household products such as cleaning agents and solvents."

"Really?" responded Katie, making some notes in her pad. "How interesting. One just takes it for granted that those items are available for purchase from a local hardware store. Of course, these products have to be created and produced in the first place."

"Yes. It often takes years of hard work and experimentation before they can be made available to the general public," replied Dr. Whitting. "And there are always safety factors that must be considered."

At that moment, daughter Elizabeth appeared, pushing a boy along in front of her. He was quite a bit taller than she was and a few years older. He was purposely dragging his feet, his hands stuffed in his pockets. "Here he is, mother," said her exasperated daughter. "I caught him trying to kiss Rosemary."

"Was not!" declared the young man. "She was trying to kiss me!"

"I don't think so, Bobby Whitting!" cried his sister, sticking her tongue out at him. "She hates your guts."

"Children!" exclaimed their distracted mother. "Enough of this silliness. It's getting late and I still need to fix dinner. Come along!" The chemist stood and extended her hand out to shake Katie's. "It was a pleasure meeting you, Miss Porter. Please give my regards to your wonderful family."

"May I give you a call if I have further questions regarding the article?" asked Katie, frowning at Bobby as he pinched his sister. Elizabeth returned the assault with a punch to his ribs.

"Yes, that would be fine," replied Dr. Whitting, busily trying to corral her progeny toward her car parked a few yards away. "I'm in the lab every day. You're welcome to contact me there. Goodbye!"

"Goodbye," Katie said with a wave. "And good luck," she added under her breath.

Katie slipped behind the wheel of her own little MG roadster and turned the key in the ignition. All the while she thought how strange it was to have a total stranger know more about her own family than she did. Over the years, she had seen her Aunt Sara infrequently, usually during the occasional holiday or Gran's birthday. Sara Timmons was a pleasant enough person, but she and her niece simply had nothing in common and, because she had no children of her own, her aunt had never been quite sure how to engage with her brother's daughter. Sad, really, since the family was so small.

When Katie arrived home, there was a telegram from Jim waiting for her on the little silver tray in the hallway.

Darling. Leaving Charing Cross Hotel. Been reassigned. Hold all mail until you hear from me. I love you. Jim

"Well, isn't that just the last straw," she muttered to herself as she took off her hat and gloves. She had been planning on writing him a long letter that evening, updating him on the new evidence in Midge's case, the amazing way Mr. Radcliff had gotten Amelia Chishelm to overcome her stutter, and her conversation with Dr. Patricia Whitting. Now it would have to wait. "Gosh it's so frustrating not to have him here!"

"Who dear?" said Gran, passing by her in the hallway and giving her shoulders a little rub. She held her reading glasses and a crossword puzzle in one hand and was making her way to the library.

"Jim," sighed Katie, following behind her grandmother. "His paper is moving him to a different location, so I'll not be able to reach him at Charing Cross. I'll have to wait to hear where he'll be before I can write to him again."

"Oh, that is too bad," replied Gran, settling down in her chair and putting on her glasses. "But I'm sure he'll let you know soon. Or at least I hope he will. I don't like seeing you so out of sorts. If this is going to happen every time the two of you are separated…"

"Gran!" exclaimed Katie, blushing. "You sound just like E.M.! It's not a matter of being separated. It's just that…"

At the moment the telephone rang and Katie, thinking it might be Jim calling from overseas, quickly returned to the hallway to answer it.

"Ruthie!" she exclaimed, hearing her best friend's voice. Ruth White had been visiting a distant relative in Canada and was now calling from New York where she was staying overnight before catching the morning train home.

The Whites lived at Sunset Hill, the estate next to Rosegate, and Katie and Ruth had grown up together. They were closer than most sisters and often spoke daily. It occurred to Katie, upon hearing her friend's voice over the phone, that not having Ruth around had added to her loneliness while Jim had been gone.

"I should have never permitted you to be gone from Fairfield at the same time as Jim," Katie added with a chuckle. "I've been in a very foul mood the entire time. When are you coming home?"

"I'll take your claim of a foul mood as a compliment," replied Ruth. "But you can return to your usual good spirits because my train arrives tomorrow afternoon around 1:00, which is the main reason I'm calling. You see, Robert's tied up at the hospital, mother and Tom have an appointment in Wakefield, and I understand Poppy is busy with some pre-trial hearing concerning a case involving your colleague Midge Pennington. So, I wonder if you would be available to pick me up from the station?"

"Yes, of course," responded Katie. "I'll be glad to! Perhaps we can stop for lunch on our way home so that I can catch you up on everything you've missed since you've been away."

"That would be nice, Katie," said Ruth cheerily. "I'm sure you've been up to all kinds of mischief without me there. I look forward to hearing all about it! See you tomorrow!"

Katie was humming when she returned to Gran in the library.

"Good news?" asked her grandmother.

"Yes. Ruth is coming home tomorrow," replied Katie. "I'm going to pick her up at the train station and then we'll grab lunch. Not having her or Jim around for over a week has been difficult even though I've enjoyed spending time with E.M. But he's not been himself either since Midge's arrest."

"Well, now that things are finally beginning to settle down, Katie dear," said Gran, her eyes twinkling as she gazed up at her only grandchild. "Perhaps you will honor me with a game of gin rummy after dinner?"

"Of course, Gran," smiled Katie, although she wasn't a fan of the game. "And this time I might actually beat you!"

"Not likely," Gran challenged. "But you can always give it a try."

They were just finishing their dinner when Andrews entered the dining room to announce that Katie had another phone call.

"The gentleman says it's very important," explained the butler. "Or else I wouldn't have bothered you."

"Surely it can't be E.M.," Katie remarked, shaking her head as she left the table. "Telling me Midge has skipped town."

"Hello honey," said the voice at the other end of the line. "I just wondered if you were free tonight?"

"Bradford Sinclair!" exclaimed Katie. "What do you want?"

"Well, that cousin of mine asked me to give you a call," said the attorney. "We're meeting tonight to go over the case and he wanted to make sure you were included."

"It's rather late," replied Katie doubtfully, glancing at the large grandfather clock that stood in the far corner of the hallway. "And I have plans tonight."

"Ah, come on, honey," pleaded Bradford. Something in his voice sounded odd. "Break them and come on over."

"Have you been drinking?" asked Katie firmly.

"Just a glass of wine with dinner," replied the attorney. "Listen, E.M. is already on his way over. We're meeting in *The Clock Room*. Do you know the place?"

"Yes. It's a bar directly across from your hotel," Katie responded.

"Good! We'll see you in 20 minutes." And he hung up the phone.

Something about the entire conversation made Katie suspicious. Perhaps it was just pure intuition or her deep distrust of Bradford Sinclair, but she picked up the telephone once again and dialed E.M.'s number.

"Well hello there, friend," said E.M. when he answered the phone. "What a pleasant surprise. Is everything all right?"

"Yes, I think so, but I just received a rather strange call from your cousin," replied Katie.

"Oh?" he asked.

"Yes," she replied. "He told me that the three of us were to meet tonight at *The Clock Room* to go over Midge's case. He mentioned that you were already on your way."

"The liar!" E.M. exclaimed. "I know nothing about this! Sounds like he's trying to get you down there on false pretenses. I have half a mind to go down to that bar and have it out with him!"

"No, wait, E.M.," Katie replied, a sudden thought occurring to her. "I have a better idea. I'll take care of Mr. Bradford Sinclair, don't you worry!" And she quickly hung up the phone.

It was nearly two hours later when Andrews appeared in the game room as Katie and Gran were playing their third round of gin rummy.

"Mission accomplished, Andrews?" Katie asked, looking up from her cards.

"Yes, Miss," replied the butler, trying very hard not to laugh. The look in his eyes, however, gave him away. "I entered the establishment and confronted the gentleman who, as you figured, was seated at the bar. He was very tipsy, I might add."

Gran looked up from her cards and glanced from Katie to Andrews. "What's this?"

"Oh, nothing Gran. I just asked Andrews to run a little errand for me," said Katie with a chuckle. Turning back to the butler she asked, "Did you deliver the message in the way I explained?"

"Yes," replied Andrews, nodding. "In the loudest voice possible I told him that the lady would not be meeting him this evening, or any other evening, until he had received his last inoculation because one can never be sure when it comes to rabies."

"Perfect, Andrews!" declared Katie, clapping her hands and smiling at him. "And how was the cognac?"

"Fine, Miss Katie," nodded Andrews, backing out of the room. "Although not up to our own standards. But watching Mr. Sinclair getting tossed out of *The Clock Room* helped ease the taste."

* * *

Katie arrived at the Fairfield train station well ahead of Ruth's arrival. She found a bench close to the platform and studied the various people that walked by. Some were struggling with overstuffed suitcases and carrying tickets. Others were, like herself, waiting for friends and family to arrive on the next train, and would soon be anxiously searching for their familiar faces.

The train from New York City was on time and Katie moved forward and waited to catch a glimpse of her friend. She didn't have to wait long as Ruth was one of the very first passengers to make her way off the train and work her way through the crowd. A porter followed close behind, carrying her large suitcase, a smaller bag, and a hat box.

"Katie!" Ruth called out, waving her hand.

"Ruth!" Katie returned, quickly moving forward and into the outstretched arms of her best friend. "Gosh I've missed you!"

"And I've missed you!" countered Ruth as the two friends linked arms and proceeded down the platform toward Katie's roadster.

"How was your trip?" asked Katie.

"Long," replied Ruth. "And tiring. I'm going to need a nap when I get home. Where are we stopping to eat?"

"Polly's?" responded Katie.

"That sounds good," nodded Ruth. "Have you heard from Jim recently?"

"Not recently," Katie said, shaking her head sadly. "He's somewhere in England. Or Europe. I don't really know. He sent me a telegram telling me that the *Times* has given him a new assignment and I'd have to wait until he knew where they were sending him."

"Ah, there's your car," said Ruth, pointing it out to the porter and then turning back to Katie. "I hope my bag will fit into your rumble seat. I should have had it shipped along with my trunk."

"Oh, I think we'll be able to cram them all in," replied Katie, glancing back at the suitcases in the porter's hand. "If not, I can always strap you to the bonnet."

Katie unlocked the roadster and opened the rumble seat allowing the porter to lift Ruth's suitcase and lower it easily into the compartment. "See, no problem Ruthie," said Katie as she watched her friend search for something in her purse.

"I seem to be a little short for a tip, sir," said Ruth to the porter. "But go ahead and kiss my friend here and that should make up for it."

"Whaaa...?" was all that Katie got out before the porter pulled her into a tight embrace and kissed her passionately.

Ruth White stood quietly and slowly counted to 15 before tapping the man on the shoulder. "OK, Jim Fielding, that's enough. Give the poor woman a chance to breath."

As Jim reluctantly let her go, Katie found herself looking up into the soft blue eyes and handsome face of the man she loved.

"Jim!" she whispered, grabbing hold of his arm as she tried to regain her balance. "How on earth..."

"Hello, darling," he replied with a sheepish grin. "I guess our little surprise worked!"

"I should say so," she replied, finally catching her breath. "You were in on this?" she asked Ruth.

"Yes, but it's a long story," nodded Ruth. "We'll tell you all about it over lunch. Here, I'll pop into the rumble seat and sit on my suitcase. You and Jim ride up front. But before we go, Jim, I suggest you change your jacket."

Katie was still in shock as she watched Jim quickly pull off the porter's jacket and hat and flip them into the rumble seat. He then opened the small suitcase and pulled out his suit jacket, buttoning it up and straightening his tie. After quickly running his hand through his light brown hair, Jim was ready to go and looked over to see Katie still standing in front of him looking as though she had just seen a ghost.

"Yes, I'm really here and gosh have I missed you!" he exclaimed, pulling her once again into his arms and giving her a gentle kiss on her forehead. "I feel as though it's taken me days to get home!"

They held hands all the way to Polly's with the few exceptions when Katie had to shift gears in the roadster and arrived within minutes at the café. Soon they were seated in their favorite booth and gave the waitress their order. Usually Jim and Katie sat across from each other but now, with Ruth accompanying them, they sat together on one side with their friend on the other. This gave Jim the opportunity to rest his arm across the back of the booth allowing Katie to sit close against him.

"Well, it all started right after you received my last letter," Jim began. "I got a long-distance call from Rosegate and, of course, thought it was you. Imagine my surprise to hear your grandmother on the other end of the line."

"Gran called you in London?" Katie asked in surprise, looking up at him.

"Yes," he replied, stifling a yawn. "She told me that she had heard that I was no longer needed in London and was just waiting for my scheduled trip back home on the Queen Elizabeth. She informed me that if I would be willing to forgo the boat ride, she would arrange to secure a seat for me on a Pan Am Clipper and pay for the ticket. I jumped at the chance of course."

"I can't believe it," murmured Katie, shaking her head.

"Neither could I at first," agreed Jim. "But before I knew it, a ticket arrived an hour later for a flight leaving at six that very evening, London time. Let's see, that would have made it only noon in New York. It's about a 20-hour flight from Heathrow to Newark Liberty so I arrived early this morning just in time for Ruth to pick me up and get us to the train station in time to catch the Fairfield express. I had just enough time to send you that telegram before leaving London although I couldn't tell you I was coming home because your grandmother wanted to surprise you."

"Well, I was certainly surprised! So, you've been awake since yesterday morning?" she asked, reaching up to stroke the stubble on his unshaven cheek.

"I did manage to catch a few short naps on the flight and then on the train but I'm afraid I haven't had a chance to shave," he replied, wrinkling up his nose and rubbing his other cheek.

"Never mind that," smiled Katie. "You are as handsome as ever. Besides, I'm just glad to have you home, no matter what you look like."

"Your grandmother spoke with my mother about her plan to surprise you and then mother called me when I arrived in New York asking if I could collect Jim when his flight arrived and get him on the train home," Ruth said, picking up the story. "I decided it might be fun to add to the surprise, Katie, so I bought the porter's jacket and hat from a costume shop on Broadway and Jim and I concocted this part."

"You could have knocked me over with a feather when I heard you tell the porter to kiss me in exchange for a tip," chuckled Katie, sliding her hand into Jim's under the table.

"Thank goodness Ruth is a generous tipper," smiled Jim, squeezing Katie's hand. "I'll carry your bags anytime for a tip like that, ma'am!" he added, giving Ruthie a wink.

Their sandwiches arrived at that moment and Katie put off updating Jim and Ruth for several minutes, giving them a chance to eat as both where quite hungry after their travels. As soon as they were nearly finished, however, she launched into what had occurred during their absence. Ruth, having not heard any of the story, listened in shock as Katie quickly told her of the five-year-old accident turned murder charge and how Midge had been the one to find the bloody body of her husband.

"We've managed to engage a top-notch attorney for her," Katie related. "You may have heard of him. His name is Bradford Sinclair."

"Yes, of course! He's quite famous!" exclaimed Ruth. "How did you manage to secure his services? I thought he only practiced law in Chicago."

"Fortunately, he's licensed to practice here, as well," replied Katie. "And, believe it or not, he happens to be E.M.'s cousin."

"Really? That's amazing!" responded Ruth, shaking her head. "What luck!"

"Yes, it is," said Katie, pausing to take a sip of her tea. "And, as you already know, Poppy is hearing the case although I suspect there will also be a jury."

"Do you think Midge has a chance?" asked Jim, poking at a piece of pie with his fork before pulling the plate closer and taking a bite.

"Yes, I think so," Katie replied. "Although there's no denying that it's going to be tough. You see, new evidence has suddenly appeared in the form of a letter. One of Midge's neighbors wrote from her death bed that she saw Midge hit her husband over the head with a hammer, killing him. She sent the letter to Midge's sister-in-law."

"Oh dear!" sigh Ruth. "That seems pretty concrete."

"Nearly," replied Katie. "But if one reads the letter carefully, it's obvious that she never actually witnessed the hitting of the head, only that she saw Midge holding her husband's head in her lap and there happened to be a hammer lying nearby."

"Did the hammer contain any blood?" asked Jim.

"I don't know," said Katie, with a shrug. "The police report doesn't mention it and they've mislaid the initial photographs taken at the scene. At the time it was assumed that Major Pennington slipped and fell, hitting his head on the concrete floor, causing him to bleed to death. Just an unfortunate accident. I suppose no one thought to handle the file that carefully."

"It probably got filed away before the photographs were developed and someone forgot to pull it out again and add them when they were delivered," said Jim, yawning. "They're probably on top of some file cabinet somewhere in a back room of the police station."

"Yes, that's most likely what happened," replied Katie, nodding. She smiled up at him. "And you are exhausted, Jim Fielding, or else I'd drag you along with me to the Little Miss Daisy Beauty Pageant, which I need to go to in the next hour."

"Yes, I suppose we'd better go," added Ruth, glancing at her wristwatch. "I'm sure there will be a million things for me to do since I've been gone for over a week. Besides, you're not the only one who's missed their beau. It seems like ages since I've seen Robert and he's coming over for dinner tonight!"

As they stood to leave the table, Katie picked up the check. "I'm paying this time. It's the least I can do now that I have you both home!"

Although it was in the opposite direction, they dropped Ruth off first at Sunset Hill and then proceeded to Jim's house which was located on the other side of town.

"I know that I'm taking the long way around to your house, Jim," said Katie guiltily. "But now that you are home, I'm rather reluctant to let go of you"

"That's quite all right, darling," he replied softly. "Perhaps I can manage to go to the pageant with you after all?"

"No, it's obvious that you're dead on your feet," she replied. "I'm just being selfish. I'll drop you home where you can take a nice long nap and then come to Rosegate for dinner."

"Sounds great, Katie," he said, smiling up at her and reaching out to take her hand.

They rode along in silence for another mile before Jim looked over at her and asked, "It was hard for you to tell Ruth about Midge holding her bleeding husband in her lap, wasn't it?"

"Yes," she replied.

"Because you once did that with me?" he added.

"Yes," she said softly.

"I've always been very sorry about that, you know," he said.

"It was all my fault," Katie reminded him. "You saved my life, remember. The least I could do was to hold you in my arms and try to save yours."

"Do you think that's what Midge was trying to do for Major Pennington," Jim asked. "Trying to find a way to save his life?"

"Perhaps," replied Katie with a sigh. "But I'm starting to have some doubts."

CHAPTER 7
PICTURES OF THE GARAGE

The Little Miss Daisy Beauty Pageant was in full swing when Katie finally arrived at the auditorium and slipped into a chair next to Lillian Chishelm. The publisher's wife gave her a warm smile and a nod and then returned her attention to the stage at the front of the room. Betsy Fitzgerald was trying to sing a rendition of *On the Good Ship Lollipop* and unfortunately managed to be off key during the entire song.

"At least she was consistent," remarked Lillian as the audience politely applauded at the end of the performance.

"And her costume was adorable although I didn't understand the hat," replied Katie, pulling out her reporter's pad.

"It was supposed to be the candy part of a lollipop," explained Lillian. "At least I think so."

"I see," murmured Katie, making a notation. "Who else did I miss?"

"Just one act," replied Lillian. "And it's too bad because I think you would have liked it."

"Really? How so?" asked Katie, tilting her head to one side and pausing her pen over her pad.

"Well it started with Patricia Vernon's tap routine to "In The Mood," chuckled Lillian. "The poor little thing managed to get on stage but then she froze. Her mother tried to coax her from the audience but to no avail. Thinking that she might have better luck running up into the wings, Mrs. Vernon started the dance herself just off stage, but still Patricia stood frozen. This made her very panicked mother inch closer and closer to her daughter, tapping the entire time, until it was Mrs. Vernon who was doing the performance while Patricia watched."

"Or how terrible!" declared Katie, shocked. "It must have been quite a disturbing spectacle to watch!"

"No, not really," replied Lillian Chishelm, smiling. "You see Mrs. Vernon was quite good. In fact, we gave her a standing ovation!"

Katie burst out laughing and was shushed by the woman seated in front of her. Regaining her composure, Katie noticed that the performers were not being called in alphabetical order and asked Lillian about it.

"Due to the number of contestants this year, they've decided to spread the talent part of the competition over two days," explained Mrs. Chishelm. "The young ladies drew numbers and half will go today and the rest tomorrow."

"What day will Amelia be performing?" Katie asked.

"Tomorrow," sighed Lillian. "She'll be reciting the poem, "The Raven" by Poe."

Katie looked at her intently but said nothing. Secretly she couldn't imagine a worse trial for young Amelia.

Amelia's mother just shrugged. "She won't be able to get through it, of course," she replied as if reading Katie's mind. "I argued with my husband about it, but he's convinced that it will be good for her to at least try."

"Perhaps he doesn't realize how challenging Amelia's affliction really is?" suggested Katie, choosing her words carefully.

Lillian Chishelm gave her a faint smiled. "No he doesn't," she replied. "But he's about to find out. I insisted that he be here tomorrow to see Amelia's performance for himself.

If the man has any heart at all, he'll stop this nonsense, thought Katie, but she remained silent, instead giving Lillian an understanding smile.

Next on stage was Eleanor Sullivan performing a ballet number from Swan Lake. It was whispered that Miss Sullivan was the odds-on-favorite to win the entire competition and her skill as a ballet dancer showed that the young lady was indeed exceptional. Katie gazed over at Mr. Radcliff from Julliard and saw that he was studying Eleanor closely.

Katie flipped through the pages of notes in her reporter's pad and saw that she had put down that Eleanor had also done well in her interview. What's more, Katie had observed that Eleanor was friendly, unassuming, and helpful to the other girls, especially those competing in their very first pageant. Although she would never admit it to Lillian, Katie secretly hoped that Eleanor Sullivan would indeed be crowned Little Miss Daisy of 1947 and Amelia Chishelm would defy her father and drop out before things proceeded much further. Only time would tell.

Much to Katie's relief the afternoon flew by quickly, and soon she was on her way home to Rosegate. She had stopped by the bakery and picked up some puff pastry filled with custard, a favorite of Grans, in gratitude for everything her grandmother had done to bring Jim home early.

She was singing to herself as she entered the large main hall of the mansion and quickly pulled off her hat and gloves, tossing them on a side table. Carrying the bag of pastries through the house and out into the sunporch, she leaned out of the open patio doors and heard Gran talking rather curtly to one of her prized rose bushes in the garden.

"I'm not going to tell you again, Thomas!" declared Gran, stooping over the bush. "You're either going to fill out properly or I'm going to have to dig you up and move you!"

Katie started laughing. "Gran!" she said as her grandmother looked up to see her standing there. "Surely you don't think that the roses listen to you?"

"Of course they do!" replied Gran sternly, but there was a twinkle in her eyes. "I speak to all of them and that's why they're doing so well." She straightened and started walking toward Katie. "I do, however, avoid singing. I will ask Jim Fielding to do that for me instead."

"Speaking of Jim," said Katie, holding up the bag of pastries. "He'll be coming to dinner tonight. I bought you these as my way of saying thank you for bringing him home early!" And she wrapped her arms around her grandmother and gave her a tight hug.

"So, I take it that he made it home safely?" asked Gran.

"Yes," replied Katie, her arms still around her grandmother. "And, yes, I was completely surprised when he and Ruth arrived together at the train station." Her eyes began to fill with tears. "I don't know how I will ever be able to thank you. You are the most wonderful grandmother a girl could ever have!"

"Now, now, Katie, dear," replied Gran, patting Katie on the arm. "It was nothing, really. And I had the help of Mrs. White, Ruth, and Jim himself. That young man jumped at the chance and most likely would have piloted the plane himself if it meant getting back sooner."

Katie smiled warmly at her grandmother who was now looking intently at the bag sitting on the table in front of them. "Puff pastry?" she asked, raising her eyebrows.

"Yes," Katie replied, releasing Mrs. Porter and reaching over to hand her the bag. "Filled with custard!"

"My favorite!" exclaimed Gran, opening the bag and pulling out a pastry. "Let's have some tea to go along with these. Unless you were saving them for dessert with Jim."

"No, Gran," Katie chuckled, ringing the bell for Gertie. "These are all yours, but I will join you for tea."

An hour later, Jim arrived for dinner. He was clean shaven and looked well rested. He held a long stem red rose in one hand and a tin of English chocolates in the other.

"Hello darling!" he said, as Katie answered the door and then stepped back to let him enter. "How's my favorite girl?" He glanced around quickly, and seeing no one in sight, leaned over and kissed her.

"Hello Jim," replied Katie, smiling and stretching up to return his kiss. "I hope I'm your only girl."

"Always," he replied softly, and handed her the rose. "These are for your grandmother," he added, holding up the tin. "A little something from London. I also have something for you, but I'll have to give it to you later."

"Did you get some sleep?" Katie asked, sliding her arm through his as they made their way to the library to join Gran for cocktails.

"Yes, for about three hours," he replied nodding. "Then I got up and called the archivist at the *Middleton Times* and asked him if he would check our files to see if our newspaper had sent over a photographer to take pictures of Major Pennington's accident."

Katie stopped abruptly just outside the library door. "Oh Jim!" she exclaimed, her eyes growing wide as she looked up at him. "Please tell me that the *Times* did exactly that!"

"OK," Jim teased. "The *Times* did exactly that!" And reaching inside his jacket, he brought out a medium size envelope and handed it to Katie.

Katie quickly flipped it open and slide out half a dozen pictures showing the bloody scene of a body lying prone against the running board of a 1933 Packard. Jim half expected Katie to cringe at their graphic nature but she was thrilled.

"These are wonderful," she exclaimed, quickly flipping through them before sliding the photographs back inside the envelope. "We'll take a closer look right after dinner."

They entered the library and joined Katie's grandmother who was sitting in her overstuffed chair, the newspaper lying across her lap and a glass of sherry on the coffee table in front of her.

"Ah, there you are," said Gran, looking up at the couple. "We're glad to see you back, Jim. How was your trip?"

"Wonderful," replied Jim, smiling at Mrs. Porter. "And these are for you in appreciation for your help."

"How lovely!" exclaimed Gran, taking the tin from him. "Between you and my granddaughter, I'm completely spoiled."

"Not at all, Gran," chuckled Katie. She slipped the rose into a flower vase nearby that already held some roses from Gran's garden until she could bring it up to her room later.

"Jim, would you like scotch or something else," she asked as she walked across the room to the liquor cart.

"Scotch would be fine," Jim replied, following a few steps behind her. She poured them both one and handed him his glass before turning to take a seat on the couch. Nugget was napping in the middle and Katie pulled him onto her lap so that Jim could sit next to her.

"Remember how scarce chocolates were during the war?" Gran reflected, opening the tin and peering inside. "And worth a king's ransom. These are lovely, Jim. Thank you."

As Jim sat down and made himself comfortable next to Katie, Nugget immediately transferred from Katie's lap onto Jim's.

"Nugget," Katie scolded the Yorkie. "Come back here. You're going to get dog hair all over Jim." But the little dog just glared at her and curled up in Jim's lap and was soon fast asleep.

"Mrs. Porter," began Jim, reaching inside the breast pocket of his jacket and bringing out what looked like a checkbook. "I would also like to reimburse you for the airplane ticket."

Katie's grandmother looked at him as though he had just suggested they set Katie on fire.

"No indeed!" Gran huffed, glaring at him. "That will not be necessary!"

"But I..." Jim began again and then caught Katie's eye. Her look told him that it was no use arguing with her grandmother.

"I gave you that ticket for Katie's sake," continued Gran, nodding at Katie. "She'd been moping the entire time you've been gone and I simply can't stand seeing her like that." And then she added, looking slyly at the two of them. "Besides, Nugget missed you also, as you can see."

"Well, in that case," smiled Jim, placing the checkbook back inside his jacket. "Thank you, ma'am. I deeply appreciate it. And I feel humbled to be missed by such a wonderful family." He winked at Katie who dropped her head slightly to hide the fact that she was blushing.

"What's that you've got there, dear?" asked Gran, looking down at the envelope that Katie had dropped on the table.

"Pictures of Major Pennington's dead body lying in his garage," replied Katie cheerily. She leaned forward to pat the packet. "Jim just brought them for me."

"I see," said Gran grimly, but her eyes were twinkling. "And all I got was a tin of English chocolates."

"Gran!" laughed Katie, getting to her feet and moving back to the liquor cart. "You're incorrigible! Can I get you more sherry? And Jim, more scotch?"

"Yes, please," replied Jim, nodding.

"Yes, I'll take another. Thank you," Gran answered, holding up her glass.

"I did bring Katie a gift from London, as well, ma'am," Jim remarked, taking the glass of scotch from Katie and then reaching into his jacket pocket. "I was going to give it to her later, but I wouldn't want you to think that I only brought her bloody crime photos."

"Oh yes?" replied Gran, looking over at him and tilting her head to one side.

Jim handed the small nicely wrapped box to Katie as she sat back down beside him. "It isn't much, really, but I hope you like it."

"I'm sure I will, Jim," Katie replied, smiling warmly at him. "Although you really didn't have to get me anything."

She carefully unwrapped the tiny box and lifted off the lid, revealing a beautiful silver brooch. "Oh Jim!" she exclaimed holding the open box up to show her grandmother. "It's lovely! Wherever did you find it?"

"In a little shop a few blocks from my hotel," replied Jim. "I saw it in the window as I was passing by and thought it matched the locket that you always wear. It's remarkably similar in design."

Katie gently lifted the brooch from the box and examined it. "It's from Asprey and Company," she said softly. "See, it's got the jewelers mark on the back."

"Yes, the shop owner pointed that out to me," said Jim. "He told me that it belonged to an elderly customer of his who died a year ago. The man bought it from his estate."

"Well, you are very observant. It is nearly identical to my locket," said Katie, holding it up against the locket she wore around her neck. "But, then again, the locket is also from Asprey. Ruthie told me that the Whites bought it in New York."

"The Whites gave you the locket?" asked Jim, leaning forward to get a better look.

"Yes, it was a birthday present," replied Katie. "For my 21st. And now I have your brooch! It's absolutely beautiful. I love it! Thank you, Jim!" She replied, looking over at him fondly as she fastened it onto her dress.

At that moment Andrews announced that dinner was ready, and Gran, Katie, and Jim made their way across the hall and into the dining room with Nugget in Jim's arms.

"Oh no you don't, you little stinker," Katie said, taking him from Jim. "You don't eat in the dining room. It's off to the kitchen for you." And she put down the little terrier and watched him scamper down the hallway in search of his dinnerplate.

As they followed Gran to the table, Katie discreetly reached over and gave Jim's hand a quick squeeze before he pulled out her chair for her. His preference would have been to take the chair beside her, but he noticed that a place across the table had been set for him. With a sigh, he walked around the table and took his seat as Andrews poured him a glass of wine.

"So your duke was found unhurt," said Mrs. Porter, spreading her napkin across her lap. Andrews held a large platter of roast beef in front of her so that she could slide a piece onto her plate.

"Yes, ma'am," replied Jim. "He had hooked up with a band of

gypsies with hopes of travelling with them but, once they discovered who he was, they dropped him off with the authorities."

"Gypsies?" asked Gran in disbelief. "Why on earth would the man do a thing like that?"

"I suppose to get away from all the responsibilities he had as an MP," replied Jim, cutting into his baked potato.

"Then he shouldn't be an MP," responded Gran pragmatically.

"I believe the gentleman also served extensively in the war," added Katie, looking over at her grandmother. "It sounds like he still carried some mental scars from that experience and needed time away."

Gran looked at her reflectively for a moment. "Yes, I can see that," she finally replied with a nod. "I suppose we all need that from time to time. Quite understandable."

"I've seen E.M. shake involuntarily, especially after experiencing a stressful situation," continued Katie. "And he was awarded the Bronze Star. I imagine some men never get over the war."

"Most do," Jim replied, looking down at his plate. "Over time."

"Do you still feel the effects of the war, Jim?" Katie asked him softly, her blue eyes looking at him intently.

"Yes, sometimes," he replied, meeting her eyes. "I have nightmares that I'm back on Omaha Beach with…" He didn't finish his sentence.

Katie subconsciously reached up and grasped her locket before dropping her hand and picking up her fork again.

"I suppose seeing me every day only serves to remind you of that terrible…" Katie began and then stopped, tears pricking at her eyes as she continued to look across the table at him.

"Quite the contrary," replied Jim softly. "Seeing you every day gives me a reason to keep going. Other men don't have that, Katie. I never take for granted how immensely lucky I am."

They sat gazing at each other for several minutes before Gran broke the spell by clearing her throat.

"Well consider yourself even luckier, young man," said Gran, reaching over to ring the bell for Andrews. "Because Gertie has baked you a pie. Apple, I believe!"

Katie and Jim both chuckled and dessert was enjoyed over much lighter conversation. Soon afterward, Gran begged off joining them in the library.

"I need to retire to my bedroom, Katie dear. I've got several letters to write," she said, giving her granddaughter a kiss on the cheek. "Besides, you and Jim will be busy studying gruesome photographs and I don't wish to be involved with that. It was nice seeing you again, Jim," she added over her shoulder as she climbed to staircase.

"Goodnight, Mrs. Porter," replied Jim. "And thanks again!"

With a wave of her hand, Gran was soon out of sight and Katie and Jim made their way into the library. Once there, Katie walked over to the large mahogany desk in the corner and, pulling out the top drawer, retrieved a magnifying glass. Jim, meanwhile, spread the photographs of Major Pennington out over the coffee table.

"The photos are numbered on the back," Jim pointed out. "One through six. It looks like our guy started with the body and then moved around the room."

"Ah," Katie replied, sitting down next to him. "These are quite good. Hopefully, we'll be able to get some information."

"Well, the first thing I notice is the hammer lying off to the side of the major's left shoulder," said Jim, pointing at the object in the first picture. "And it definitely has blood on it."

"So it does," replied Katie grimly. "What's that next to it?"

"Looks like a screwdriver," said Jim, holding the picture a little closer.

"Does one usually use a hammer while fixing a car?" asked Katie.

"Not that I'm aware of," replied Jim. "But, then again, I don't work on cars."

"Well Midge does. And this would be a good question to ask her," remarked Katie. "There's certainly quite a lot of blood."

"Yes, but then again head wounds tend to bleed profusely," replied Jim.

"True," agreed Katie, picking up the second photograph. This one was a closeup of Major Pennington's body. Katie picked up the first picture again and held them side by side, comparing them to each other. "Jim, do you notice anything strange?"

"No, not in particular," replied Jim, looking at both photos.

"We just said that there's a lot of blood, correct?" she asked.

"Yes," replied Jim, nodding.

"Then why isn't there blood spatter?"

"You're right!" exclaimed Jim, leaning forward to take a closer look.

"If Midge Pennington clobbered her husband over the head with a hammer, there should be blood spatter all over the place," Katie declared. "There's no blood even on the side of the car."

"One would have expected it which is why the police probably discounted murder in the first place," replied Jim. "Do we know if there was a wound to the back of his head?"

"I don't think so," replied Katie, shaking her head. "I didn't see it in the police report when E.M. and I met with Bradford. The only obvious injury is the cut on his forehead, but it looks too small to have been made by a hammer."

"Besides, Pennington would have seen his wife coming towards him," Jim pointed out. "And would have been able to ward off her attack."

"True," murmured Katie, laying down both pictures and moving on to the third one. "Gosh, this is a mess."

The third photograph showed a worktable with several items strewn about. The shelf directly above it was partially down, with one end resting on the top of the table and the other end still attached to the wall. A jar of screws, a container of fluid, and a bottle of rum were laying on their side halfway down near the broken end of the shelf. Katie and Jim could see that the contents of each had spilled over from the shelf, to the worktable, and onto the floor. Forming an outline, the ring of a cup could be seen where it had previously been placed.

"Look at this, Jim," said Katie, pointing to the outline. "I wonder if this was made by the same cup that we can see next to the body?"

They looked at the first two pictures. "Yes, I believe you're right," replied Jim. "I didn't notice the cup before." Next to the elbow of Major Pennington lay a peculiar looking coffee mug.

"So I suppose the dear Major was taking a sip from the mug when he slipped on the grease spot and fell," Katie theorized.

"Or at least he was carrying the mug in his hand," added Jim. "It looks like the handle broke off when it hit the floor."

"Yes," nodded Katie. "But this also shows that he and Midge kept a messy shop proving that Pennington could have slipped or tripped over something, hit his head, and bled to death."

"I think that shelf must have collapsed fairly recently, darling," countered Jim. "The screw jar, fluid, and rum are still on their sides although I believe that item right there might be a rag or something."

"Yes, I see it," said Katie, picking up the magnifying glass and peering through it. "It is a rag! I wonder if the major started to clean up the mess and, perhaps on his way across the garage to grab an extra towel, slipped and fell, knocking himself out. That might explain why the jar, fluid container, and bottle are still on their sides."

"How long did you say the major had been dead before Midge found him?" Jim asked.

"15 minutes, at least," replied Katie, placing the magnifying glass down on the table. "According to the coroner."

Jim picked up the fourth photograph. It showed Midge speaking with one of the police officers. Her dress was covered in blood and she looked upset. They both studied the photograph silently before Jim placed it back down on the table and picked up the fifth one.

"That's the door leading from the house into their garage," said Katie, pointing to the picture. "It fits Midge's description. See, the car extends out past the door and she would have had to step inside the room and around it in order to find her husband."

"Did Midge say anything about the broken shelf and the mess it created?" asked Jim. "She would have seen it as soon as she opened the door."

"No," replied Katie thoughtfully. "She never mentioned it."

The final picture was the same shot as the first two except the body and surrounding items had been removed. The only thing remaining was the Packard and the blood. Katie and Jim could see the outline of the cup, hammer, and screwdriver.

"I suppose this was taken just before the blood was cleaned up," said Katie softly.

"Yes," replied Jim. "The police probably collected the cup and other articles as potential evidence and Midge would have had the terrible task of cleaning up."

"What an unpleasant..." Katie suddenly stopped in midsentence and looked up at him. "Jim, the blood!"

"Yes, she would have had to clean up the blood herself," he repeated, somewhat confused.

Katie leaned forward and picked up the picture of Midge in the bloody dress. "Midge said that she got the blood on her dress by kneeling to assess her husband's condition. She said that she saw right away that he was dead which led her to call for the police instead of an ambulance."

"So?" Jim asked.

"So," continued Katie, looking closely at the picture. "How would the cut over his eye still be bleeding if he was dead, and for at least 15 minutes, as the coroner stated in the police report?"

"That's right!" exclaimed Jim, his eyes opening wide. "Even for a head wound, that's not possible once the heart stops beating! A little residual dribble for a second, maybe, but not this much. So, how is it that so much of it got on Midge, especially if she was just kneeling beside him?"

"Because she wasn't and he wasn't," Katie replied. She paused for a moment and took a deep breath. "When you...after you had been stabbed...I sat on the ground and held you in my lap," she continued. "The only thing I could think of was trying to keep you from dying. I kept telling you to hang on and then, quite instinctively, I rolled you onto your side to look for your wounds. I pressed my hand against what looked to be the worst one and tried to stop the blood. I ended up with just slightly more on my dress than Midge has on hers."

"Katie," replied Jim, looking from her to the picture. "I was stabbed twice. Our major here only has a cut on his forehead."

"Yes, that's true," said Katie, nodding. "And Midge downplays the trauma of finding her husband. To hear her speak of it, finding him dead was going to screw up their dinner plans. Even E.M. alludes to the idea that their marriage was one of convenience."

Jim looked at the picture. "Katie, Midge looks very distressed in this picture."

"Exactly," replied Katie. "Here's what I think really happened. Major Pennington sustained a cut on his forehead which means he would have landed face down. Unless he rolled over on his own, which I admit is possible, Midge must have found him that way. She didn't just kneel next to him to check his pulse. I believe she rolled him onto her lap, turning him face up, and held him for several moments, which is why she's covered in so much blood."

"You mean while he was still alive?" asked Jim.

"Yes, although he may have been seconds away from death already," replied Katie, looking directly into his eyes. "His heart had to be beating for him to still be bleeding. It's the only way it makes sense."

"Yes, I see," nodded Jim.

"I remember feeling your life starting to slip away," said Katie softly. "And that just made me hold you tighter. It was as though my being alive might transfer over to you and keep you alive. They had to pull you out of my arms to get you into the ambulance."

Jim leaned forward and placed his forehead against Katie's. "Are you saying that Midge Pennington held onto her dying husband because she loved him and couldn't let him go?"

"Yes," replied Katie, bringing her arms up and sliding her hands around the back of his neck. "She loved him. Perhaps nearly as much as I love you."

CHAPTER 8
THE ONLY BOY

"You know this doesn't bode well for Midge," said Jim, as he and Katie drove to the auditorium the next morning. Since he didn't have to report back to the *Middleton Times* until the following week, Jim was tagging along with her so they could spend as much time together as possible, even if that meant enduring the Little Miss Daisy Beauty Pageant.

"I know," replied Katie, gazing out the window at the passing landscape. "The death bed letter from the neighbor stated that she witnessed Midge holding her husband and watching him die which, in fact, is most likely exactly what happened. The only difference being that Midge didn't kill him."

"So we've ascertained," smiled Jim. "Let's just hope a jury agrees."

"Which is why I'd like to do some poking around to see if I can find out what happened," Katie added, nodding.

"It's a bit of a cold case, don't you think?" Jim remarked, pulling into the large parking lot of the auditorium. "It will be difficult to discover any new evidence."

"Yes, that's true but it's worth a shot," she replied and then let out a sigh. "I can't wait for this pageant to be over. Thankfully, that will be early tomorrow. They'll finish up with the talent program today and announce the winner in the morning."

Jim parked the car and then came around to open the passenger side door for Katie.

"By the way," she said, looking up at him as she stepped out of the car. "You may remember that my publisher's daughter is named

Amelia Chishelm and we'll be sitting with her mother, Lillian."

"How nice," replied Jim, taking her arm. "But I have the distinct feeling that there's a reason you're telling me this."

"Yes indeed," smiled Katie, a twinkle in her eye. "My publisher is supposed to be attending Amelia's talent performance as well so behave yourself, young man."

"Katie Porter, I always behave myself!" exclaimed Jim, pretending to be affronted. "I don't believe I've ever even held your hand in public!"

"Oh, holding my hand is fine," teased Katie, sliding hers into his. "But from what I've been able to surmise, Mr. Chishelm doesn't treat his wife or daughter very well and you may be inclined to punch him in the nose."

"I see," smiled Jim. "Yes, I would be inclined to do that. But I'll try to refrain for your sake although I can't stand a man who mistreats women and children."

"I know, darling," Katie whispered as they approached the front door. "Neither can I."

Katie immediately spotted Lillian as they entered the main room of the building. The publisher's wife had saved a seat for her and, noticing Jim following close behind, scooted one over to make room.

"You're just in time," said Lillian. "Norma Murphy is about to start off the program. She does this baton twirling routine every year, which is quite good."

"Wonderful," replied Katie, sliding in beside her as Jim took the aisle seat next to Katie. "Lillian, this is Jim Fielding. Jim, Lillian Chishelm."

"How do you do?" they both responded in unison and nodded to each other.

"Lillian," said Katie smiling. "Jim is my beau."

"And drop dead gorgeous at that," Lillian whispered in Katie's ear just as Rachel Webster started playing the pageant's theme song to announce the beginning of the day's program.

"Good morning everyone," announced Mrs. Webster into the microphone as the last note on the piano fell silent. "To start off the second half of the talent competition is Miss Norma Murphy. You may recall that Norma usually ignites each end of her batons during her routine. However, I'm sad to announce that our Fire Marshall has forbidden it this time after last year's little mishap."

"She accidently set fire to the curtains," Lillian quietly informed Katie and Jim. "Caused considerable damage to the auditorium and the evacuation of the entire block."

Katie and Jim chuckled but said nothing as the young lady stepped onto the stage and began her routine. Lillian was right. The youngster was quite good as were the next three competitors who came after. All the while, Lillian glanced toward the auditorium door while checking her watch.

"Are you looking for your husband?" asked Katie, gazing at the back of the room and realizing that the publisher had failed to show up.

"Yes," she replied, chagrined. "And he swore to me that he would be here."

"And next up is Amelia Chishelm," announced Mrs. Webster. "Amelia, are you ready?"

Amelia stepped onto the stage and nodded. She took her place in the center and waited until the judges gave the signal to start.

"There he is!" Lillian suddenly exclaimed as a stout man with thinning black hair hurried down the aisle in her direction.

"I'm sorry I'm late but I got caught in a meeting," replied Mr. Chishelm, stepping over Jim, Katie, and Lillian and plopping down in the seat on the other side of his wife. "But no harm. I see she's getting ready to start her recitation now."

"Yes," his wife answered just as the judges nodded to Amelia.

"You may begin," said Mrs. Bonifay.

Katie crossed her fingers as Amelia took a deep breath and opened her mouth. She stared wide eyed out into the audience, her eyebrows raised in desperation, and her hands clasped tightly in front of her. Not a sound came out.

"Take your time Amelia," said Miss Owens, nodding in encouragement from the judges table.

"Take a big breath and try and sing it if you can't say it," reminded Mr. Radcliff, but all little Amelia could do was make a "ca...ca...ca" sound.

"Recite, Amelia!" came a loud voice from the audience as Mr. Chishelm stood up and bellowed out the command. "Do you hear me! Recite, now!"

The audience gasped and Katie sensed Jim growing tense. He straightened in his chair and she reached over and gently placed her hand over his.

"Amelia, damn you!" shouted her father. "I said…"

But before he could continue, a beautiful male voice rose from beside Katie and before she knew it, Jim was standing and had started to sing.

"If you were the only girl in the world," he sang to Amelia, stepping out into the aisle and walking slowly towards the stage.

Amelia's expression suddenly brightened and, smiling, she walked over to the edge of the stage. "And I were the only boy," she sang, picking up the next line.

Katie recognized the song. "If you were the only girl in the world" had been published in 1916, at the peak of World War I, and was one of Gran's favorites. It had just been re-released last year and was still very popular even now. Still, Katie was amazed that young Amelia Chishelm knew the words.

Jim and Amelia continued singing the song together, as a duet, with Jim handling the harmony. Suddenly Rachel joined them on the piano and soon the three had the audience completely mesmerized. Amelia's voice was pitch perfect and outstanding in quality, matching perfectly with Jim's. The audience swayed along and then, unable to resist, joined in on the final words, "and I were the only boy," before jumping to their feet in applause.

"Bravo!" they shouted, clapping loudly. "Brava!"

Jim, standing near Rachel at the piano, held out his hand, first in the direction of Amelia, and then to Rachel, as the audience enthusiastically applauded each. Then, giving a slight bow, he walked back to his seat beside Katie.

"I'm sorry, Katie," he began as he sat down and looked over at her. "I just couldn't sit here and…"

"That was the most wonderful thing I've ever seen anyone do in my entire life," she interrupted, with tears in her eyes. "You saved that little girl from…" she couldn't finish but, instead, threw her arms around him and hugged him tightly.

Suddenly the audience grew quiet as they realized that the three judges were huddled together in quiet conversation. Then Mrs. Bonifay wrote something down on a piece of paper and handed it to Miss Owens who handed it up to Mrs. Webster on the stage. Mrs. Webster glanced down at the note and, nodding to the judges, moved over to the podium.

"Your attention please," she said loudly into the microphone. "I have received a note from the judges. It seems that Amelia Chishelm has broken a Little Miss Daisy Beauty Pageant rule that states that no contestant may perform their talent routine with the assistance of another person except for the designated pageant accompanist. Since the gentleman is not a designated accompanist, the judges have no choice but to disqualify this competitor from the talent portion of the competition."

An angry murmur arose throughout the auditorium. "Besides," the pageant director added defensively, fearing the possibility of a riot, "Amelia did not perform the routine she had listed on her form for the judges. She was supposed to recite the poem, "The Raven," by Edgar Allen Poe."

Boos could now be heard from the crowd and one lady stood up and yelled, "what kind of outfit is this when a young girl with a voice like an angel gets disqualified over a little help from the audience!"

"This is all your fault," yelled Mr. Chishelm, red faced and jumping to his feet to point his finger at Jim.

"Hey, wait a minute buddy," said Jim, putting up both hands in surrender. "I was just trying to help. Can't you see that Amelia suffers from a stutter. There's no way she was going to be able to recite a poem."

"I'm going to punch…" huffed Mr. Chishelm, stepping over his wife and moving towards Jim.

"Wait a minute, Richard," Lillian Chishelm pleaded, grabbing hold of his arm to keep him away from Jim. "Jim was only trying to help. How were we to know that Amelia would be disqualified?" Her husband, however, payed no attention and quickly shook off her grasp.

"That's true," remarked Katie, stepping in front of Jim. "Besides, your daughter has an amazing voice. We would have never heard it if Jim…"

"And who do you think are you!" interrupted Chishelm, pushing past Lillian and coming to a stop in front of Katie. He glared down at her.

"I'm Katie Porter," she replied, looking back up at him. "Your reporter at the *Gazette*."

"Well not anymore, Miss Porter," shouted the publisher, his breath blowing in her face. "You're fired!"

"Now wait just one minute," declared Jim, stepping around Katie and standing nose-to-nose with Chishelm. "This is not Katie's fault. She had nothing to do with this. If you want to blame anyone, then blame me!"

"OK!" replied Mr. Chishelm. "Then you're fired, too!"

"You can't fire me!" Jim shouted back at him, prodding the other man's chest with his finger. "Because I don't work for you!"

"Apparently neither do I," added Katie, gathering up her purse and jacket and turning to leave. She tugged at Jim's arm, pulling him away from the Chishelms and towards the door of the auditorium. As they made their way up the aisle, Katie looked briefly over her shoulder just in time to see that Lillian Chishelm was crying.

"Well, that went well," said Katie grimly as they slid into Jim's car.

"Oh, Katie, I'm so sorry!" he replied, grasping the steering wheel tightly. "I should never have tried to help. I just felt so badly for that little girl."

"Please don't apologize, Jim!" exclaimed Katie, trying to regain her composure after what had just happened. "That man is a tyrant!"

"But your job!" Jim replied. "It's all my fault that you got fired!"

"Let's not think about that," said Katie, although she was heartbroken. "Anyway, now I'll have time to concentrate on Midge's trial and you can cover it for the *Middleton Times*!"

Jim gave her a weak smile. "I'll see if we have room for another reporter at the newspaper. The least I can do is to try and get you another job."

"Not before lunch, OK?" Katie replied sadly. Then she leaned over and kissed him.

"What was that for?" he asked, smiling fondly at her.

"That was for trying to help someone in trouble," she replied softly, resting her hand on his cheek and gazing into his beautiful blue eyes. "And for always doing the right thing."

* * *

"So who's this guy?" asked Bradford, looking up as Katie and Jim walked through the front door of Midge's home. After they had eaten lunch at Polly's, they had driven up to Rosegate to call E.M. and collect the photographs. It was E.M. who had arranged the meeting with Bradford and Midge.

"I'm Jim Fielding," replied Jim, extending his hand out to shake Bradford's. "I'm a reporter with the *Middleton Times* although I'm not here to cover the story. At least, not now."

"Jim's paper has furnished us with pictures of the scene of the accident," added Katie, holding up the envelope as she flopped down on the couch in the living room. "His newspaper managed to send a competent photographer, unlike the *Gazette*."

"Well, I don't like it," remarked Bradford, looking intently into Jim's eyes as he shook his hand tightly. Jim returned the firm handshake and then joined Katie on the couch.

"How are you doing, E.M?" Katie asked her friend as he entered from the kitchen carrying a pitcher of iced tea.

"Swell, so far, although it's early yet," he joked. "Did I hear you mention accident photographs?"

"Yes," said Katie. "And they're particularly good. Jim and I studied them last night and think we may have discovered a few clues."

"I still don't think we should discuss anything in front of Tom here," insisted Bradford, nodding over at Jim. "He's not part of the team."

"He is now," said a voice coming into the room. They looked up to see Midge carrying a tray of cookies and small cakes. "And his name is Jim, not Tom. He's Katie's friend and he's staying. I have a right to decide who's on my defense team, don't I?" she added, glaring at the attorney as she placed the tray down on the table in front of them and then sat down in a chair close to E.M.

"Yes, of course," replied Bradford, although his tone indicated that he wasn't at all happy about it.

"So Katie," said E.M. "What did you two find out? Is Midge cleared?"

"Well, yes and no," replied Katie, glancing at Midge. "These pictures prove that Major Pennington wasn't hit with a hammer or anything else that would cause great impact."

"What made you conclude that?" asked Bradford, picking up the envelope and pulling out the pictures. He flipped through them, stopping to study one or two more closely.

"Well, for one thing," replied Katie, relieved that he wasn't spreading them out around the cookie tray on the table. "You can see that there is no blood spatter. A blow to the head with a hammer would have definitely produced some."

"Does the police report indicate that there was another wound at the back of the head?" Jim asked Bradford.

"No," the attorney replied, taking the file from his briefcase and handing it to Jim. "Here, you can read it for yourself."

Jim opened the file and began to look through it. "No," added Midge. "Bill had only one wound and that was the one on his forehead."

"Which reminds me," said Katie suddenly. "Midge, would someone ever use a hammer and screwdriver while working on a car?"

"A screwdriver, yes, but not usually a hammer, although Bill sometimes found one useful to break off radiator caps or rusted bolts and screws," replied Midge. "I prefer to use a wrench or pliers, myself."

"So a hammer would not be readily visible to an intruder?" Bradford asked, suddenly looking over at his client. "You know, someone walks into the garage and perhaps gets into an argument with Major Pennington. They're real angry, you see, and they look around and spot the hammer and pick it up to give him a good whack. Then they drop it on the floor and take off."

"We have a hammer, of course, but it is usually kept in a drawer," replied Midge evenly. "It would not be laying around in view unless Bill was using it at that moment. And, no, I did not use it to kill him."

"Well then, what did you use? Because, according to these photos, your husband was using the hammer at that very moment," challenged Bradford. "And no one else was in the garage but you and now we have a witness who saw you hit him!"

"Hey, wait just one minute!" exclaimed E.M., jumping to his feet and taking a step towards Bradford.

"Easy E.M.," muttered Katie, reaching out and grabbing his arm. "Bradford is just demonstrating what the prosecuting attorney will ask Midge if she's on the witness stand."

"Yes, that's exactly right," said Bradford, nodding. "This is not going to be easy for Madge here…er…I mean Midge. And, remember Dapper, I'm on her side so you can go ahead and sit down now," he added with a dismissive wave of his hand.

Katie continued. "The letter from the witness only *alludes* to the idea that Midge hit her husband. Our dying neighbor never admits to actually seeing her do it, just that Midge was seen holding her husband in her arms."

"And about that," continued Bradford. "You said that you just knelt down to check his pulse. Yet the neighbor says she saw you holding your husband in your arms. Is that why you're covered in so much blood?"

"I knelt down, damn you, to check his pulse," replied Midge, getting angry. "How am I to know how I got covered in blood? As I'm sure you can see by the pictures in your hand that there was quite a lot of it around!"

"I think I can shed some light on that, Bradford," said Katie, looking apologetically at Midge. "Any wife who loved her husband would naturally drop down to the ground to cradle the dying man in her lap."

"Dying?" repeated the attorney, glancing over at Midge. "But I thought he was already dead?"

"He was!" declared E.M., reaching over and covering Midge's hand with his.

"No, E.M., he wasn't," replied Katie gently. "You see, Major Pennington had to be alive for the wound on his head to still be bleeding so badly. If he slipped and fell, the premise we're all going for here, Midge most likely would have found him face down. She couldn't truly know his condition unless she turned him over, which I think is what you did, Midge."

Midge just looked at her and did not answer. "Your husband was not a small man and would have been hard to move. Besides, you were deeply concerned, so you dropped to the ground and rolled him over onto your lap. He was barely alive and still bleeding from the head wound so you held him for a few seconds perhaps trying to decide how to save him. But it was too late and he died in your arms. That's when you got up and called the police. And that's why your dress was covered in blood."

"Ah, gee, Midge baby," moaned Bradford. "Please don't tell me that Bill Pennington was still alive when you found him? Please don't tell me that you held the man and watched him die?"

Midge looked over at him, tears running down her face. "Yes," she replied, nodding sadly. "Katie's right. Bill was alive when I found him and he died while I was holding him in my lap."

"This doesn't prove anything," declared Jim, leaning forward.

"This doesn't mean that Midge had anything to do with her husband's death."

"Well, let's just hope the jury agrees with you, Tom," replied Bradford, slipping the photographs back inside the envelope. "But this does lend credibility to the death bed letter."

"His name is Jim," said Katie, looking at Bradford and pointing to Jim sitting beside her. "But the death bed letter does bring up another question. Why was this lady apparently out to get you, Midge, and, more importantly, why is your sister-in-law so bent on pursuing the matter?"

"Because of the affair," Midge replied softly.

"Oh dear god," muttered Bradford, placing his forehead in his hand.

"You were having an affair?" Jim asked, looking at Midge in disbelief.

"No," Midge answered. "He was."

"Midge, don't," whispered E.M. tightening his hold on her hand. "You don't need to explain."

"Yes, she does," insisted Bradford, looking up. "The prosecutor will bring it up and the jury will most likely think that Midge killed Pennington because she was jealous, angry, or wanted to punish him. Maybe all three. This is not good, Madge."

"Her name is Midge," said the others in unison.

"Whatever," muttered her attorney.

"Midge, are you sure Bill was having an affair?" Katie asked, leaning towards the woman.

"His sister and my neighbor believe so," Midge replied with a shrug. "And they think it was my fault. They believe that I wasn't showing enough affection towards Bill so that he had to seek it elsewhere."

"But you don't really believe that, do you?" asked Katie.

"No," said Midge firmly. "We even talked about it when Pamela accused him of it. That's his sister. It was supposed to be with one of the female officers at his post in California. The entire thing is ridiculous!"

"Women are so gullible," remarked Bradford. "So this neighbor of yours. Was she friends with your sister-in-law?"

"Yes," Midge replied in disgust. "More like a spy, really. Mildred Willow took great pleasure in peeking through windows and hiding behind bushes, the nosy old bitty. I'm glad she's dead."

"I advise you not to say that in court," warned Bradford, removing a legal pad from his briefcase and jotting down a few notes.

"I like her kid, Thomas," Midge continued, gazing out the window at the house next door. "He's a good sort. Works as a stock boy at the drug store and on weekends helps some of the older folks on the street by mowing their grass and running errands. His parents left him the house and he lives there now with his grandmother."

"His father is dead?" Katie asked.

"Yes, heart attack nine years ago," replied Midge, then added scornfully. "Perhaps that why his wife spent most of her time butting into other people's business. Had nothing better to do."

It was nearly dinner time when Katie glanced at her watch and announced that she should be getting home. The only thing that they seemed to have accomplished was to uncover proof of Midge's guilt and upset her with each passing minute.

"This certainly didn't get us anywhere," Katie whispered to Jim as they stood to leave.

"Well, I suppose it's better to clear things up before she goes to trial," he responded.

E.M. offered to stay behind and help clean up the dishes as the others collected their coats and walked towards the door.

"So, when Midge said that Tom here is your friend," said Bradford, turning towards Katie as Jim helped her on with her coat. "Did she mean "friend-friend" or something more."

"She meant that I'm Katie's boyfriend," replied Jim. "And, for the last time, my name is Jim."

"Well then, honey," said Bradford smoothly, ignoring Jim completely. "We could still have some fun, you and me. After all, boyfriends come and go."

"Not this one," replied Katie, taking Jim's hand. "And most certainly not for you."

Bradford only chuckled as he put on his hat and turned toward the driveway where his rental car was parked. Katie and Jim turned away from him and walked in the opposite direction where Jim's car was parked around the corner.

"Oh, just a minute, darling," Jim said as he held the passenger side door open for her. "I think I left my notepad at Midge's. Go ahead and wait for me in the car and I'll be right back. It'll only take me a minute."

Katie settled inside and was just going over Midge's story in her mind when, true to his word, Jim reappeared only seconds later.

"False alarm," he declared, sliding into the driver's seat next to her and turning on the ignition. "It was in my jacket pocket the whole time."

He pulled away from the curb and turned the corner, passing Midge's house just in time for Katie to see Bradford Sinclair sitting on the ground by his car. His legs were splayed out in front of him and his hat was lying in the grass several feet away. He was rocking back and forth and covering his right eye with his hand.

Katie paused for a moment before glancing over at Jim. He was looking straight ahead, his hands holding tightly to the steering wheel.

"Jim?" she asked.

"Yes, Katie?"

She glanced in the side mirror at the shrinking figure of Bradford struggling to his feet and turning to search for his hat.

"Oh nothing," she replied, looking down at her hands to hide her smile. "Never mind."

CHAPTER 9
THE TRIAL

Katie and Gran were just sitting down to breakfast the next morning when Andrews entered the dining room and solemnly announced that a Mr. Connor was there to see Katie.

"Mr. Connor of the *Fairfield Gazette*?" exclaimed Katie in surprise. With all that was happening with Midge, she had nearly forgotten that she had been fired yesterday morning.

"Yes, Miss," Andrews confirmed. "I told him that you were at breakfast, but he was rather insistent that he speak with you."

"Well, show the gentleman in, Andrews," Gran instructed. "Perhaps he'll have a cup of coffee with us."

Katie rose to her feet as the butler left the room to retrieve her former boss. "Gran," she began. "There's something I forgot to tell you."

"There usually is, Katie dear," replied Gran dryly, as she poured some cream into her coffee cup.

"But you see…" continued Katie just as Mr. Tom Connor entered the dining room.

"Katie!" exclaimed Mr. Connor, coming toward her with his hand extended and a smile on his face. He grasped her hand and shook it firmly. "How do you do, ma'am," he said, looking past Katie and nodding to Gran.

"Mr. Connor," said Katie, somewhat confused and overwhelmed. "This is my grandmother, Mrs. Agatha Porter. Gran, this is Mr. Connor from the *Gazette*."

"Formerly from the *Gazette*," corrected Mr. Connor.

"Mr. Connor, please join us for breakfast," said Gran, pointing to a chair across from Katie. "Andrews, please get our guest a plate and some silverware."

"Thank you, Mrs. Porter," replied Mr. Connor, taking his place at the table. "Don't mind if I do. Gosh it's nice to see Rosegate again. It's been quite a while. And a perfect time of year! I bet your gardens are in full bloom right now."

"Yes, indeed, Mr. Connor," said Gran, passing him the sugar bowl. "Are you interested in gardening?"

The two of them continued in pleasant conversation for several minutes as Katie sat staring at them, her jaw hanging open.

"Katie, dear, eat your eggs and toast before they get cold," said Gran, finally gazing over at her. "While Mr. Connor tells me what you did yesterday to get yourself fired."

"How on earth did you know that?" responded Katie with surprise.

"Lillian Chishelm," replied Gran calmly. "She's an old friend of mine. She told me all about it when she stopped here yesterday afternoon on her way to catch a train to New York. Young Amelia was with her. She's left her husband and has gone to live with her sister in the city. Amelia will go to school there and begin therapy for her speech impediment. When she turns 16, she'll attend Julliard on the scholarship she was awarded at the Little Miss Daisy Beauty Pageant. Mr. Radcliff was quite taken with her after hearing her performance with Jim."

"Oh how wonderful!" exclaimed Katie, clapping her hands together. "Amelia's therapy and scholarship, that is. Not the fact that Lillian has left her husband."

"Drastic actions are sometimes needed," replied her grandmother mildly. "Besides, I believe it's gotten the attention of her husband, isn't that right Mr. Connor?"

"Yes, indeed," agreed Tom Connor, taking a bite of toast. "Especially when he realized that he had fired the *Gazette's* most talented reporter and was now without someone to cover the pageant story."

"Of course, the story would have been about Amelia and the scholarship," added Gran. "And not the winner of the competition."

"Since you know so much, Gran," teased Katie. "Would you happen to know who won?"

"Yes, of course," Gran smiled. "It was Eleanor Sullivan, of course. And that spunky little girl, Elizabeth Whitting, was runner-up."

"Wonderful," Katie replied and then sighed. "Well at least something wonderful came out of all that craziness! I almost wish I had been there to see it."

"Well, if it's that important to you, I can give you the same assignment next year," said Mr. Connor.

"You seem to forget, sir," replied Katie sadly. "I no longer work for the *Gazette*."

"Neither do I, come to think of it," chuckled her former editor. "You see, I've resigned from the paper."

"What?" exclaimed Katie.

"Yes," replied Mr. Connor. "When Richard Chishelm called me up to tell me that he had fired you and Jim Fielding, even though Jim's with the *Times*, over something as silly as helping his daughter at the pageant, well, I guess I lost my temper and told him I quit."

"Oh no! Mr. Connor, please tell me you didn't!" replied Katie.

"Yes, I'm afraid so," he replied chuckling. "When I announced it to the pressroom, E.M. Butler stood up and announced that he, too, was quitting."

"No!" cried Katie, looking at Mr. Connor in shock.

"Oh, yes!" replied Mr. Connor and then he started counting on his fingers as he recited the names. "Then Max Browning and Helen Murphy, our two financial reporters, quit as well as our receptionist Nancy Applegate, Mel Barkley in sports, and Patrick Grant, our Archivist. The next thing I knew, nearly the entire staff had quit, including Midge Pennington who submitted an actual letter of resignation since she's at home. I think the only people left are Jane Milligan, our advice columnists, who doesn't get along with anyone anyway, and Paul Murray, who is away on vacation and probably hasn't heard the news yet. So, basically, our publisher woke up this morning and found that he has no paper to publish."

"Oh dear!" replied Katie, heartsick and worried. "I'm terribly sorry to cause so many people such distress but I stand by what Jim did! He stood up for the little girl and…"

"Now don't get excited, Katie," said Gran, holding up her hand. "We all know what Jim did and we applaud his actions. It was the right thing to do and Richard had no reason to fire you."

"Yes, it's the unfairness of it all that has everyone upset," added Mr. Connor. "And the fact that you are a member of our *Fairfield Gazette* family. We protect each other and stand up for one another in times like these. Besides, Richard Chishelm has always been a bully and it's about time he gets what's coming to him!"

"What do you mean?" asked Katie, thoughts of violence running through her mind.

"This evening there will be a meeting of all the *Gazette's* shareholders," replied Gran, spreading a healthy helping of strawberry jam on her toast. "I don't like to mention it, of course, but I happen to own shares in the newspaper."

"You never told me that, Gran!" exclaimed Katie. "Is that the real reason I got the job at the newspaper?" she asked, turning to Mr. Connor.

"No, indeed!" exclaimed the editor. "You got the job because you were able to prove to me that you were a good reporter. I'll never forget the articles you wrote about Sunset Hill. I didn't even know your grandmother was a shareholder until very recently."

"The majority shareholder," murmured Gran grimly. "And I intend to take care of Mr. Richard Chishelm and his tyrannical behavior toward my friend Lillian, and his daughter Amelia, and my granddaughter. You mark my words. Everyone will be back at the *Fairfield Gazette* by this time tomorrow!"

"I can't wait to see his expression when he sees you at the meeting, Mrs. Porter," chuckled Mr. Conner, reaching over for another piece of toast. "But, then again, I won't be there, will I? I don't think they allow former employees to attend."

"Gracious!" exclaimed Katie, shaking her head. "This certainly has been an interesting way to start the day!"

* * *

The expression on the faces of the jury were solemn as they entered the courtroom and took their seats. Not one of them looked at Midge Pennington sitting at the defendants table next to her attorney.

"That's not a good sign," Ruth whispered to Katie who was seated next to her in the visitor's section. "Poppy always says that a jury that doesn't look at a defendant doesn't want to feel empathy for that person."

"I believe that's only after they've decided on the verdict," replied Katie. "Or I hope that's the case," she added, looking intently at them.

"All rise," shouted the bailiff and everyone stood as the Honorable Judge James White, known affectionately as "Poppy" to Katie and his family, strolled into the room and took his chair behind the judge's bench, which loomed three steps up above the courtroom floor. He wore his black judicial robe and held several notebooks in his arm which he then placed gently on the desktop in front of him. His expression was grim as he looked over and nodded at the bailiff.

"You may be seated," said the officer and then, looking down at a document in his hand, turned to the judge and announced, "Your Honor, this is case number 3180, The State vs. Mrs. Margaret Louise Pennington on the charge of murder in the first degree."

"Thank you, Officer Kennedy," said Poppy, nodding once again to the bailiff. "Will the Clerk of the Court now read the charge."

"Your Honor," said the middle-aged woman seated behind the small table next to the judge's bench. "On the evening of November 8, 1942, at or about 6:00 pm, Mrs. Margaret Pennington murdered her husband, Major William Odom Pennington, in cold blood by striking him in the head with a hammer while he was working in the garage of their private residence at 1033 Second Street in Fairfield. Major Pennington was declared dead at the scene."

"Thank you, Miss Jones," replied Poppy. "The court now recognizes the defense council. Please rise and identify yourself for the record."

"Bradford Sinclair, Attorney at Law, Your Honor, from Chicago, Illinois," declared Bradford, rising to his feet. He was immaculately dressed in a dark blue pinstriped suit and gray tie. He was freshly shaven, and his hair neatly combed back against his head. The only thing strange about him was the black eye he was sporting but those in the courtroom seemed to take no notice.

"Thank you, Mr. Sinclair," nodded Poppy. "And may I add that the court is familiar with your reputation."

"Thank you, Your Honor," replied Bradford.

"Will the defendant now rise," Poppy ordered, and Midge rose to her feet. "Mrs. Pennington, how do you plead?"

"Not guilty, Your Honor," responded Midge firmly, her hands

folded in front of her.

"Very well," replied the judge. "The defense may be seated. The court recognizes the state prosecuting attorney to make his opening statement followed by the defense. You may begin, Mr. Martin."

"Thank you, Your Honor," began the prosecuting attorney, standing and moving from behind the prosecutor's table to better address the jury. "Ladies and gentlemen of the jury, the prosecution will prove beyond a reasonable doubt that the defendant, Margaret Pennington, despised her husband and intended to divorce him. The State also contends that Mrs. Pennington knew that her husband was having an affair and, when he refused to give her a divorce, she flew into a rage, picked up a hammer, and hit him in the head in an attempt to murder him. Sadly, the blow didn't kill him immediately, so Mrs. Pennington waited for her husband to bleed to death before calling the police."

A gasp could be heard throughout the court room and the state attorney paused for a moment to let his words sink in with the jury members who sat motionless, hanging on his every word.

"The State will enter into evidence testimony from Dr. Henry Winfield, the coroner who examined the body of Major Pennington at the scene, Mrs. Robert Elliot, a next door neighbor of several years, and Detective Harrell Cunningham of the Fairfield Police Department, who was called to the Pennington home and conducted the initial investigation. Additionally, during the trial we will enter in evidence a letter from Mrs. Matthew Willow, now deceased, who wrote from her deathbed to Mrs. Pamela Percy, Major Pennington's sister, stating what she witnessed inside the Pennington garage on the night of the murder."

"Objection!" shouted Bradford Sinclair. "The defense objects to such evidence since we have had no prior opportunity to determine the authenticity of the letter or the ability to cross-examine the writer."

"Overruled," said Judge White. "But the court reserves the right to refuse the admission of the letter into evidence at the time it is presented.

"I wonder what that means," E.M. whispered to Katie. He was seated on her other side, opposite of Ruth.

"It most likely means that Poppy wants to wait and see how the prosecutor intends to use the letter," Katie whispered back.

"We maintain, ladies and gentlemen, that the defendant not only had the motive, she also had the means as the hammer, that we contend is the murder weapon, was discovered only inches away from the body. Mrs. Pennington picked up the weapon and hit her husband in the head and then sat and watched him die. It was the first time that Major Pennington was home on leave and his wife saw her opportunity and took it!"

And, with that, the state prosecutor returned to his table and took his seat.

"Your turn to make your opening statement, Mr. Sinclair," said Poppy White, looking over at Bradford.

"Thank you, Your Honor," replied the attorney, standing and buttoning his jacket. He paused for a moment before strolling around the defense table and coming to a stop several feet away from the jury.

"Ladies and gentlemen of the jury," Bradford began, placing his hands behind his back. "It's only been two years since the end of the war and who can forget our brave men and women who served our country? Risking their lives on the front lines so that we can enjoy the freedom we have today. I'm sure that many of you here answered the call when your country needed you!"

The jury straightened in their chairs as the men, who made up all but two of the seats, nodded their heads.

"So did Major Pennington. He enlisted in the Army and left behind his wife and home soon after the attack on Pearl Harbor…"

"To a cushy assignment in California," E.M. whispered in Katie's ear.

"What you may not know is that Mrs. Pennington also served her country," continued Bradford. "Oh, not in the armed forces, mind you, but to report the war as a civilian war correspondent for the *Associated Press* and for your very own paper, the *Fairfield Gazette*. She didn't have the protection of fellow soldiers, tanks, or planes. Heck, she didn't even carry a sidearm. While we were here, safe and sound enjoying the comfort of our own homes, Mrs. Pennington was dodging bullets so that her friends and hometown neighbors could know what their loved ones were fighting for! What America was fighting for!" And here, Bradford turned and waved his hand dramatically at Midge.

"She didn't have to serve," Bradford reiterated, holding up his hands. "She didn't have to place her life in danger for us all, but she did."

"He makes it sound as though she fought Hitler single handed," said Ruth, a bit chagrined.

"Perhaps it was Midge who gave him that shiner," added E.M. noting his cousin's black eye. "It's a doozy!"

"Hush you two," admonished Katie, although she was smiling. She leaned forward to listen more intently to Bradford. She had to admit that, so far, he seemed to be doing quite well.

"Then finally, she and her husband managed to get their leaves at the same time," the attorney continued. "God only knows how long it had been since the couple last saw each other. They had one lovely week back home together. What bliss! Mrs. Pennington made their supper every night as Major Pennington turned on the radio and poured the wine. Who knows, perhaps they even stepped away from their meal to enjoy a dance or two when they heard one of their favorite songs."

Katie saw Midge begin to roll her eyes and then catch herself when she realized that the jury might be looking.

"Why then, on that tragic Sunday evening, would Mrs. Pennington suddenly take it upon herself to hit her husband in the head with a hammer? Would this truly be the actions of a woman newly home from the war who hadn't seen her husband in several years? No, I say! Not Midge Pennington, war correspondent!"

Bradford paused and walked over to the defense table. He picked up two sheets of paper and glanced over them before addressing the jury once again. "Ladies and gentlemen, I'll tell you exactly what happened on the night of November 8, 1942. Dinner was running a little late, so the Major decided to go into his workshop in the couple's garage to look at the vintage car he had been working on before going off to war. He strolled around the vehicle, coffee cup in hand, when suddenly he stepped on a tiny spot of grease and slipped and fell, hitting his head on the concrete floor and cutting it. It was a small cut but still, like most cuts on the head, it bled profusely. He had landed so hard that he lost consciousness. His wife went out into the garage to summon her husband for dinner only to find him lying there. He was close to death by that time but Mrs. Pennington, overcome with panic and grief, couldn't tell and held him in her arms until finally coming to her senses and running back into the house to call the police."

The two women on the jury gave Midge a sympathetic look. Midge, herself, glanced down at the table.

"My esteemed colleague, here, says it was cold blooded *murder*," declared Bradford, emphasizing the word. "But the defense, ladies and gentlemen, will prove that it was only an unfortunate accident leaving yet another widow during a time of war. Thank you, Your Honor."

One almost expected those in the courtroom to burst out in applause and perhaps Poppy thought so, too, because he quickly called for a 15-minute recess.

"Well, that was rather riveting," declared Ruth, as she and E.M. stood with Katie in the lobby of the courthouse. "It's a shame that Robert had a full schedule in surgery today. But where is Jim?"

"He called me this morning and told me that he'll meet us for lunch at Polly's," Katie replied. "The *Times* brought him back to work earlier than expected to cover the demise of the *Fairfield Gazette*."

"May it rest in peace," smiled E.M., glancing down at his watch.

"Which reminds me," said Katie, throwing her arm around his shoulders. "You didn't have to resign on my account, dear friend. It was awfully sweet of you but what are you going to do for a job?"

"I thought I might come and live with you at Rosegate and become a man of leisure," he teased. "But if that option isn't available, I can always go back to bartending."

"You are always welcome at Rosegate," smiled Katie, giving him a hug. "You could be the brother I never had."

"I would be honored if you would consider me your brother anyway," replied E.M. softly, giving her hand a squeeze. "But I believe that things will work out at the *Gazette* and we will all be happily employed once again."

At that moment, the doors re-opened and court was called back into session.

"Mr. Martin, you may call your first witness," said Judge White, once again seated behind the large judge's bench.

"Thank you, Your Honor," replied the prosecutor. "The prosecution calls Fairfield Police Detective Harrell Cunningham."

Detective Cunningham had been with the Fairfield police department for over 20 years and was well liked in the community. He was a tall, gentle man, married, with six children. He was also an exceptionally good detective and now seemed a bit annoyed at having to rehash a case that was, in his opinion, put to rest five years ago.

"We arrived at the defendant's home at 6:07 pm on the evening of November 8, 1942," stated the detective, reading from his notes. "That was a Sunday and my wife was just putting dinner on the table when I got the call around 6:00 pm."

"What did you find when you arrived at the scene?" Mr. Martin asked.

"Mrs. Pennington was standing in the middle of her driveway and the garage door was open," said Office Cunningham. "She informed us that her husband was dead. Officer Hadley and I entered the garage to find Major Pennington lying on the floor next to an old Packard. There was quite a lot of blood around."

"Did you see anything else? Any tools, for instance?" asked the prosecutor.

"Yes, sir, of course," replied the detective calmly. "Lots. It was a garage with a worktable in it. What else would we see?"

Several of the courtroom spectators chuckled. Katie could see that Detective Cunningham was not going to make the state prosecutor's task an easy one.

"What I mean to ask," said Mr. Martin patiently. "Is whether there was anything close to Major Pennington's body other than the vehicle."

"Yes," replied Officer Cunningham. "There was a hammer, a screwdriver, and a broken coffee mug."

"Thank you, Detective," said the prosecutor, giving him a smile. "Now then, did you speak with Mrs. Pennington?"

"Yes."

"And what did she say?" asked Mr. Martin.

"She told me that she had been fixing dinner and that her husband had gone out to look at the Packard," Officer Cunningham replied, once again looking down at his notes. "When she stepped into the garage to call him in, she found him dead on the ground. She stooped down to check his pulse and then called the police."

"Not an ambulance?"

"No," replied the detective. "She told us that when she saw that he was dead, she decided it better to call the police since an ambulance would be of no use to him."

"Interesting. I imagine Mrs. Pennington was upset. You know, crying and fainting and such," said Mr. Martin.

"Not crying or fainting, sir, like most women," noted Detective Cunningham, casting a glance at Midge. "She was upset, of course, but not hysterical. More on the shocked side I would say."

"Objection!" cried Bradford Sinclair, jumping to his feet. "The witness is not a psychologist or psychiatrist so cannot testify to my client's mental state."

"Overruled," said Poppy. "The witness is an experienced police officer of over 20 years and has interviewed many a distraught person in his time. I'm sure Detective Cunningham knows a hysterical woman when he sees one."

This caused laughter in the court room and the witness chuckled and replied, "You're right about that, Your Honor!"

"Now then, Detective, did you notice anything about the defendant's dress?" Mr. Martin asked him.

"She was pretty much covered in blood," replied the officer.

"Isn't that rather unusual for someone who says she just knelt down to check a pulse?"

"Objection!" called Bradford again. "That calls for conjecture."

"Sustained," ruled Poppy.

"I withdraw the question, Your Honor," stated Mr. Martin, walking back to the prosecutor's table and picking up a piece of paper. "Detective Cunningham, the case has been reopened, is that correct?"

"Yes, sir," replied the officer. "Your office called me last week."

"And what did my office ask you to do?"

"Your office asked me to investigate an argument that had occurred on the afternoon of November 8, 1942, at Fairfield's downtown supermarket."

"And did you do that investigation?" continued Mr. Martin.

"Yes sir, I did."

"And who did you discover was involved in this argument?" asked the prosecutor.

"Mr. and Mrs. Pennington," replied the detective.

"And this was on the same day that Major Pennington was found dead, was it not?"

"Yes, it was on the same day," confirmed Detective Cunningham.

"And, even though it's been five years, were you able to find witnesses to this supermarket argument?" Mr. Martin asked.

"Yes," replied the detective. "A Mrs. Sarah Haverson. She remembered clearly because she got pelted with a tomato thrown by Mrs. Pennington."

This produced more laughter from the spectators and this time Judge White had to pound his gavel.

"Quiet, please," he shouted, although he, himself, was trying hard not to laugh. "There will be quiet in the courtroom."

"Thank you, Detective," said Mr. Martin, returning to his seat behind the prosecutor's table. "I have no further questions for this witness."

"Mr. Sinclair," Poppy began, glancing up at the large clock in the courtroom. "It is nearly noontime. Are you agreeable to postponing your cross-examination of this witness until after lunch?"

"Yes, certainly, Your Honor," replied Bradford.

"Thank you," said Poppy. "Then we are adjourned until 1:00." And he gaveled the courtroom into recess.

* * *

"So they've found out about the supermarket tomato assault, hey?" Jim remarked, as he, Katie, Ruth, and E.M. seated themselves in their favorite booth in Polly's Café.

"Yes," chuckled Katie. "You know, I've always wondered about that."

"What? Whether Midge is capable of nailing someone with a tomato?" Jim asked, chuckling.

"Oh, she's quite capable of that!" declared E.M., glancing over the menu.

"No, not that silly," replied Katie. "How the prosecutor's office found out about it? Someone must have told them. After all, it's not something that would have necessarily made the papers."

"Especially if Mrs. Haverson was involved," Ruth agreed. "People like that try and avoid publicity. Perhaps that same nosy neighbor that wrote the letter found out about it and told Midge's sister-in-law just to add fuel to the fire."

"You're forgetting that our notorious letter writer is dead," Katie replied. "The letter most likely arrived after she was gone and before Pamela could squeeze more ammunition from her. And I think that if Pamela knew about the argument earlier, she would have used it five years ago."

"Speaking of ammunition," said Jim. "It looks like quite a lot of it was flying at the *Gazette's* shareholder's meeting last night. I got only a few words out of the recording secretary in the form of 'we anticipate that there will be some changes' and 'the official word will be made public soon' but I was able to interview your grandmother."

"Gran gave you an interview?" exclaimed Katie, somewhat surprised.

"Well, perhaps calling it an interview is a slight exaggeration," Jim replied. "She only said that the meeting was full of lively debate and that the results turned out to be quite satisfying."

"That doesn't sound like much," remarked E.M. pouting slightly. "Do we still have our jobs or not?"

"Mrs. Porter said she will tell us everything tonight at dinner and we're all invited!" Jim exclaimed, smiling broadly. "My gut tells me that your publisher got the boot!"

They paused for a moment when the waitress appeared to take their order and then returned to the topic of the trial.

"It will be Bradford's turn to question Detective Cunningham when we return," Katie remarked. "And I must say that, so far, your cousin's done a good job, E.M."

"Yes, I have to agree with you," replied E.M. "Especially turning Midge into a war widow."

"Well she is, in a manner of speaking," said Ruth, smiling. "She did become a widow during a time of war. Just not in the way his opening argument implies."

"That's just like an attorney," grumbled Jim, but then smiled as the waitress began to place their sandwiches on the table in front of them.

"Your pie, sir," she added, sliding a large slice of apple pie alongside his plate.

"Funny, I don't recall you ordering pie," said E.M. looking over at him.

"It comes automatically whenever Jim enters Polly's," replied Katie, giving Jim an affectionate nudge.

"You're just jealous," he replied, wrinkling up his nose at her.

"Can we continue with Midge's case, please, before you two get out of hand?" E.M. teased, lifting his sandwich and taking a bite.

"I was wondering," Ruth said, continuing with their previous conversation, "whether Midge got any financial compensation from the army since her husband was in the service at the time of his death.

"Hm, interesting point," said Jim, shaking his head. "I'm pretty sure she would have received some sort of survivor's benefit, but all bets would be off, of course, if she was the one who killed him."

"Except that his death was originally deemed an accident," replied Katie thoughtfully. "Making it rather inconvenient if she's found guilty now although I can't believe army compensation would have ever entered Midge's mind when she lost her husband."

"And surely she wouldn't kill him and then make it look like an accident just for the survivor's benefits," Ruth added.

"Certainly not," agreed E.M. "I'd be willing to bet she never even filed for it. And remember, Midge wouldn't have needed it anyway. She had her own income as a war correspondent."

"She may not have needed the small amount given by the army," Katie said suddenly, dropping her sandwich back on her plate. "But the amount from a life insurance policy would certainly go a long way!"

"Katie, how could you even think that!" cried E.M., putting down his glass and glaring at her.

"E.M., I don't really believe for one minute that Midge killed her husband," Katie assured him, reaching over and squeezing his hand. "But, as we talked before, it would be nice to know if she had a policy on the major and, if so, for how much."

"The prosecutor will definitely bring it up if she did," added Jim.

"Yes, I suppose that's true," replied E.M. frowning. "As you well know, Midge is a very private person, not that I would have asked her about such a thing anyway. I remember there was a small funeral made up of the staff from his bank and a few of her colleagues from the *Gazette*. And I was there, of course. I picked up the tab for the flowers, but Midge paid for everything else: the casket, hearse, the priest, and the gravestone. All without so much as a penny of help from his sister...the old bat!"

"Didn't the military help out in any way?" asked Jim, raising his eyebrows. "Send an honor guard or at least a flag for the casket?"

"No, Midge said that she rejected their offer," E.M. replied with a shrug. "She said that Pennington specifically told her that he didn't want such a fuss when he died."

"Now that's rather odd," remarked Jim, gazing out the window. "But I suppose a fancy funeral isn't everyone's cup of tea."

"Would you want a military funeral, Jim?" Ruth asked, glancing over at him as she pushed her empty plate to one side. "After all, you served your country and in one of the most important battles."

Jim had his hand resting in his lap under the table and he felt Katie slip her hand into his and grasp it tightly. Neither of them looked at each other. "No, I don't think so, Ruthie," he replied after a moment. "I'll save that for the real heroes like your brother and E.M. here."

"And I'm never going to die," E.M. announced. "So there's no use making any plans other than we'd better get a move on. The trial is scheduled to start again in ten minutes!"

They made it back to the courthouse, and into their seats, just as Ruth's father was entering from the side door that led from his judge's chambers. Jim was with them this time and wedged himself in between Ruth and Katie.

"All rise!" announced the bailiff. "The court is now in session, the Honorable Judge White presiding."

"Thank you, Officer Kennedy," said Poppy, settling in behind the bench. "You may be seated. Mr. Sinclair, I believe it is your turn to cross-examine the witness. Bailiff, would you please recall Detective Harrell Cunningham to the stand."

"Thank you, Your Honor," replied Bradford, standing as Detective Cunningham stepped back into the witness stand and took a seat.

"Remember, Harrell," said Poppy from above. "You're still under oath."

"Yes, Your Honor," replied the detective, nodding his head. "I remember."

"Now then," began Bradford, coming forward to stand by the witness. "Since you are a police officer of long standing and considered an expert by the court, I'd like to ask you about what you observed at the Pennington home on Sunday, November 8, 1942. Most specifically at the scene of the accident."

Detective Cunningham nodded. "Yes, sir," he mumbled.

"Good," replied Bradford. "You told the court that you noticed Mrs. Pennington's dress covered in blood, is that correct?"

"Yes, sir," replied the witness. "She had quite a lot of blood on her."

"And how much blood would you say was on the floor of the garage?" asked Bradford.

"Oh, quite a lot sir," said the detective, nodding.

"By quite a lot, would you say enough to cover her husband's clothing?"

"Yes, especially his shirt," replied Harrell Cunningham.

"I see," said Bradford. "How about the hammer, screwdriver, and coffee mug? Were those covered with blood. After all, they were lying on the floor next to Major Pennington's body."

"I don't honestly remember about the hammer and screwdriver," replied the detective, glancing down at his notes. "I see that I didn't make any notes about those. I did note that the handle of the coffee mug was broken off."

"Well perhaps I can refresh your memory," said Bradford. "If it pleases the court, Your Honor, I would like to enter into evidence pictures 1-a through 1-f, 6 pictures in all, of the accident scene at 1033 Second Street, Fairfield, the residence of Major and Mrs. Pennington." Bradford handed the pictures up to the judge who glanced through them briefly.

"Any objections, counselor?" Poppy asked Mr. Martin, looking over at the prosecutor.

"No objections, Your Honor," replied Mr. Martin.

"The court will accept the photos into evidence, Mr. Sinclair," replied Poppy White, handing them down to the clerk of the court to record.

"Thank you, Your Honor," nodded Bradford. "Now for purposes of clarity, I have had each photograph enlarged and mounted on poster board so that they can be displayed properly for the jury. These are the exact same pictures, Your Honor, so I am not requesting that these copies be placed in evidence."

Judge White raised his eyebrows and looked over at Mr. Martin.

"Oh, we have no objections," said the prosecutor, waving his hand in the direction of Bradford Sinclair. "We are indeed grateful for the efforts towards clarity made by the defense."

Bradford nodded toward the bailiff who quickly brought forward an easel, placing it near the witness stand and in view of the jury. The attorney then walked over and placed the first picture on the easel and stepped to one side. It was the one showing the bloody image of the body lying next to the Packard. Some of the spectators cringed but the members of the jury sat looking on without emotion.

"Is this the body of Major Pennington in his garage at 1033 Second Street, Fairfield?" Bradford asked.

"Yes sir," nodded Detective Cunningham. "That's him."

"For the record, the defense agrees that there is indeed quite a lot of blood," stated Bradford, looking in the general direction of the court reporter. "Now then," he continued, placing the second picture on the easel, over the first picture. This one was the broader angle which showed more of the scene. "Is this the same scene as shown in the first picture?"

Detective Cunningham leaned closer. "Yes, sir," he replied. "The photographer just stepped back a few feet to get a broader shot."

"Yes, thank you Detective," responded Bradford.

"What is he doing?" whispered E.M. "Trying to shock the jury?"

"No," replied Katie, whispering back. "Just wait and see. I think I know where he's going with this!"

Bradford then put up picture number three, showing Midge in the bloody dress. "And who is this woman in the photograph?"

"Why, that's Mrs. Pennington," declared Harrell Cunningham. "The defendant."

"And is this woman now present in the courtroom?"

"Yes, sir," replied the detective, nodding to Midge. "That's her over there."

"Let the record show that Detective Cunningham has identified the defendant as Mrs. Margaret Pennington," said Bradford. "And I would agree with you, Detective, there is certainly a lot of blood on Mrs. Pennington's dress." he added.

"Yes, sir," nodded the officer.

Bradford Sinclair then removed the picture of Midge, showing once again the broad picture of Major Pennington and the scene in the garage.

"So, with so much blood around," said Bradford, strolling away from the witness, his hands behind his back. "Where is the blood on the walls and on the side of the car?"

"Bingo!" whispered Katie, smiling. "There it is, E.M."

"There isn't any," replied Detective Cunningham, smiling. "Or not enough for the human eye to see."

"But surely if Mrs. Pennington had whacked her husband in the head with a hammer there would have been blood spatter all over the walls, would there not, Detective Cunningham?" Bradford asked, turning to the witness.

"Yes sir," replied Harrell. "There should have been blood spatter all over the place, but we didn't find any."

"Interesting," said Bradford. "Is that why you ruled it an accident?"

"Objection, Your Honor," shouted Mr. Martin, jumping to his feet. "Mr. Sinclair is leading the witness!"

"I'll rephrase the question," smiled Bradford. "Did you draw any conclusions from this lack of blood spatter?"

"Yes," replied the detective. "We concluded that the victim must have started bleeding after he hit the concrete floor of the garage due to slipping and falling."

"I see," nodded Bradford. "And what made you think Major Pennington slipped and fell?"

"Because the workshop was a mess, Mr. Sinclair," replied the detective. "I nearly slipped and fell a few times myself."

Bradford walked over to the easel and placed the fifth picture, showing the worktable and broken shelf, in front of the others.

"Is this what you mean?" he asked the detective.

"Yes, that's it," replied Cunningham. "That's what we found when we did our investigation. There were containers of stuff leaking all over the place and a dirty rag where someone had started to clean up."

"I see," replied Bradford, placing the final picture on the easel. "This picture shows that the body has been removed as well as the hammer, screwdriver, and coffee mug. Can you tell us what happened to these items?"

"The body was sent to the morgue and the other items collected as evidence," replied the detective. "However, we returned them to Mrs. Pennington two weeks later at her place of employment, the *Fairfield Gazette*."

"Why the *Gazette*?" Bradford asked.

"Because Mrs. Pennington had already returned to France to cover the war," replied Detective Cunningham, giving Midge an admiring glance.

"Indeed," murmured Bradford. "Now, Detective Cunningham, I won't keep you much longer but I'm curious as to why the prosecuting attorney's office would want to reopen the case after you and your team had done such a thorough job in determining it to be an accident? Would you please tell the court what you know?"

"I received a call from Mr. Martin's secretary about a week ago," replied Harrell Cunningham. "She informed me that Mr. Martin had received a call from Mrs. Pamela Percy, Major Pennington's sister, requesting that the case be reopened."

"Did she say on what grounds?"

"Yes, she told me that Mrs. Percy had been sent a letter from one of the Pennington's neighbors saying that she had witnessed Mrs. Pennington murdering her husband."

"Ah, you didn't mention that when asked by Mr. Martin," Bradford remarked. "And you were also asked to investigate the argument in the supermarket, is that right, Detective?"

"Yes sir," replied the officer, glancing over at the prosecutor. "I was told that an argument had taken place between Major and Mrs. Pennington in the downtown supermarket on the afternoon of the major's death and Mr. Martin wanted me to see if anyone at the store remembered it."

"Thank you," said Bradford. "No further questions, Your Honor."

"You may step down," Poppy directed, and the detective left the stand quickly. "You may call your next witness, Mr. Martin."

"Thank you, Your Honor," said Mr. Martin. "The prosecution calls Dr. Henry Winfield."

Dr. Winfield was the Fairfield Police Department's Coroner. Katie had met him just two months earlier when she was nearly killed by a sociopath named Dorothy Smith who had hurled them both over the side of a cliff. Katie had fortunately managed to grab hold of a tree root stopping her plummet to the ground 100 feet below. Dorothy, however, had not been so lucky and it was Dr. Winfield who had examined the woman's body and pronounced her dead at the scene.

"Doctor," began Mr. Martin. "How long have you been the police coroner here in Fairfield?"

"12 years this March, except for my service in the navy during the war," the doctor replied.

"Were you the one who examined the body of Major Pennington and certified that he was dead?" asked Mr. Martin.

"Yes," nodded Dr. Winfield.

"And to what do you attribute the cause of death?" asked the prosecutor.

"Major Pennington bled to death from a deep cut on his forehead."

"Dr. Winfield, can you tell us, based on your expertise, how long the victim had been dead?"

"Around 15 minutes making the time between 5:45 pm and 6:00 pm," replied Dr. Winfield.

"Really? You can be that precise?"

"Not normally, no," replied the coroner. "But in the case of the major, his wife told us that she had sent him out to the garage as she was trying to finish fixing their meal and he was underfoot. She told us that he left the kitchen no earlier than 5:45 pm and she found him dead at approximately 6:00 pm."

"Do you always take the word of a witness? Especially a spouse?"

"Not entirely, of course," smiled Dr. Winfield. "I took the temperature of the body."

"Please explain to the jury why taking the temperature of the corpse would be pertinent in establishing time of death," remarked Mr. Martin, stepping away from the coroner and pausing in the center of the room.

"Mr. Martin," interrupted Poppy. "I'm going to ask that you be a little less descriptive and refer to Major Pennington as "the deceased" or "the body." After all, his widow is in the room and she is innocent of the charge unless you can prove that she's guilty."

The prosecuting attorney turned and looked at Midge sitting behind the defense table as if he just now realized that she was, indeed, in the courtroom. "My apologies, Your Honor," he replied, and then nodding to Midge added, "ma'am."

"Thank you, counselor," said Poppy. "You may proceed, Dr. Winfield."

"Well you see, a cor…I mean…well, let me start by saying that a normal temperature for a living human is 98.6. When we die, our body stops producing internal heat and it gradually begins to gain or lose heat until it reaches equilibrium with the temperature around us. This change occurs by one and one half a degree per hour. So, if a witness saw a man at 1:00 and then the man was found dead at 4:00, we would multiply 1.5 degrees by 4 hours, which comes to 6 degrees of temperature loss. We simply subtract 6 degrees from the normal temperature of 98.6 and then check to see if the deceased's temperature is 92.6. If so, that would tell us that the man was most likely dead for the entire 4 hours he was missing."

"Very interesting, Doctor," replied Mr. Martin. "Would that gain or loss in temperature also depend on the temperature surrounding the body?"

"Yes," nodded the doctor. "We have to allow some variance in our calculations if the body is found in extreme environmental conditions."

"What was the temperature at 6:00 pm on Sunday, November 8, 1942?" asked Mr. Martin.

"Well, let's see," answered Dr. Winfield, glancing down at his notepad. "Yes, here it is. Being that it was November, it was cold, but around 63 degrees which we don't consider an extreme condition."

"So, what was the temperature of the cor…I mean the body when you took its temperature?"

"It was 98.0, Mr. Martin," replied the coroner. "Indicating that the victim had been dead for no longer than one hour."

"I see," replied the prosecutor, nodding. "And how long does it take for a person to bleed to death under normal conditions."

"Around five minutes, sir," replied Dr. Winfield.

"Thank you, Doctor," said Mr. Martin. "I have no further questions. Your witness, Mr. Sinclair."

"Dr. Winfield," began Bradford, barely looking up from his notes. "Detective Cunningham stated that Major Pennington's body was sent to the morgue. Was there an autopsy performed?"

"No sir," replied the coroner.

"Really? Why not?" asked Bradford.

"Because the morgue is part of the hospital, sir, and they're always very busy over there."

"Busy or not, surely all bodies found in such circumstances undergo an autopsy?"

"Only about 50 percent of bodies sent to the hospital morgue *are* autopsied, sir," replied Dr. Winfield defensively. "And even fewer in cases of an accident, which was deemed the case with Major Pennington."

"Yes, indeed," replied Bradford. "Thank you, doctor. I have no further questions, Your Honor."

"Well then, Dr. Winfield," said Poppy, leaning slightly toward the witness. "You may step down. Ladies and gentlemen, it has gotten rather late so we will continue tomorrow morning at 10:00 am. Court is adjourned until tomorrow."

"Why all that fuss about body temperature?" E.M. asked as they gathered up their coats and turned to leave.

"Because if Major Pennington died during that very short period of time," Katie answered grimly. "It puts Midge as the only person at the scene of the crime."

CHAPTER 10
MR. CHISHELM

"Something's not right about this whole thing," said Katie, taking a glass of sherry from the tray held by Andrews. "I have this feeling that the key to Midge's innocence is staring us right in the face, but for some reason we're not seeing it."

"You'll figure it out, Katie," said Jim, looking over at her fondly. "You always do."

"I think you're a bit biased, sir," she replied, smiling. She slid down on the couch next to him. "But let's review what we already know and see if any of us can figure it out."

The group had left the courthouse and driven over to Rosegate for their dinner meeting with Gran. Katie and E.M. were especially anxious to find out whether they had gotten their jobs back at the *Fairfield Gazette*. Gran had met them at the door and asked them to enjoy cocktails in the library while she made a phone call and waited for a few more guests, including Mr. and Mrs. Connor.

"We know that Midge is innocent," said E.M., strolling over to the fireplace with his drink in hand.

"No, we assume she's innocent," said Jim. "We don't actually know that for a fact."

"She's innocent, Fielding, and you know it!" declared E.M., turning swiftly to face Jim.

"Now, now, you two," said Katie, holding up her hand. "Let's just say we'll work on the premise that she is. What do we know for certain as fact?"

"Major Pennington was found lying on the floor in his garage at 6:00 pm," said Ruth.

"Yes, good, Ruthie," replied Katie, putting down her drink and getting up from the couch to retrieve some paper from the desk in the corner. "We know that there was a lot of blood around and that there was a cut on his head."

"We know that there was no blood spatter," said Jim, watching Katie jot down the notes.

"We know that Midge's dress was covered in blood," added Katie. "And we know that it was Midge who discovered her husband."

"And that he was dead," added Ruth.

"He wasn't," replied Katie, shaking her head. "Midge told the police that he was, and he was when they arrived. But she admitted to us that he was alive when she found him and that he died in her lap."

"Oh, dear," muttered Ruth softly.

"We know that the worktable was a mess and that a shelf was broken," said Jim.

"And the shelf broke recently because there were several containers lying on their sides with their contents leaking out," added Katie, writing quickly.

"And there was a rag on the bench that may have indicated the beginnings of a cleanup," added Jim.

"I'll give you the rag, but we don't know if it was being used to clean up the spilled liquids," Katie pointed out.

"We know that he died between 5:45 and 6:00 pm," said Ruth. "And that a person can bleed to death within 5 minutes."

"And we know, for certain, that Midge was alone and in the house during that time," Katie said softly.

"We know she was in the house," said E.M., joining in for the first time. "But do we know for certain that she was alone? She only mentioned she was alone after the police came if you recall."

"Yes, that true!" remarked Katie, nodding. "Great point, E.M.! That's something we'll definitely need to find out! A visitor could provide Midge with an alibi."

"Lastly, we know that the Penningtons had an argument in Fairfield's downtown supermarket," said Jim. "And that Mrs. Haverson witnessed it."

"What I don't understand is why the state attorney thinks Midge killed her husband when the blow was to his forehead," said Ruth.

"One would think that a wife would sneak up behind her husband if she wanted to whack him with a hammer."

"Hmm, that's true," replied Katie thoughtfully. "I certainly would kill my husband that way."

"Really? What a thought!" exclaimed Jim, his eyes twinkling. "You'd sneak up and hit the poor unsuspecting man in the back of the head?"

"Well, she'd have to," remarked E.M. "Otherwise, you'd see her coming and stop her. I mean, her husband would. I think that's why most wives use poison instead. Doesn't require them to fend off their stronger husbands."

"What if Midge was able to surprise him?" Ruth continued. "You know, sneak up on him with hammer in hand, tap him on the shoulder, and then wham!"

"I'm beginning to have serious concerns for Robert's safety," joked Jim. "Shall I warn him before your wedding?"

"Maybe," chuckled Ruth. "But I do agree with E.M.'s method. Poison is much less troublesome and doesn't leave such a mess."

"I think that Major Pennington would have heard Midge walking across the concrete floor," Jim pointed out. "Even in bare feet."

"Let's try an experiment," said Katie, jumping up from the couch and walking over to pick up Gran's newspaper. "Jim, stand over here by the back of Gran's chair. You are the major and the chair is the Packard."

Jim got up from the couch and walked over to the chair, facing the back of it. Katie stepped several feet away, rolling up the newspaper and holding it in her hand.

"Are you ready Major?" she asked Jim.

"Yes, you can kill me whenever you're ready," he chuckled.

They repeated the exercise several times but each time, as Katie silently crept towards him, tapping him on the shoulder and attempting to hit him in the forehead, Jim was quick enough to spin around and grab her wrist or the newspaper. They even tried it without the tap. Still, he was able to fend off her attack.

"It's because I either hear a rustling behind me or sense someone coming," he told them.

"But if that someone was your wife, you might be used to having her come up behind you," said Ruth. "And not be alarmed by her approach."

"Yes, that's true," replied Katie, nodding. "But even then, I just didn't have enough time to get in a good swing before Jim turned and grabbed my wrist. Perhaps I should come across the room with the hammer already raised?" She walked back to her starting point and Jim once again turned his back on her.

This time she snuck across the room with the newspaper raised high above her head. Nugget, who had been sitting in Gran's chair witnessing the whole scene, started to growl.

"It's OK. friend," Jim said, smiling down at him. "It's just my crazy wife…," and then, suddenly, TAP and WHACK!

"Got 'em!" cried Katie in delight as Jim fell dramatically to the floor. Nugget gave a sharp bark and jumped off the chair to give his face several licks.

"Hey, no fair!" Jim yelled, laughing as Nugget leapt onto his chest. "I was distracted!"

"Roll over, Fielding," instructed Katie. "You're not supposed to be face up. Remember, Midge found the major face down."

Jim dutifully rolled over, much to the disappointment of Nugget.

"Now Midge, still holding the hammer in her hand, would have sat down…" continued Katie, looking down at Jim. She suddenly froze and her voice started to quiver. "Would have…she would have…"

"Here let me," said Ruth, quickly stepping forward. She gently moved her friend to one side and took the newspaper from her hand. "Midge would have dropped down on the ground and rolled her husband onto her lap to see if she had succeeded in killing him."

Ruth dropped down next to Jim and, with the newspaper still in her hand, tried unsuccessfully to roll him over and onto her lap.

"I can't do it without putting down the hammer," explained Ruth, setting the crumpled rolled up newspaper to one side.

"Oh!" gasped E.M. "That's exactly where the hammer ended up in the photographs. Right next to the body."

"Now I can do it," continued Ruth, rolling Jim's head and shoulders onto her lap. "All I have to do now is wait until he dies," she added, unconsciously running her fingers through Jim's hair. He relaxed and closed his eyes.

"You don't mind if I take my time, do you?" he said, smiling. "This feels rather nice."

"What on earth are you children doing?" came a voice from the doorway. They looked up to see Gran standing with her hands on her hips. "And what happened to my newspaper?"

Jim quickly rolled off Ruth's lap and jumped to his feet, bending to give Ruth a helping hand. Meanwhile Katie, regaining her composure, bent down and picked up the newspaper.

"We were demonstrating how a wife might murder her husband," said Ruth, blushing slightly at the admission.

"And this was the murder weapon," Katie added, placing the newspaper back on Gran's side table.

"I see," replied Gran, a twinkle in her eyes. "Well I hope you and Ruthie figure out which husband is which before the killing starts." Now it was Katie's turn to blush, and she did so down to her roots.

"She could have done it," E.M. whispered in Katie's ear, moving over to her. His hands were shaking.

"No, E.M.," Katie responded firmly. "There's no way and we're going to prove it!"

"I see our guests have arrived," said Gran, glancing out the window. "Shall we go greet them?" she added, stepping out into the hallway as Andrews made his way to the front door. Ruth and E.M. turned and followed her, but Jim caught hold of Katie's arm, pulling her back for a moment.

"Darling," he said, wrapping her in his arms. "It's over and I'm very much alive."

"I know," she mumbled into his chest. "It was silly of me but when I realized that I would be pulling you onto my lap…"

"You don't need to explain anything to me," he interrupted, holding her close. "I, of all people, know what it's like to suddenly relive a bad memory."

"Ah, there you are," they heard Gran exclaim from the hallway. "Please come in. It's nice to see you again."

Katie and Jim joined Ruth and E.M. just in time to see a handsome young man enter the house and reach out to gently shake Mrs. Porter's hand. He had wavy black hair and dark brown eyes that held an expression of amusement as he turned toward the group standing a few feet away.

"Peter, please allow me to introduce my granddaughter, Katie Porter," said Gran, holding her hand out in the direction of Katie.

"So nice to meet you," Katie replied, not having the least idea if it really was.

"The pleasure is all mine, Miss Porter," said Peter, giving her a slight bow.

"And this is Katie's best friend and our neighbor, Miss Ruth White," continued Gran. "And Mr. E.M. Butler, our good friend from the *Gazette* and Mr. Jim Fielding, our good friend from the *Middleton Times*."

"A pleasure to meet you," smiled the young man, nodding at each in turn. "And all good friends! How fortunate."

"Yes, we are very fortunate," replied Gran. "Please come and join us for a glass of sherry. Or do you prefer scotch?"

"Sherry would be fine, Mrs. Porter," replied Peter, following her down the hall.

At that moment, the front doorbell rang and Katie, being the closest to it, turned to answer it. On the doorstep were Mr. and Mrs. Connor.

"Hello!" Katie said, greeting them. "Please come in! We've been enjoying cocktails in the library!"

"Has Mr. Chishelm arrived yet?" asked Mr. Connor anxiously.

"Excuse me? Mr. Chishelm?" asked Katie, nearly recoiling at the thought. "I thought he was on his way to New York to try and reconcile with his wife?"

"No, not Richard Chishelm!" said Mr. Connor, taking Katie by the arm. "Mr. Peter Chishelm, his nephew."

"Oh!" exclaimed Katie. "Yes, he's just now arrived. He's in the library with the others. Gran just introduced him as Peter."

"Yes, he seems rather hesitant to use his last name here in Fairfield," replied Mr. Connor. "I met him last night. He stopped by the house after the shareholder's meeting to introduce himself and ask me to return to the *Gazette*. He even added a raise in pay. He seems like a very modest young fellow."

"So have you accepted his offer?" Katie asked, walking them down the hall towards the library.

"I told him I'd think about it," smiled Mr. Connor. "A lot depends on what happens during our little meeting here."

The doorbell rang again, causing Katie to exclaim, "Gracious! That may be more guests. It appears that Gran has invited all of Fairfield!" She turned and headed toward the door. "Please go on in and grab a drink," she added, over her shoulder. "I'll be right with you."

She opened the door to find Midge Pennington and Bradford Sinclair standing there. Midge looked tired but relaxed. Bradford, however, stood with an expression of complete awe on his face. "Nice digs you have here, hon…er…Katie," he said, stepping inside and handing Katie his hat.

"Hello, Katie," said Midge, coming in behind him. "It was awfully nice of your grandmother to invite me especially under my current circumstances."

"Well of course," Katie replied, taking her arm. "You are always welcome at Rosegate. I hope you know that. And, now that you're here, I want to thank you. I've been quite taken aback by the support I have received from my newspaper colleagues, especially you, Midge, who has so much to contend with right now. I'm just sorry that everyone felt compelled to resign from their jobs."

"Well, let's hope that's been rectified," replied Midge. "Although I doubt I'll be able to keep my job in jail."

"No one's going to jail, Madge," said Bradford. "I'll get you off, just you wait and see. Well, hello there Dapper!"

E.M. had stepped into the hallway to greet Midge.

"Hello Bradford," he said dryly and then came over and hugged his friend. "Hello Midge! Gosh it's great that you're here! Come, let me get you a drink," he added, wrapping an arm around her shoulders and leading her into the library. Bradford reached to take Katie's arm but she side-stepped him and quickly walked on ahead, entering the library just as Gran was welcoming all their guests.

"Well," Gran was saying. "Now that we're all here, I'd like to introduce our special guest, Mr. Peter Chishelm. I've asked him to come to dinner tonight to discuss what happened at last night's shareholder's meeting of the *Fairfield Gazette*. Peter?"

"Thank you, ma'am," said Peter, stepping forward and standing in front of the room. "Well, first, I'd like to thank Mrs. Porter and Miss Porter for inviting me into their home. It gives me a chance to meet all of you, many of whom are valued members of the *Gazette* staff, as well as inform you of several decisions that were made last night concerning the paper."

Katie sat down next to Jim and he reached over and took her hand.

"I will begin by telling you that my uncle, Mr. Richard Chishelm, has stepped down as publisher of the *Gazette*. To be more accurate, you still have the same publishing firm, but my uncle will not be overseeing the account. You may not know it but the Chishelm, Banks, and Clifford Publishing Company has been publishing the *Fairfield Gazette* for nearly 75 years and we don't plan on giving that up for at least another 75."

Peter paused and glanced around the room before picking up his glass of sherry and taking a sip.

"I have been asked by the shareholders to take over the account and I have gladly accepted. The *Gazette* has always been one of our most stellar newspapers. Of course, in order to continue to publish it, we need the newspaper to exist," he continued, putting down his glass. "Now I could hire all new reporters and staff. I've even had several folks approach me about taking on the job of editor. But I firmly believe that the *Gazette* is the excellent paper it is because of the people who work there. You care about getting the story. And you care about each other. That's why it was no surprise when the entire staff resigned in support of Miss Porter. We don't see that type of loyalty very often in this business, especially when the reporter is relatively new to the organization. So, I am humbly offering every one of the reporters and staff their jobs back."

Peter Chishelm looked over at Mr. Tom Connor standing next to Gran. "I have already offered your editor his job back but he has delayed accepting until he hears from all of you. Oh, and I don't want to forget, the offer comes with pay raises all around. Compensation for the inconvenience you have all suffered.

"Well what do you say?" asked Mr. Connor, glancing around the room. "E.M., Midge, Katie? Should we rejoin the madness and bring the *Fairfield Gazette* back to life?"

The three reporters looked at each other. "Well, I don't know," said E.M. rubbing his chin. "I was hoping to take on a life of leisure...oh, well...why not! I'm in!"

"So am I," replied Katie, smiling.

"Me as well," said Midge. "Hopefully."

"But only if Mr. Connor accepts as our editor," added Katie, glancing over at him as the others nodded their heads.

"Well, if you all will then so will I!" he declared. "After all, why should you have all the fun?"

"Wonderful!" exclaimed Peter, raising his glass in the air. "A toast! To the best newspaper in Fairfield!"

"Wait just a minute," said Jim, putting down his glass. "I can't drink to that!"

"Oh, Mr. Fielding, I almost forgot," replied Peter. "You were the one who caused the entire incident in the first place! My uncle told me all about it."

"Look here..." Jim began, getting to his feet. "I didn't mean to cause..."

"Please, don't misunderstand me," Peter interrupted, holding up his hands. "My family and I are eternally grateful. My little cousin Amelia has an amazing voice, one that we hope will take her far professionally as well as help with her affliction. The scholarship to Julliard, which you helped her get, and the recognition that it brings will help enormously," Peter added, stepping over and shaking Jim's hand. "Uncle Richard is a terrible bully and always has been. He used to pick on my father when they were children. It's only right that he should pay for his behavior. My Aunt Lillian is a remarkable woman. It's a wonder that she stayed with him for nearly a dozen years. He lost the support of his family long ago and now he has lost his job, his wife, and his daughter."

"Such a tragedy," remarked Gran, shaking her head. "He had all the benefits that come with growing up in a good family."

"Even the best of families can't undo a bad temperament," said Katie.

"Very true," Peter replied, nodding. And then he turned back to Jim. "I'm in a position to offer you a job at the *Gazette*, Mr. Fielding. And at a substantially higher salary than you are currently making at the *Middleton Times*."

Everyone in the room looked at Jim and held their breaths. Jim looked down at Katie as she looked up at him. They stayed like that for several seconds and then Jim turned back to Peter.

"That's very kind of you, really," he said softly. "But I'm quite happy at the *Times* and I feel I owe them. You see, about a year ago they took a chance on a stranger from out of town and gave me a job. That enabled me to move to Fairfield and follow up on a situation that had been bothering me since the war." He sat back down on the couch and took Katie's hand. "And, because of that I was able to find Katie. No, I'm sorry Mr. Chishelm. I appreciate the offer but I'm very happy with the ways things are now."

Katie smiled at him and squeezed his hand.

"That's too bad," replied Peter, smiling. "But I understand. Please know that the offer stands if you ever change your mind."

"Thank you, sir," replied Jim. "I'll remember that."

"Well, with all this wonderful news, I think we'd better have dinner," announced Gran, turning towards the library door. "I, for one, have worked up quite an appetite!"

"All that beauty wasted," muttered Bradford Sinclair scornfully.

"Who?" asked E.M. coming up alongside him as the group entered the dining room and found their places around the large table.

"Katie Porter, of course. I always figured Jim Fielding for a fool," Bradford replied, sliding into his chair. "Why not jump at a job that offers to pay so much more. He could really spoil that beautiful babe if he had money in his pocket."

"You may not have noticed, dear cousin, but Katie Porter doesn't need to be with someone who has a lot of money," replied E.M. taking the seat beside him. "She has quite enough of her own. Besides, it can be awkward for a married couple to work for the same newspaper."

"But they're not married, Dapper," responded Bradford, glancing across the table at Katie and Jim. "Not even engaged."

"That's true," replied E.M., placing his napkin across his lap. "But you have to admire a man who keeps his options open."

CHAPTER 11
FAMILY HISTORY

"Gran, if I remember our lineage correctly," said Katie to her grandmother the next morning. "Wasn't great-great-grandfather Maine a newspaper publisher?"

They were enjoying a late breakfast of ham and eggs after being up quite late the night before. The announcement that they were rid of their former publisher and would all be getting their jobs back at the *Gazette* led to a celebration that lasted into the wee hours of the morning. Even Gran had stayed up to enjoy the fun.

"Yes, Katie dear," smiled Mrs. Porter, cutting into a thick slice of smoked ham. "Grandfather Maine was co-owner of the firm Maine and Fitzgerald."

"Ah," replied Katie. She paused in thought for a few minutes and then looked over at Gran, her eyebrows raised. "And wasn't great-great-grandmother Maine a Fitzgerald before she married? Isn't that where you get your middle names?"

"Yes, granddaughter," Gran replied innocently but there was a twinkle in her eye.

"So, grandfather Maine met grandmother Fitzgerald because he and her father owned the publishing company?"

"No," replied Gran, reaching over to take a sip of coffee. "Your great-great-grandfather Reginald Maine and your great-great-grandmother Augusta Fitzgerald started the publishing firm together. They weren't married at the time but, between them, had just enough money to start the business so they decided to establish a professional partnership. A very unusual arrangement for a woman back then. But, then again, the women of my family never felt inclined to follow social norms when they didn't make any sense. Good thing, because Maine and Fitzgerald became highly successful, becoming the publisher of at least 20 small town newspapers across the country. During that time, my grandparents fell in love, married, and had six children, one of whom was my father."

"Oh, Gran!" exclaimed Katie. "A thought just occurred to me! Did Maine and Fitzgerald ever publish the *Fairfield Gazette*?"

"Yes, Katie," chuckled her grandmother. "I must say you have a mind equal to Sherlock Holmes! Yes, Maine and Fitzgerald were the original publishers of the *Gazette*. After several years, the company grew so large that my grandparents decided to sell some of the accounts to other firms. That is how Chisholm, Banks and Clifford ended up with your newspaper."

"But Maine and Fitzgerald keep ownership of several shares of the *Gazette*," said Katie, her eyes twinkling. "Which is why you have them now."

"Yes," replied Gran, smiling. "They really didn't want to let it go completely. Even back then, the newspaper was quite successful. I inherited the shares from my grandmother and then bought up several more, over the years, eventually becoming the majority shareholder."

"Gran, you are simply amazing!" declared her granddaughter.

"You will eventually inherit my shares, of course, which might make things complicated if you're still working as a reporter for them," Gran pointed out. "Although your colleagues now know that I have some involvement with the paper, they don't know how much. And I have sworn Mr. Connor to secrecy!"

"I suppose I could always transfer over to the *Middleton Times*," Katie teased. "To avoid any difficulties."

"No, sorry Katie," replied Gran, shaking her head as she rang the bell for more coffee.

"You're not saying you own shares in that newspaper as well!" exclaimed Katie in surprise.

"I'm afraid so, dear," replied Gran, nodding.

"Well, it certainly is interesting to be so well connected," replied Katie, chuckling.

"Yes, indeed," said Gran. "Which reminds me. Peter Chishelm is very well connected. If I wasn't so fond of Jim Fielding, I might be pushing you in his direction," she teased, glancing fondly at Katie. "But, then again, I've never been able to push you in any direction, have I?"

"No Gran, I'm afraid not," replied Katie, giving her grandmother a sweet smile. "But who can blame me? It's in my blood. I'm a Porter, Maine, Fitzgerald, after all."

* * *

"Please state your name and address for the record," Mr. Martin instructed the witness.

"Rosemary Elliott, 1031 Second Street, Fairfield," replied the nervous woman on the witness stand.

The trial was just beginning as Katie made her way to a seat next to Ruth. "Did I miss anything?" she asked her friend.

"No, the first witness is just now being sworn in," replied Ruth. "She's Midge's neighbor."

"Mrs. Elliott, you are Mrs. Pennington's neighbor. Is that correct?" asked Mr. Martin, leaning against the railing of the witness stand.

"Yes, that's correct," nodded Mrs. Elliott. "We've been neighbors for about seven years now."

"I see," replied the prosecutor. "Would you consider yourself and Mrs. Pennington good friends?"

"I wouldn't say we're good friends, really," said Mrs. Elliott hesitantly. "We're more like good neighbors."

"And what in your opinion makes for a good neighbor?"

"Well, sir," replied the witness. "I suppose a good neighbor is one who is there when you need them and minds their own business when you don't."

Several people in the courtroom nodded their heads and two ladies near the back nudged each other and smiled.

"I see," said Mr. Martin, giving Mrs. Elliott an encouraging smile. "Now on the evening of November 8, 1942, did you go over to the Pennington home?"

"Yes," replied Mrs. Elliot. "I was in the middle of making a cake for my husband, Robert, when I realized I didn't have enough milk. Well, that put me in a bit of a panic seeing that milk was on the ration, so I went over to see if Midge might have some extra, seeing that she and Mr. Pennington had no children. Besides, they'd both been gone for months and most likely hadn't used up their cards. So, off I went with my little pitcher in hand."

"What time was that?" asked Mr. Martin.

"Well, let's see," said Midge's neighbor. "It must have been around 5:55 or so because I was listening to the news on the radio and decided to rush over when they went to air one of their sponsor messages."

"Was Mrs. Pennington home?" asked the prosecutor.

"Yes," replied Mrs. Elliott.

"Then what happened?"

"She gave me the milk and I went home," replied Mrs. Elliott, an expression of confusion on her face.

"Yes, of course," said Mr. Martin gently. "But could you perhaps give us a little more detail. For instance, how did Mrs. Pennington seem to you? Was she nervous or upset, anything like that?"

"Oh I see," replied Mrs. Elliot. "Well, Midge seemed a bit upset, I'd say. You see, she'd been listening to the same radio program. It was the John Daly show and he was reporting that American forces had just invaded Algiers and Casablanca. She was worried because she knew several of the officers who would be in the battle. She told me that she should have been there covering the story instead of home on leave. I remember telling her that I thought she'd be happy to be home with her husband since it'd been months since they'd seen each other."

"And how did she respond to your comment?" asked the prosecutor.

"I don't recall her saying anything at all. Just shrugged her shoulders and poured the milk into my pitcher."

"Was Major Pennington in the house?"

"No, I didn't see him at all," replied Mrs. Elliot.

"Now, Mrs. Elliott," continued Mr. Martin. "Do you remember the dress that Mrs. Pennington was wearing?"

"Well now, it was five years ago but I seem to remember that it was the blue one with the white collar," recalled Mrs. Elliot. "Yes, I believe she wore that one. She's always looked very nice in it."

Mr. Martin walked over to the evidence table and picked up the picture of Midge in the bloody dress. "I'll spare you the enlargement, Mrs. Elliot, but would you please look at this picture and tell the court if this is the dress that you remember Mrs. Pennington wearing on the evening of Sunday, November 8, 1942."

Mrs. Elliot took the photograph and glanced down at it. She cringed for a moment before handing it back to the prosecutor. "Yes, that's the one," she replied softly. "It only had a tiny blood stain on it when I saw it."

Mr. Martin had started to return the photograph to the table when her comment made him suddenly stop and turn. "What do you mean when you say the dress only had a tiny blood stain on it when you saw it?"

"I mean there was only a tiny smear when I saw her in it, not all of that blood in the picture," replied Mrs. Elliot. "Of course she was wearing her apron so I didn't see the whole front. She was in the middle of cooking, you see, and it's always best to wear an apron. But I remember asking her about it."

"And what did she say about the blood when you asked her about it?"

"Well, I said something like 'Midge, bicarbonate soda will take that stain right out' and she said something like 'never mind, it's only blood. It will come right out with a little scrubbing.' Then she held up her finger and showed me the band aid and said she had cut it chopping an onion."

Mr. Martin had the look of a cat who had just swallowed the canary when he looked back at Midge Pennington seated at the defense table and said, "I have no more questions, Your Honor. Your witness, Mr. Sinclair."

"No questions," replied Bradford, looking down at some notes in front of him.

"No questions, counselor?" asked Poppy from the bench.

"That's correct, Your Honor. No questions," repeated Bradford.

Poppy paused for a moment and then looked down at the witness. "You may step down, Mrs. Elliot. Mr. Martin, you may call your next witness."

"Your Honor, the state calls Mr. Marshall Baker," announced the prosecutor.

A small man wearing a worn brown suit and horn-rimmed glasses entered the courtroom and made his way to the witness stand. He held a manila folder in his right hand and had to shift it over to his left when the bailiff swore him in for his testimony.

"Mr. Baker," began Mr. Martin. "Please tell the court your title and the name of the business you represent."

"I'm a senior account agent with the Mayfield Insurance Company. We're based out of Seattle Washington," replied Mr. Baker.

"And how long have you been with the Mayfield Insurance Company, Mr. Baker?"

"Fifteen years," answered the insurance agent.

"What types of insurance do you sell, sir?" asked Mr. Martin.

"All types," responded Mr. Baker, his eyes lighting up. "Home, Auto, Life, Farm Equipment…"

"Thank you, Mr. Baker," interrupted Mr. Martin. "I believe we get the idea. Do you remember selling an insurance policy to a Major William Pennington and his wife Margaret during the war?"

"Well not from memory, mind you. I sell quite a lot of policies," replied Mr. Baker. He then opened the file he had been holding in his lap. "But when I got your call, I looked through my files and here it is. The policy was purchased on September 27th, 1942."

"I see," nodded Mr. Martin. "Please tell the court what type of policy it is that you sold to Major and Mrs. Pennington."

"It's a life insurance policy," replied Mr. Baker, glancing down at the document. "But it wasn't for them both. The policy was taken out by Mrs. Pennington on her husband."

"Really? And how much was the policy worth should Mrs. Pennington's husband die?"

"Half a million dollars," replied the insurance agent proudly.

Katie heard gasps from those seated in the room as Mr. Martin paused to let the amount sink in with the jury. She looked over at Midge and saw that she was sitting motionless and staring straight out in front of her.

"Your witness, Mr. Sinclair," said the prosecutor, returning to his chair.

"Thank you, Mr. Martin," responded Bradford, slowly standing and picking up a document from the defense table. He walked over to the witness and smiled. "Mr. Baker, do you see Mrs. Pennington here in the courtroom?"

"Yes, sir," replied Mr. Baker, nodding. "That's her at the defense table."

"Thank you," responded Bradford. "Do you recall if Mrs. Pennington's husband was with her when you sold her the policy?"

"No, I don't believe he was," answered Mr. Baker. "In fact I have a written note here in the file that says he was stationed in Los Angeles at the time and that he and his wife had talked about getting the policy should he be killed in action."

"I see," said Bradford. "Did Mrs. Pennington happen to file a claim on this policy five years ago when her husband died?"

"Well, let's see," replied the agent. "No sir, no claim was ever filed."

"How very interesting," said Bradford, turning slightly to glance at the jury. "Now Mr. Baker, I wonder if you would clarify something for me since you are an insurance agent with fifteen years of experience with the Mayfield Insurance Company. Is there a waiting period from the time the policy is sold and the time it takes effect?"

"Oh yes," nodded Mr. Baker. "It's 45 days for all of our policies."

"And why implement a waiting period, Mr. Baker?"

"It's so that folks can't take out the policy and then collect on it the very next day," replied Mr. Baker. "Let's say I sell you an accident policy on your automobile. We wouldn't want you to drive it into a tree right after that so that you can get some money. You'd be surprised. Some folks are in desperate need and will try and do something like that. So, the 45 day wait discourages them from taking advantage of the insurance company."

"Very sensible," replied Bradford nodding. "Did Mrs. Pennington know of the 45-day waiting period?"

"She checked the box and initialed it, sir," replied the agent, looking down again at the policy. "To indicate that she was told and understood that the policy would not be good until that time."

Bradford Sinclair nodded and then handed Mr. Baker the piece of paper that he had been holding. "Now Mr. Baker, are you familiar with this document?

"Yes," responded the agent. "It's a death certificate. We see these all the time."

"Really? Why?"

"Because they're needed when a claim is filed to collect the money on a life insurance policy," explained Mr. Baker. "We can't very well send out a check on a person who might still be alive."

"No, of course not," smiled the attorney. "Would you read the name on the certificate and tell the court, please?"

Mr. Baker glanced over the document and read the name out loud. "William Odom Pennington."

"And the date of his death?" asked Bradford.

"November 8, 1942," replied Mr. Baker.

"Thank you," said Bradford. "Now referring back to Mrs. Pennington's policy on her husband. On what date did you say she purchased it?"

"September 27, 1942," replied the insurance agent.

"So, given the 45-day waiting period required by your company," Bradford asked. "On what date would the policy have gone into effect?"

"Well let's see," answered Mr. Baker, looking up at the ceiling as he made the calculation. "It would have gone into effect on November 10 of that year."

"So, if Major Pennington died on November 8..."

"Oh dear, oh dear!" exclaimed Mr. Baker, suddenly realizing the situation. "The policy would not have been active, and Mrs. Pennington would not have been able to make a claim and collect."

"Perhaps Major Pennington should have waited two more days to be killed," remarked Bradford Sinclair, turning and walking back to his table.

"Your Honor, please!" shouted Mr. Martin, jumping to his feet.

"My apologies, Your Honor. I withdraw the comment," Bradford replied, giving Poppy a slight bow. "I have no more questions for this witness."

* * *

"Not that I'm complaining about having lunch alone with you," joked Jim, sitting next to Katie on a bench in the city park across from the courthouse. They had picked up sandwiches from the deli and were now enjoying eating lunch outside. "But where are E.M. and Ruth?"

"Ruth had some errands to run for her mother," replied Katie, smiling at him. "And Bradford sent E.M. to the train station to pick someone up for Midge's trial. So, I'm afraid it's just you and me."

"A circumstance I'm enjoying immensely," said Jim, winking at her as he bit into his sandwich. "I'm sorry I missed the trial this morning, but I had to get out my article on the revival of the *Fairfield Gazette*. And after the party at your place last night, I overslept and arrived late to the office."

"Well, you missed the testimony of the Pennington's neighbor who spotted a blood smear on Midge's dress several minutes before Midge told us she actually found her husband, and that of Mr. Marshall Baker, the insurance agent who sold Midge a life insurance policy on her husband with a payout of half a million bucks," replied Katie.

"Oh boy," muttered Jim. "This sounds bad."

"Well, it wasn't good although Bradford did take some of the sting out," replied Katie, sighing. "You know, we keep going around and around on this thing and don't seem to be getting anywhere. Major Pennington's cut on the forehead and all the blood, Midge being the one to find him…"

"And did she really hit him with a hammer and then watch him die?" added Jim, holding up his index finger.

"And who hits their husband with a hammer in order to kill him and then holds him in their lap tightly enough to end up with all that blood on them?" questioned Katie, taking a sip of her tea.

"And did Midge really love him or not?" asked Jim, smiling at Katie as she handed him a small cardboard container with a piece of pie in it.

"And how about the neighbor?" continued Katie. "She says that Midge claimed to be upset about her friends fighting in Algiers and Casablanca but has a blood smear on her dress that could belong to her husband. And then there is the life insurance policy that Midge can't use because the major happened to die two days before it went into effect. She knew that so, if she is the killer, you'd think she'd wait two more measly days before bumping him off so that she could collect half a million dollars."

"Add a nosy neighbor and a spiteful sister-in-law and what do you have?" asked Jim, rhetorically.

"The same situation that existed five years ago when the poor man fell and busted his head open," replied Katie soberly. "And to think that the police sent his body to the morgue and no one there performed an autopsy. So many questions could have been answered and Midge might never have been arrested!"

"Well, like the coroner testified, everyone thought his death was an accident and, besides, the hospital was busy during the war. Remember, the man said only 50 percent of bodies underwent autopsies," said Jim, digging his fork into his pie. "I'm sure the morgue didn't want to hold onto the body any longer than they had to and Midge, herself, was running out of time. She had to get the major buried before she could go back on assignment."

"Yes, I suppose...hey, wait a minute!" exclaimed Katie, looking over at him. "That's right! There wasn't time *then* but there is now!"

"Katie Porter, what are you saying?" asked Jim, his fork pausing in midair. "We should have the major dug up and examined?"

"Yes! I'll ask Bradford to petition the court to have Major Pennington's body exhumed," replied Katie, jumping to her feet and looking over at the courthouse. "Midge can ask to have it done as his next of kin. We'll find out what killed Major Pennington once and for all! And I bet my bottom dollar that a little blow to the head and some blood didn't do it!"

"I don't think a bottom dollar exists in the Porter world, but I get your point," Jim chuckled. "I do hope this doesn't backfire on us, though. As my mother often says, be careful what you wish for."

* * *

"Your Honor, may we approach the bench?" asked Bradford Sinclair when the proceeding resumed two hours later in the courtroom of the Fairfield Courthouse.

"Yes, counselor," replied Poppy, nodding to both Bradford and Mr. Martin. The two attorneys came forward and Bradford leaned toward the judge, spoke for a few minutes, and then handed him a piece of paper. Poppy read the document and handed it to Mr. Martin, who read over it and nodded. Then the two attorneys returned to their respective tables and remained standing.

"Mr. Sinclair, you are free to make your request to the court," announced Poppy, glancing over at the clock on the wall.

"Thank you, Your Honor," replied Bradford. "If it pleases the court, the defense is requesting, on behalf of his widow, the exhumation of Major William Pennington so that his body may be autopsied. Mrs. Pennington has signed the necessary papers and is requesting that the pathologist at Fairfield Hospital perform the procedure."

"Mrs. Pennington, is it your wish to have your husband's remains exhumed and autopsied?" Poppy asked Midge.

"Yes, Your Honor," replied Midge somberly.

"Do you have any objections, Mr. Martin?" Poppy asked, turning to the prosecutor.

"No, Your Honor," Mr. Martin replied. "The prosecution has no objections."

"Then the court so orders," declared Judge White. "The remains of Major Pennington will be exhumed no later than Sunday, the day after tomorrow. This trial will continue as we wait for results. However, neither side will rest its case until the autopsy report has been delivered. Is that clear to both parties?"

"Yes, Your Honor," replied the attorneys in unison.

"Very well," said Poppy. "Mr. Martin, please call your next witness."

"The state calls Mrs. Sarah Haverson," announced the prosecutor and the courtroom door opened to reveal a stout woman in her fifties wearing a tailored suit and modest hat. She held her pocketbook up in front of her as she walked to the witness stand and proceeded to sit down.

"Just one moment, ma'am," said the bailiff. "You must be sworn in."

"Oh, of course," replied Mrs. Haverson, a little flustered. "I beg your pardon," she added, holding up her right hand and taking the oath.

"Mrs. Haverson," began Mr. Martin. "You were in the Fairfield's downtown supermarket on the afternoon of November 8, 1942, were you not?"

"Well, I don't remember the exact date, Peter, but if that's when the argument between the Penningtons occurred then I suppose you are correct," replied Mrs. Haverson, tilting her head to one side.

"Yes, well," said Mr. Martin. "Doesn't really matter. The important thing is that you heard the Penningtons arguing. Is that correct?"

"Yes, and they were rather loud about it!" declared Mrs. Haverson. "She was yelling her head off at him and he was yelling right back at her. And in the middle of the vegetable aisle!"

"And do you recall what it was Mrs. Pennington was yelling?"

"Oh yes, she was very harsh," explained the witness. "She said 'if you keep doing it, I swear I'll kill you' and he said something like, 'you know I don't mean anything by it' and that's when she picked up a tomato and threw it at him."

"Is that when it hit you by mistake?" asked the prosecutor.

"Yes. Major Pennington ducked and the tomato sailed over his head and hit me in the chest!" replied Mrs. Haverson, dramatically. "Would have ruined my new blouse had I not gotten it to the drycleaners right away."

"Thank you, Mrs. Haverson," said Mr. Martin. "Your witness Mr. Sinclair."

As Bradford got to his feet and was approaching the witness stand, Mrs. Haverson cast a glance over the spectators and saw Katie and Ruth sitting with Jim a few rows back. Recognizing her neighbors, she gave the young women a little wave, causing Bradford to turn and look in their direction before continuing forward toward the witness.

"Mrs. Haverson," Bradford began. "Do you know the defendant, Margaret Pennington?"

"No," the witness replied, squinting her eyes to get a better look at Midge.

"I see that you know two women in the courtroom today," Bradford continued. "Miss Porter and Miss White. Is that so?"

"Well, yes of course," replied Mrs. Haverson, nodding. "The White family lives next door to us and the Porters next door to them. We are all neighbors."

"I see," nodded Bradford. He gave Mrs. Haverson a knowing smile. "I imagine it's very nice to have such fine neighbors."

"Yes, indeed," the lady replied, straightening a bit in the witness stand. "The Whites and the Porters are two of the finest families in Fairfield," she added, giving Poppy a nod.

"When you say that you are neighbors with these fine families, Mrs. Haverson, you don't actually mean in the same sense that the Penningtons are next door neighbors to, say, Mrs. Rosemary Elliott. Isn't that true?"

"I don't know Mrs. Rosemary Elliott or the Penningtons so I would say that was true," replied Mrs. Haverson. "You see, there are only a few families left in Fairfield that own estates and my husband and I know them all because their properties border on our own."

"Objection, Your Honor!" exclaimed Mr. Martin. "The defense council is trying to discredit the witness."

"Not at all, Your Honor," replied Bradford calmly. "I'm just trying to figure out why a woman who owns an estate north of town and has such fine, and wealthy neighbors, would insist on taking money from a front line war correspondent to pay the dry cleaning bill on a blouse."

"I didn't want to take the money," said Mrs. Haverson rather hastily. "But Peter insisted. He said that people like the Penningtons need to show more respect for families like mine."

"Your Honor!" continued Mr. Martin. "I don't see…"

But Bradford Sinclair interrupted and came in for the kill. "When you say 'Peter,' are you referring to Mr. Martin, the prosecutor?"

"Yes, that's right," replied Mrs. Haverson smugly. "And he should know! He was there in the supermarket when Mrs. Pennington hit me with the tomato! He saw the whole thing!"

"Thank you, Mrs. Haverson," said Bradford, glancing over at the prosecutor who now had his forehead resting in his hand. "I have no more questions for this witness."

"So that's how we know about the argument in the supermarket!" exclaimed Katie, leaning against Jim and whispering in his ear. "The prosecutor was there at the time and must have remembered it when the major's sister asked him to open the case."

"Adding a little bit more fuel to the fire," Jim remarked, nodding.

"I can't wait to tell E.M.!" exclaimed Katie, looking around the courtroom. "I wonder where on earth he could be?"

"You told me that Bradford sent him to the train station to pick up someone," Jim reminded her. "Maybe the train was late."

"Yes, but that was hours ago," Katie replied. "Surely the train can't be that late!"

"Your Honor," said Mr. Martin as Katie and Jim turned their attention back to the front of the courtroom. "The state calls Mrs. Pamela Percy to the stand."

Major Pennington's sister was a small attractive woman of indeterminate age and not at all what Katie expected. She wore an inexpensive but well-fitting ready-to-wear dress with matching shoes and hat. Although her demeanor appeared calm, her eyes kept shifting from face to face as she made her way through the spectators to the witness stand. The only person Pamela Percy did not look at was her former sister-in-law, Midge Pennington.

"Mrs. Percy," began Mr. Martin, giving the witness a warm smile. "You are the sister of the late Major William Pennington, is that correct."

"Yes," Mrs. Percy replied. "He was my older brother."

"How many siblings do you have?" asked the prosecutor.

"I have a sister and I had two brothers," replied Pamela. "Both my brothers are now gone. You know about Bill, of course. My other brother, Phillip, was killed at Midway."

"You know the defendant, Margaret Pennington," Mr. Martin continued. "Is that correct?"

"Yes," responded the witness.

"She is your sister-in-law?"

"She was," replied Mrs. Percy.

"Yes, of course," said Mr. Martin, nodding. "How long have you known Mrs. Pennington."

"She was married to my brother Bill for ten years," Pamela Percy replied. "I knew her then."

"Would you say that you and the defendant got along?" Mr. Martin asked, glancing back at Midge.

"No, I would not say that," Mrs. Percy answered.

"I see," replied the prosecutor. "Would you say that your animosity toward the defendant stemmed from her behavior toward you or your brother?"

"It has to do with the way she treated my brother," replied the witness evenly. "She never did anything toward me, but she could be downright rude to him. Was embarrassed just because he had a drink or two. She was always telling him to behave himself."

"Did you often witness this treatment by Mrs. Pennington toward your brother?"

"No, but I didn't have to," replied Mrs. Percy. "Bill told me all about it. He didn't put it in exact words, mind you, but I got the impression that she never paid much attention to him in a way a wife should," continued Pamela, now glaring at Midge. "My poor brother was driven to look for affection elsewhere, if you know what I mean."

"Look elsewhere?" Mr. Martin repeated. "You mean your brother was having an affair?"

"Yes," said the witness. "I heard from one of his pals at the post in California. He said that Bill was having an affair with a female officer although he didn't give the lady's name."

"I see," said Mr. Martin, nodding. "Do you know if your sister-in-law was aware of the affair?"

"I wouldn't know," replied Mrs. Percy, shrugging her shoulders. "As I said, she and I didn't get along so she certainly wouldn't have admitted something like that to me. But wives always know. We have an intuition about such things."

"Yes, I can imagine. Now, moving on, Mrs. Percy. Who was Mildred Willow?" asked Mr. Martin, switching tactics.

"She lived next door to Bill and Midge," explained Pamela Percy. "And she was my good friend."

"Four weeks ago you received a letter from Mrs. Willow. Is that right?"

"Yes. Mildred wrote to me just days before she died," replied Mrs. Percy. "She wanted the case of my brother's death reopened."

"Your Honor," said Mr. Martin, walking over to the prosecutors table and picking up a piece of paper. He looked up and addressed Poppy. "At this time, the prosecution would like to enter into evidence this handwritten letter from Mrs. Mildred Willow."

"Does the defense counsel have any objections at this time to this letter being entered into evidence?" Poppy asked Bradford.

"No, Your Honor," replied Bradford. "The defense has no objections."

Poppy paused for a moment and raised his eyebrows. He looked intently at Bradford Sinclair before declaring, "the letter from Mrs. Willow is entered into evidence as exhibit M-1."

"Thank you, Your Honor," continued Mr. Martin. "So Mrs. Percy, what does the letter say?"

"It says that Midge killed my brother. That Mildred had witnessed Midge holding Bill on her lap and that there was a bloody hammer lying next to her. Mildred assumed that Midge had hit him in the head with it and was watching him die. She wrote to me because she knew that I would insist the case be opened. As Mildred said, Midge shouldn't get away with it."

"Thank you," said the prosecutor. "I have no further questions."

"Mrs. Percy," Bradford began, moving over to the evidence table and picking up the letter. He handed it to Pamela. "Does this letter from Mrs. Willow say that she saw the defendant strike your brother with the hammer?"

"No, not exactly," replied Pamela.

"What does she say she saw," Bradford prodded. "Exactly?"

Pamela Percy sighed. "She writes that she saw Midge through the window holding Bill in her lap and that there was a bloody hammer nearby."

"And that, in Mildred's opinion, your sister-in-law must have hit him," said Bradford. "Is that correct, Mrs. Percy?"

"Yes, that's correct," replied Pamela softly.

"Did you know Margaret Pennington before she married your brother?" Bradford asked suddenly.

"No," replied Mrs. Percy, somewhat surprised at the change in questioning.

"Ah, perhaps you met your future sister-in-law when you attended your brother's wedding?"

"No, indeed!" replied Pamela. "I didn't attend the wedding!"

"Oh no?" asked Bradford. "You didn't approve of your brother's future bride even though you hadn't met her yet?

"You are making it sound so spiteful Mr. Sinclair but it was more complicated than that," replied Mrs. Percy.

"Please explain, then, ma'am," Bradford requested. "It's important that we get to the truth in these matters."

"Well, you see, Bill was supposed to marry Silvia Martin," replied Pamela, leaning slightly forward. "Her father was the president of the bank where Bill worked. Silvia and I had it all worked out. I was to marry her brother and Bill was to marry her. Then that woman came along and ruined our plans. She stole my brother away from his career and his family!"

"So, your family really didn't have anything against Midge Pennington, per se," Bradford pointed out. "Except that she wasn't the right woman according to your plans. How unfortunate that the wrong woman stayed married to your brother for 10 years."

"Yes," replied Mrs. Percy softly.

"Now did you and Mr. Peter Martin, the prosecuting attorney, end up getting married?" Bradford asked.

"No, we split up after that because…" Pamela began and then stopped when she heard the gasps from the spectators in the courtroom.

"Objection, Your Honor!" shouted Mr. Martin, jumping to his feet. "My past relationship with this witness has nothing to do with this case!"

"Doesn't it?" replied Poppy from the bench. He thought for a moment and then said, "I'm going to overrule your objection and allow the witness to finish her answer."

"Your Honor," interjected Bradford, smiling. "I'll go ahead and withdraw the question. The defense doesn't wish to have past associations reflect badly on the prosecution in any way. I have no further questions for this witness."

"Wow!" Jim whispered.

"Yes," Katie whispered back. "Wow, indeed!"

CHAPTER 12
THE RADIO BROADCAST

"E.M.!" Katie exclaimed into the phone later that evening. "Where have you been? You're missing some real excitement at Midge's trial!"

"I know!" E.M. lamented. "I've just been called as witness! I can't be in the courtroom until I testify."

"What?" replied Katie. "By whom? Mr. Martin?"

"No, by my cousin!" said E.M. in a huff. "Bradford wants me to tell the court about Midge's war record and some of the trauma she endured. You know, stuff like that."

"Why would he want to dredge all that up?" Katie wondered. "Goodness, you don't think he's trying to portray Midge as having lost her mind due to battle fatigue and that made her kill her husband, do you?"

"I don't know, Katie dear," replied E.M. "But I don't like it. I don't like it at all!"

"Tell me what you know about battle fatigue, E.M." Katie asked. "I know the doctors call it Combat Stress Reaction but, other than that, I don't really know much about it."

"Well there's nothing much to tell, really," replied her friend softly. "It comes from being in battle for a long period of time. Soldiers just get worn out, exhausted. Their reflexes and even their speech slow down and they have a hard time focusing. They disengage from their surroundings. Not a healthy thing to happen when they're in the middle of a battle. As soon as they can, the unit commander will get the guy out and to medical help. You can spot someone when they're suffering from CSR. They just sit with a blank stare on their face. The military calls it the thousand-yard-stare."

"How long does it last?" Katie asked.

"Usually only a couple of days. Once they get the soldier well rested and relaxed, they return the guy to his unit."

"Gosh, that quickly," replied Katie thoughtfully.

"The military found that men usually didn't want the stigma. Battle fatigue could be judged as a weakness. You know, the guy was not tough enough to hang in there and protect his buddies. So it was best to get them back in the fighting as soon as possible," E.M. explained. "Of course, it was better understood as the war went on."

"But what about after?" Katie asked. "You still have the shakes sometimes and Jim just admitted to having nightmares. Heck, even a British Member of Parliament tried to drop out for a few days."

"Sometimes the trauma of war has little to do with exhaustion," replied E.M. almost in a whisper. "Sometimes it runs much deeper. In my case, the fear of having looked death in the face. For Jim, it's the guilt of not dying. I imagine he may still be struggling with the idea that it should have been him killed and not Ruddy."

"And Midge?" asked Katie. "Could she still be suffering from being at the front lines covering the war?"

"Possibly but nothing that would drive her to kill Pennington," E.M. insisted. "Downing several whiskeys is how Midge usually handles the aftereffects of the war. As tough as she may seem, Katie, I have never seen Midge Pennington come close to hurting another living soul. Deep down, she has a heart of gold."

Katie paused for a moment thinking about their newspaper colleague. Midge could come across as a tough customer. But Katie also knew that Midge could be counted on when one needed help. Just months ago, Midge had been one of the first people to volunteer to help Katie with a project to save the Pearson Playhouse. It was Midge who had sprung into action to rescue Ruth after a bad fall. And, like Katie, Midge was fiercely protective of E.M. In fact, that was the major thing she and Midge had in common. Now, through this very public ordeal, Katie was seeing yet another side of the Midge Pennington that E.M. was so loyally defending.

"You know something, pal?" she finally said. "I'm thrilled that you looked the Grim Reaper in the eye and made him blink. I love you to

The Murder of Major Pennington

pieces and it would have been terrible if I had never gotten a chance to know you!"

"I won't argue with the illogical nature of that statement, Katie Porter," chuckled E.M. "And I love you, too. Now, call that boyfriend of yours and reassure him that he was the one meant to come home to you! I will see you from the witness stand tomorrow. Goodnight, Katie."

"Goodnight, E.M." she replied, disconnecting the call and then placing her finger on the dial to call Jim. However, a thought suddenly came to her and instead she dialed the number of Jake Ross, an old friend of Ruddy's. Jake ran the local radio station that broadcast in Fairfield and the surrounding area.

"Hello, Jake?" she said into the telephone when she heard his voice. "This is Katie Porter."

"Well hello Katie!" exclaimed Jake with delight. "It's been a while! How are you?"

"I'm fine, Jake. And you? How are Jane and the children?"

"Oh, just great, Katie," replied Jake. "We're all well. So, what can I do for you?"

"I'm calling to find out if your station keeps tape recordings of all of the broadcasts," said Katie. "Not just the local ones but ones that you transmit from the larger stations like CBS in New York."

"Yes, as a matter of fact we do," replied Jake. "Are you looking for one in particular?"

"Yes," Katie replied. "I'm interested in getting hold of a copy of CBS World News Today with John Daly. The one aired on November 8, 1942."

"Got it!" Jake said, jotting down the information. "John Daly's broadcasts are always popular so we most likely also have a transcript. Would you like that as well?"

"Yes, that would be wonderful!" replied Katie.

"I should have everything ready for you by tomorrow morning," said Jake. "Can you stop by the station, say, around 10:00 am?"

"Yes, absolutely!" Katie exclaimed. "See you then!"

"You bet," replied Jake, ending the call.

After pausing for a moment to write down the time of the appointment, Katie finally dialed Jim's number.

"Hello handsome," she said when she heard his deep wonderful voice on the other end of the line.

"Well, hello beautiful," Jim responded. "I've been trying to call you all evening but your line's been busy."

"Yes, I've been tying up the phone line talking to other men," she admitted, teasing him a little.

"I see," he said calmly. "Should I be jealous?"

"No," Katie replied. "Not in the least."

"Glad to hear it," Jim said chuckling. "So, I take it you've been working on some angle concerning Midge's situation."

"Yes, I wonder if you would help me conduct a little experiment tomorrow before we go to the courthouse?"

"Sure," he replied. "Mind telling me what you have in mind?"

"I've been able to wrangle a copy of the radio broadcast that Midge and her neighbor Rosemary Elliot were listening to on the night Major Pennington died. We won't have time to listen to it until later, but my friend Jake is going to give us a transcript as well. I'd like to see just how long it took Rosemary to cross over to the Pennington's and how long she stood in the kitchen with Midge."

"Thus potentially providing Midge with an alibi," Jim added.

"Exactly," Katie replied.

* * *

At 10:00 the following morning, Katie, Jim, and Ruth pulled up in front of the Fairfield radio station and parked along the curb. Jake Ross was waiting for them in the lobby, with the box containing the broadcast recording in one hand and a manila envelope in the other.

"There you are!" exclaimed Jake, leaning over to give Katie a kiss on the cheek. "And Ruthie! How wonderful to see you!" he added, kissing Ruth as well. "Well, this is just like old home week!"

"Jake, this is Jim Fielding," said Katie, introducing Jim, who stepped around her to shake Jake's hand. For a split second, Katie hesitated. Ruddy had been her fiancé and if he had survived the war, Jake most likely would have been one of the groomsmen at their wedding. But perhaps it was time to finally move on. "Jim is my boyfriend," she added, smiling warmly. "He's helping us gather information to help my colleague, Midge Pennington, who has been arrested for murder."

"Really?" Jake replied. "Is that why you wanted this recording?"

"Yes," Jim replied, nodding. "One of the people who could possibly supply Midge with an alibi was listening to this broadcast with her during the time of the alleged murder."

"Well, I hope this helps," replied Jake, handing the box and envelope to Katie. "Just make sure you get these back to me in one piece, OK Porter?"

"You bet!" Katie chuckled, looking at the box in her arms.

"Nice meeting you, Jim," said Jake smiling. "Don't let these two get you in any trouble."

"Too late for that, Jake," joked Ruth, giving him a hug goodbye. "Please give our love to your family."

They left the building and returned to Katie's car. She handed the keys to Jim as he helped Ruth into the rumble seat and then opened the passenger side door for her. As he started up the MG roadster and pulled away from the curb, Katie opened the manila envelope and pulled out the transcript.

"Oh, how wonderful!" she exclaimed. "Not only does this show what was said during the broadcast but has the times listed along the margin. It even tells when the sponsor ads came on."

"I imagine that the station manager needed that so that he could make sure the broadcast fit into the time allotted and could make adjustments," replied Ruth. "Someone probably sat on the other side of the studio with a stopwatch and signaled Mr. Daly when to slow down or speed up."

"Yes, you're probably right," Katie agreed. "But this is also going to help us with our little experiment. You see, we're going to time how long it takes you, Ruthie, to walk from the Elliot house to Midge's. That's why I asked you to come along. Jim could have done it, but his legs are much longer, and he would have travelled the distance faster."

"Good point," nodded Jim, turning right at the corner. "So what do I get to do, other than enjoy the company of two smart and attractive young women?"

"You're going to act out the part of John Daly and read the transcript out loud, so we have an idea when things started to happen based on what Mrs. Elliott told the court she heard," replied Katie.

"And you, Detective Porter?" asked Jim, chuckling. "What's your assignment?"

"I'll be timing the whole thing, of course" replied Katie, reaching into the glove box. "See, I've even brought a stopwatch."

When they arrived at Midge's house, they noticed Bradford Sinclair's car parked in the driveway.

"Looks like your friend is making sure Midge shows up for court this morning," teased Jim, opening the car door for Katie and Ruth.

Katie wrinkled her nose at him. "You know perfectly well that Bradford is not my friend," she replied, giving him a playful poke in the ribs. "But I'm glad he's here. He can witness the experiment and Midge can verify what was being played on the radio during the time Rosemary Elliott appeared at her doorstep with milk pitcher in hand."

It took only a few minutes for Katie to explain to Midge and her attorney what she and her friends were up to.

"Midge, Mrs. Elliott testified that she left her house to walk over to yours when the sponsor message came on," recalled Katie. She studied the transcript, turning several pages. "She thought it was around 5:55 but here it is! The commercial started at 5:50 indicating that she might have been with you five minutes longer. We'll start Ruthie walking at that point in the transcript. If you could please keep your front door open and listen, you'll be able to tell us what you heard on the radio as your neighbor started over. Bradford, as an officer of the court, you'll be able to verify what we discover during this experiment."

"Whether it helps me or not," Midge cautioned, looking over at him.

"Indeed," nodded Bradford, stepping off to one side. "Please, let the proceedings begin!"

They watched as Ruth made her way over to Mrs. Elliott's front porch and turn and wait. Meanwhile, Midge stepped inside her house, leaving the front door open. Jim found the spot in the transcript where the sponsor ad began and waited for Katie's signal. Katie held up her hand and readied the stopwatch.

"Everyone ready?" she asked, looking around. "And go!" she shouted, dropping her hand.

"Continental Radio and Television Corporation, makers of Admiral radios and a variety of house- hold appliances, are proud sponsors...," Jim began reading and Ruth started her journey down the Elliott's porch and across the yard. "...of CBS's World News Today with John Daly," Jim continued.

Katie kept her eye on the stopwatch, and Ruthie, as she strolled up the walkway to Midge's and onto the porch.

"...Admiral radios are simply the very best money can buy..." read Jim.

Ruth knocked on Midge's door and Midge pretended to open it and greet her guest.

"Stop!" shouted Katie, clicking off the stopwatch. "That took one minute exactly, bringing our time that evening to 5:51. Midge, do you remember hearing the commercial that Jim just read?"

"Yes, strange but I do," replied Midge, looking over at Katie. "I remember thinking that here men were dying overseas and all people were supposed to worry about was Admiral radios and appliances!"

"It still took money to broadcast the news, Midge," interjected Bradford. "No matter what's going on in the world."

"Yes, well," Katie interrupted. "What do you remember hearing next?"

"Let's see, Rosemary and I entered the kitchen just as John Daly was talking about General Eisenhower."

"Jim," said Katie, turning to him. "How soon from this point in the transcript is there a mention of General Eisenhower?"

"Ah, here he is," replied Jim, looking through the next few lines. "He comes up in only four lines from now."

"Perfect," said Katie. "That should just be enough time to get us down the hall and into the kitchen. Ruth, when I give the signal, please explain to Midge that you are making a cake and have realized that you don't have enough milk. Ask her if she can spare some. And then Midge will say "yes," and we'll proceed down to the kitchen. Everybody got that?"

Everyone nodded yes. Jim found his place in the transcript and, when Katie gave the signal, he continued to read, a little more softly this time, as Ruth went through the motions of asking Midge for milk. Katie, having started the stopwatch again, followed along.

"...forces, under the command of General Dwight Eisenhower..." read Jim, reaching the kitchen right on cue.

Katie signaled Jim to keep reading as Midge and Ruth listened. "Tell me at what point of the broadcast you remember walking Mrs.

Elliott back to the front door on her way out," Katie whispered to Midge.

"...labeled Operation Torch, Allied amphibious landings by the Western Task Forces captured Casablanca quickly although control of Oran and Algiers was a bit trickier due to bad weather and some unexpected resistance from the enemy..." Jim read on through the transcript until he reached the end of the broadcast announcing the purchase of war bonds. "...remember every United States War Bond goes to support the efforts of our gallant men fighting for our freedom in lands faraway."

"There!" exclaimed Midge. "That's when I switched off the radio and walked Rosemary to the front door."

Katie clicked off the stopwatch. "Exactly nine minutes. So, if it took Mrs. Elliott one minute to cross over to Midge's house and then listen to the radio broadcast until the end, which is another nine minutes, that's a total of ten minutes in coordination with points heard in the CBS broadcast."

"That means that instead of the five minutes Rosemary Elliott thought she was with Midge," summarized Bradford. "our witness was actually here closer to ten."

"Wait a minute," Jim argued. "You can't count the minute it took the neighbor to cross the lawn. Although it tells us at which point in the broadcast Mrs. Elliott started over, she didn't actually see Midge until she reached the door."

"And there's the five unaccounted minutes within our 15-minute timeframe," Bradford reminded them. "Midge could have been just returning from murdering her husband in the garage when Rosemary knocked on the front door."

"True," Katie agreed. "But it does drastically cut it down. I would imagine that it takes more than five minutes to hit someone in the head with a hammer and then hold them in your lap until they die."

"The dying part only takes five minutes, hon...er...Katie," replied Bradford, shrugging.

"Perhaps Katie can time me trying to kill you, counselor?" remarked Midge sardonically.

"As fun as that sounds," responded Bradford, chuckling as he glanced at his watch. "It's time we get to the courthouse."

"I'll get my hat," Midge replied and turned to leave the kitchen.

The Murder of Major Pennington

"Before you go, Midge," said Katie quickly. "Would it be all right if Ruth, Jim, and I stay here a little longer? I would like to look at the layout of your garage. We'll make sure to lock up when we leave."

"Yes, certainly," said Midge. "The garage is that way," she added pointing across the way. She then turned and left the kitchen with Bradford following close behind.

"So what is it we're looking for?" asked Jim, stepping through the doorway and into the garage. An old Buick was parked inside with its hood open and an oily rag draped over its grate. A small wooden toolbox was sitting on the worktable and the shelf, which appeared broken in the photographs, was now up and in place. The worktable was clean and organized and the items on the shelf were arranged within reach, including the jar of screws and the windshield wiper fluid. The only thing missing was the bottle of rum.

"I'm not quite sure what we're looking for exactly," replied Katie. "I suppose I just want to get a feel for the place."

"Well, I must say that Midge keeps a cleaner shop than her husband did," observed Ruth, walking to the right side of the garage and looking at the neatly arranged shelves.

"Yes, indeed," agreed Katie. She pulled open one of drawers in the worktable. Inside were several wrenches lined up in order of size.

"I suppose this is where the major died?" asked Jim, standing next to the car.

"Yes," Katie replied, nodding. She looked over and noticed that a window was located directly across from where he was standing, affording in a clear view of his body to anyone peering in.

"Nice car," murmured Jim, running his hand along the side as he moved back towards Katie at the worktable. "I suppose Midge is working on it."

"Yes," replied Katie. "Midge is quite knowledgeable about cars."

"Hey look at this!" Jim exclaimed. He reached over and took a coffee mug from the far end of the shelf. "It looks like the same mug that was in the pictures. I wonder why Midge has kept it?"

"Because it can be hard to let go of things that once belonged to someone who has died," replied Ruth, looking across the room at them. "Especially if it was someone you loved."

"Yes, I suppose you're right," replied Jim softly. He did not look at Katie, who was standing next to him, and instead placed the mug back on the shelf. Suddenly it gave way, dumping the mug back into his hands and tossing the screw jar and wiper fluid container down on the workbench below.

"Yikes!" Katie exclaimed, jumping back as the items hit the bench. "It's a good thing these are closed tightly. They might have spilled otherwise."

"Just like in the photos," said Jim, reaching over to put his arm around her. "Are you all right?"

"Yes, I'm fine," replied Katie. "It just startled me for a moment." She looked over at the shelf. Just like in the photographs, the end closest to Jim was still attached to the wall but the end near Katie had collapsed and was resting on the top of the table.

"You barely touched it, Jim!" declared Ruth, coming over. "It looks like Midge just stuck this piece of wood underneath to brace it."

"You're right, Ruthie," Katie agreed, examining the shelf. She picked up the collapsed end and wedged the piece of wood back into place. "I guess this is just a temporary fix."

As they were carefully placing the spilled containers back onto the shelf, Katie turned and caught a glimpse of someone peering through the window.

"Hey!" she yelled, running over to it. "Wait!" She quickly opened the garage door and ran around to the side of the house. Jim was right behind her and he ran past and easily caught up with the young culprit.

"Stop!" Jim commanded, grabbing the young man by the collar. "We just want to talk to you for a minute."

Katie caught up with them and, catching her breath, asked the fellow his name.

"Thomas Willow," he replied. "I didn't do anything. I was just wondering if Midge was home. I wanted to return this," he added, holding up a wrench.

"Ah, you must be her neighbor," said Katie, giving Thomas a warm smile. "We didn't mean to frighten you. We're Midge's friends. Can I ask you a few questions?"

The man shrugged his shoulders as Ruth came over and joined them.

"It will only take a minute," Ruth assured him softly. "And it could help Midge. She's in quite a lot of trouble, you know."

"Yeah, she told me," said Thomas. "I want to help but I didn't see a thing. I wasn't even around when her husband got bumped off."

"Did you know Major Pennington well?" Katie asked casually.

"A little," replied Thomas. "I know Midge better."

"Yes, of course," Katie remarked. "And she says she knows you. In fact, she's quite fond of you."

"Oh yeah?" Thomas asked, his expression brightening. "Well I think she's swell. She helps me work on my car and even lets me borrow her tools."

"Did her husband also let you borrow tools?" Jim asked, bending over and picking up the young man's cap and handing it to him.

"Sometimes," replied Thomas. "When he remembered that he had them."

"What do you mean?" asked Katie.

"Nothing," Thomas quickly replied, shrugging his shoulders.

"How long have you lived next door to Midge?" asked Katie.

"Gosh, my whole life," replied Thomas. "That would be seventeen years, Miss."

"So you're seventeen now?" asked Jim.

"Yes, sir. That's right. Or I will be next month, that is," the young man replied.

"Did you drop this just now?" asked Ruth, holding up a long screwdriver.

"Yeah," replied Thomas, reaching out and taking the tool from her. "I was returning it to Midge along with the wrench."

"Is that why you were looking in the window?" Katie asked. "To see if Midge was home?"

"Yeah," nodded Thomas. "I do it all the time. Midge often works on the Buick with the garage door closed. I tap on the window and she lets me in. That way, I don't track grease through her house."

"I see," replied Katie. "And did you look through the window on the night Major Pennington was killed?"

"No!" declared Thomas Willow, stepping away from them. "I told you. I wasn't even around. I never saw him in the garage and I never saw the shelf fall!"

"That's fine," said Ruth gently. She glanced at Katie who nodded slightly. "That's all we wanted to ask you! We've got to go now but we'll let Midge know that you were looking for her."

"Thanks!" replied Thomas, somewhat relieved. "Tell her I have her tools and I'll give them back to her when she's home."

Jim slid his arm through Katie's and the three of them walked back into Midge's house. They made sure to lock the front door before getting into the car and heading to the courthouse.

"Too bad the kid couldn't tell us anything," sighed Jim.

"Oh, he told us quite a lot," murmured Katie. "Quite a lot indeed!"

CHAPTER 13
THE AUTOPSY REPORT

Bradford Sinclair handed Katie a note as she, Jim, and Ruth entered the courtroom just minutes before the beginning of the trial.

Keep the results of your experiment on ice until after we get the results of the autopsy, it read.

"I wonder why?" Ruth whispered, glancing at Bradford as he made his way back to the defense table and took his seat next to Midge.

"I don't think he wants to go out on a limb about Midge's alibi if the autopsy reveals that the major died of something like a heart attack. After all, we still can't prove that Midge didn't whack her husband over the head during the five minutes preceding Mrs. Elliott's visit, although I admit it wouldn't give her much time."

"That's right," added Jim, leaning toward them. "She'd have to kill him, make sure he was dead, perhaps by checking his pulse so as to get as little blood on her dress as possible, hear Mrs. Elliott knock on her door, rush out of the garage and through the house while putting on her apron and listening to the radio broadcast. I suppose it's possible but not probable."

"We should have tested that by letting me kill you again," chuckled Katie, looking up at him fondly. "But we ran out of time talking to Thomas Willow."

Jim just slid his arm around her shoulders and pulled her a little closer.

"Your Honor," began Mr. Martin, addressing Poppy after the judge had entered the courtroom and took his seat behind the bench.

"The prosecution rests for now, pending the outcome of the autopsy as formerly agreed upon."

"Very well," replied Poppy. "The defense will now present its case."

"Thank you, Your Honor," said Bradford, coming to his feet. "The defense calls Lt. Colonel Silvia Ellsworth."

Lt. Colonel Ellsworth entered the courtroom in full military attire and a determined expression on her face. She seemed to take command of the room just by walking through it on her way to the witness stand. After being sworn in and taking her seat, she glanced over at Midge and gave her a quick nod.

"Colonel Ellsworth," Bradford began. "You are currently stationed at Fort Ord in Monterey California, is that correct?"

"Yes sir," replied the colonel.

"In 1942, you were stationed with Major William Pennington, is that correct?"

"Yes, sir," replied Colonel Ellsworth.

"Was this at Fort Ord as well?" asked Bradford.

"No, sir. We served together at Mines Field in Los Angeles."

"Mines Field? Is that now the Los Angeles Airport?" asked Bradford.

"Yes, sir. That is correct," remarked the colonel. "The airfield had just been purchased three years prior by the City of Los Angeles and construction to expand the site was just beginning. The military still maintained a small outpost there but was in the process of shutting it down. Major Pennington was not scheduled to return to Mines Field after his leave."

"And you were reassigned as well, isn't that true Colonel?" Bradford asked.

"Yes, sir," replied Colonel Ellsworth. "I was transferred to Fort Ord at that time."

"Were you and Major Pennington close friends?"

"Close friends, sir?" responded the colonel. "We were friends, but I wouldn't say we were particularly close. It was a small post, sir, so we all knew each other fairly well."

"Interesting," murmured Bradford, tilting his head to one side. "Someone in your outfit has accused you and the major of having an affair."

"That is ridiculous," said Colonel Ellsworth firmly.

"Really?" replied Bradford. "People have affairs all the time. Why not you and Major Pennington?"

"Because I lived with my husband and two small children when I was stationed at Mines Field, sir," replied the colonel. "And, because I love my family, I went home to them every night."

"And Major Pennington?"

"He often spoke with fondness of his wife and we all assumed he loved her," replied Colonel Ellsworth. "Besides, he seemed more interested in rum than in women."

"You would have considered him a drinker then?" asked Bradford.

"Let's just say we all handled the pressures of our wartime enlistment in different ways."

"I see," replied Bradford, nodding his head. "Now on the night of November 3, 1942, you were called to a nearby hotel concerning a situation involving Major Pennington and several other officers. Please tell us what happened."

"I was on duty that evening and received a call from the hotel manager telling me that several of the officers in our unit were drunk and causing damage to the hotel's bar and restaurant. He asked that I send over some MP's and remove them," explained Colonel Ellsworth. "When I arrived with two trucks and a dozen MP's, I found a dozen of our officers drunk and disorderly as the hotel manager had described. They had practically destroyed the ground floor of the building."

"Was Major Pennington one of them?" Bradford asked.

"Yes," replied the colonel.

"Was a Lt. Johnson one of them?"

"Yes, sir," replied Colonel Ellsworth.

"What happened next?" asked Bradford.

"All the men were confined to quarters for three days, except for Major Pennington and Lt. Johnson who were charged and jailed."

"Why single out Pennington and Johnson?"

"Because this was not their first offense," explained the colonel. "In fact, the major had just received his silver oak leaves a month before and then got into a bar room fight a week later. The Army busted him and he lost the rank. Lt. Johnson was on his fourth offense and was immediately dishonorably discharged."

"And Major Pennington?"

"I believe his case was still pending when he was sent home on leave, sir," replied Colonel Ellsworth.

"Colonel, you will not be surprised to know that it was Lt. Johnson who reported to Mrs. Pennington's sister-in-law that you and Major Pennington were having the affair. Why do you think he would do such a thing?"

Colonel Ellsworth grinned for a moment. "I suppose it's because I was the one who pressed the charges and made sure the Lieutenant was booted out of the Army."

"I see," replied Bradford, smiling. "And did you do the same to Major Pennington?"

"No, sir," responded the colonel. "I believe that Major Pennington had a drinking problem, but I recommended that he get help. The military has great programs to help officers like Bill Pennington. But General Dennis thought differently. He said that the stakes were much higher in war time. He felt that the misconduct of a young Lieutenant was one thing, but a high-ranking officer should have known better. It was the General who was pushing for the dishonorable."

"Thank you, Lt. Colonel Ellsworth," said Bradford, giving her a nod. "I have no further questions. Your witness, Mr. Martin."

The prosecutor stood and studied the witness for a moment. Something about the silver oak leaves on her epaulets or all the ribbons on her chest must have convinced him that this was not a witness to be challenged because he suddenly seemed to change his mind.

"I have no questions for this witness, Your Honor," he told the court, sitting back down in his seat.

"Very well," replied Poppy. "You are free to step down, Colonel Ellsworth. And thank you for travelling all the way from California. I hope the journey wasn't too taxing?"

"No, sir, the flight to New York was fine and the train ride to Fairfield uneventful," replied the colonel, stepping from the witness stand. "I must say that the young man who picked me up at the station was very entertaining."

"Mr. Butler? Yes, he certainly is that," smiled Poppy, glancing briefly at Katie and Ruth in the spectator section.

"Your Honor," began Bradford, once again jumping to his feet. "The defense calls…"

Poppy suddenly put up his hand to stop Bradford as the bailiff reached up and handed him several documents. He glanced over them briefly and then made an announcement to everyone in the courtroom. "The report from the hospital pathologist has just arrived. The court will recess for ten minutes while both counselors meet with me in my chambers." He pounded the gravel and then stepped down from the bench, leaving by the side door with Mr. Martin and Bradford following close behind.

"I wonder what's in the report," Katie pondered out loud. "Poppy seemed very concerned about it."

"Yes, I agree," replied Ruth. "I'm not sure I like this at all, Katie."

"Perhaps Bradford has had some suspicions all along," Jim whispered.

"Perhaps," Katie nodded. "But his suspicions are wrong. Midge didn't do it. I just know it!"

"What do you think Bradford will do next?" asked Ruth, giving her friend a worried look.

"Well it all depends on what's in the autopsy report, of course," replied Katie. "But I have a bad feeling that he's going to try and plead that Midge was not in her right mind when she killed her husband."

"A plea of temporary insanity?" Jim asked, looking over at her.

"Yes, exactly," said Katie.

"Oh dear," muttered Ruth under her breath.

At that moment, Judge White returned to the bench as the two attorneys filed in behind him and returned to their respective tables.

"Ladies and gentlemen," Poppy began. "The court is taking the liberty of entering into evidence the autopsy report submitted by Fairfield Hospital pathologist, Dr. John Winston. The clerk will label the document as R-1. Dr. Winston completed an autopsy on William Odom Pennington's remains yesterday. Although the entire report is entered, I will only read the summary into the court record."

Poppy turned to the last page of the document in front of him. "The summary of the report is as follows. The remains of William Pennington displayed a deep cut on the forehead. This is the only impact wound present on the body. The police coroner's report indicated that the temperature of the deceased at the time of initial examination was 98.0 and that the victim was dead for no longer than one hour. The autopsy results bear out these findings. However, in addition to the cut on the head, food particles were found in the victim's esophagus. This prompted lab analysis of tissue from several organs which indicated a significant presence of the chemical methanol…"

"What does that mean?" Ruthie whispered to Katie.

"Oh no!" Katie exclaimed, shaking her head.

"Due to these findings," continued Poppy. "It is the opinion of this physician that Mr. Pennington did not die from the cut on the forehead and loss of blood, as previously determined by Dr. Henry Winfield, but of methanol poisoning. The report is signed, Dr. John Winston, Chief Medical Pathologist, Fairfield Hospital."

There was a loud gasp from the occupants in the courtroom and Midge placed her face in her hands.

"That's why Bradford wanted us to hold back on the results of our experiment," declared Katie. "He wanted to make sure that Midge didn't have time to murder her husband by a different means! We would have proven that she could have!"

"Yes. It only takes a second to poison someone," sighed Jim. "And you don't have to be present after you do it."

"Giving Midge more than enough time to drop the poison into his cup and send him out into the garage, leaving her to wait in the kitchen," added Katie, shaking her head. "The visit by Rosemary Elliott was just a bonus."

"You and Ruthie both mentioned that wives would most likely use poison to kill their husbands," Jim reminded them.

"Yes, we did say that," agreed Ruth reluctantly.

"Jim!" exclaimed Katie, looking up at him. "Surely you don't believe that Midge did such a thing?"

"No," he replied, shaking his head. "But it certainly doesn't look good for her."

"No, it certainly does not," Katie sadly agreed.

They saw Bradford lean over and say something to Midge who shook her head.

"Mr. Sinclair," said Poppy. "In view of this new development, does the defense wish to proceed with its case at this time or do you need a recess to confer with your client?"

"We'd like to proceed, Your Honor," replied Bradford, much to everyone's surprise. "The defense calls Mr. E. M. Butler."

The courtroom door opened and E.M. stepped inside and made his way to the witness stand. As usual, he was dressed suitably for the occasion in a dark pinstriped suit and gray bowtie. His hair had been freshly trimmed and his shoes shined so thoroughly that one could see the lights of the courtroom reflected in them. He carried a fedora in one hand and a pair of gray gloves in the other.

"Your Honor," said Bradford as E.M. took the stand. "If it pleases the court, I would like to state for the record that this witness is related to me. Mr. Butler is my first cousin, but that relationship has no bearing on this case. He is being called due to his friendship with my client and their experiences during the war."

"Does the prosecution have any objection?" replied Poppy, his eyebrows raised.

"No, indeed," smiled Mr. Martin. "The prosecution doesn't wish to have the fact that Mr. Sinclair has relatives inhibit the defense's case in any way."

"Thank you," replied Bradford, giving Mr. Martin a sly smile.

"Now Dap…er…Mr. Butler," began Bradford. "How long have you known the defendant?"

"Five years," E.M. replied.

"So you met during the war?"

"Yes, in London."

"You were both war correspondents, is that right?" asked Bradford.

"Yes, that is correct. I was with *Stars and Stripes*," replied E.M. "And Midge was with the *Associated Press* and the *Fairfield Gazette*.

"Both in the military?"

"No," said E.M. "I was but Midge was a civilian."

"I see," said Bradford. "And your military rank and branch of service?"

E.M. paused for a moment as if to ask what that had to do with anything. "Captain," he finally replied. "United States Army."

"Thank you," replied his cousin, smiling at him. "Now, would you consider Mrs. Pennington a close friend?"

"Yes," replied E.M.

"In fact, it was Mrs. Pennington who got you your job at the *Gazette*," Bradford remarked.

"Yes."

"It sounds like you owe Mrs. Pennington quite a lot," said Bradford.

"I owe Midge Pennington my life," E.M. answered softly.

"Really? How so?" Bradford pushed.

"Midge saved me, and the life of another correspondent, while we were under enemy attack and experiencing machine gun fire," explained E.M. and then he described in detail the same account of Midge's bravery that he had already related to Katie.

"Quite impressive," remarked Bradford, nodding his head. "Were any of you injured?"

"Yes, Miss Miller and I suffered concussions and Midge received a cut on her forehead and leg," replied E.M.

"Where you hospitalized?"

"Yes, Miss Miller and I were in the hospital for three days," said E.M. "But Midge was treated and released."

"Now, Dap…er…Mr. Butler," Bradford continued. "Do you know what Combat Stress Reaction is?"

"Oh no, here it comes," whispered Katie to Jim and Ruth. "I can't believe Bradford's going to do this!"

"It may be the only way he feels he can save her, Katie," Ruth whispered back. "But I hope it isn't."

"It's another name for Battle Fatigue," replied E.M. softly, looking sadly up at his cousin.

"In your role as a reporter for *Stars and Stripes*, you visited the front lines often, did you not?"

"Yes," replied E.M. "Often."

"Did you ever witness soldiers suffering from Combat Stress Reaction?"

"Yes."

"Is one of the symptoms of CSR mentally disengaging with one's surroundings," asked Bradford. "And exhibiting a blank stare?"

"Yes," E.M. answered.

"Did you ever see extreme cases where a soldier was hallucinating or having difficulty sleeping?" continued Bradford, looking intently at his cousin. E.M.'s hands began to shake and he placed them in his lap so that they were hidden from view behind the panel of the witness stand.

"Yes," nodded E.M.

"And are these soldiers removed from combat so that they don't present a danger to themselves or anyone around them."

"Yes, but the removal is only temp…" began E.M. before Bradford cut him off.

"And have you ever witnessed your close friend, Midge Pennington, exhibiting any of these symptoms?" pressed Bradford. "And remember Mr. Butler, you are under oath!"

Katie felt the almost overwhelming urge to leap to her feet and run up to the front of the courtroom so that she could throttle Bradford Sinclair within an inch of his miserable life for what he was doing to her friend. Ruth and Jim, seated on either side of her, must have sense her internal struggle because Katie suddenly felt them both gently clutch her by the elbows as if to hold her back.

E.M. sat silently and looked pleadingly up at Bradford. He could not fathom why his cousin was pursuing this line of questioning. It was as though he wanted Midge to be found guilty of murder. And it was clear that Bradford wasn't about to show his cousin any mercy either.

"Well, Mr. Butler?" asked Bradford gruffly. "Have you? Answer the question!"

"Yes," mumbled E.M. "But that was during the war…"

"You've never known Midge Pennington to have trouble sleeping?" Bradford continued. "You don't recall her ever disengaging from her surroundings, staring blankly?"

"No!" shouted E.M. jumping to his feet. "No!"

"Thank you, Mr. Butler," said Bradford suddenly. He turned his back to the witness and calmly walked towards the defense table. "I have no further questions." Midge glared at her attorney, but Bradford just gave her a shrug.

"Mr. Martin?" said Poppy, addressing the prosecutor but glancing down at the witness in hopes that E.M. might be spared. But the reprieve was not to come.

"Thank you, Your Honor," replied the prosecutor. "I just have a few questions for this witness."

He stood and walked over to E.M., who had shrunk back down in the witness chair, and gave him a reassuring smile. "My goodness, Mr. Butler," Mr. Martin teased. "With questioning like that, I hope your family doesn't get together often for holidays."

Chuckling could be heard from the spectators in the back of the courtroom.

"Now then," continued Mr. Martin. "I realize that you are not a doctor, Mr. Butler, but you are an experienced war veteran. In your opinion, does Mrs. Pennington currently suffer from CSR?"

"Objection, Your Honor!" exclaimed Bradford.

"Sustained," said Poppy.

"I'll rephrase the question," smiled Mr. Martin. "Mr. Butler, have you ever witnessed Mrs. Pennington exhibiting CSR symptoms since you both returned from the war?"

"No," replied E.M.

"Really? Not even a little from time to time," asked Mr. Martin.

"We all have trouble sleeping now and again," replied E.M. "But I swear to you, Midge Pennington was over her battle fatigue! She would never hurt a fly much less murder her husband!"

"You seem very sure of that, Mr. Butler," said Mr. Martin, leaning slightly into the witness stand.

"I am," replied E.M., casting a glance at Midge.

"Would you say your friend has a temper?"

"No," E.M. answered. "Well, no worse than anyone else."

"I see," replied the prosecutor. "Have you ever heard her yell?"

"Well yes, of course," answered E.M. "We all yell at times…"

"Has she ever threatened you, Mr. Butler?" interrupted Mr. Martin.

"Well, I wouldn't say that exactly," replied E.M. shrugging. "Sometimes Midge gets a little…"

"How about throwing things?" asked Mr. Martin.

"Never," replied E.M.

"Not even a tomato?" asked the prosecutor.

"Well, I…" E.M. began.

"Mr. Butler, I notice that your hands are shaking," remarked Mr. Martin, looking over the panel and into E.M.'s lap. "Are you all right?"

"Yes," E.M. replied. "Sometimes I shake when I'm stressed."

"Oh, too bad," responded Mr. Martin, shaking his head. "A result of the war?"

"Yes, you see I have…" E.M. began and suddenly stopped realizing that he had walked into a trap.

"Combat Stress Reaction?" Mr. Martin prodded.

E.M. stared at the prosecutor and said nothing.

"I'm sorry Mr. Butler," said Poppy from above. "But you must answer the question."

"A form of it, yes," replied E.M. softly.

"Perhaps that's why you are so quick to imagine you see it in others," responded Mr. Martin, turning towards his table.

"Objection!" yelled Bradford.

"I withdraw the comment, Your Honor," said Mr. Martin, taking his seat. "I have no further questions."

"Mr. Martin, Mr. Sinclair," said Poppy solemnly. "You have both thrown out some rather offensive comments for the sole purpose of letting the jury hear them and then withdrawing them so that you do not get reprimanded by the court. Let me remind you that this is hardly my first case. I have been a judge for a very long time. I am aware of this type of judicial trickery and I will not tolerate it in my courtroom. The next time either of you make an inflammatory comment like the one I just heard, you'll be held in contempt. Do I make myself clear?"

"Yes, Your Honor," both attorneys replied in unison.

"Good," replied Poppy. "Mr. Sinclair, I believe it's your turn."

"Before we let this witness go," said Bradford. "I'd like to ask him some questions on re-direct."

"Oh gee whiz!" muttered Katie softly. "Please let E.M. go! He looks like he's about to faint!"

"Mr. Butler," began his cousin. "You are the recipient of a rather significant medal for your actions during the war, is that correct?

"Yes," replied E.M.

"What is the name of the medal you were awarded?"

"The Bronze Star," replied E.M.

"And how does one earn a Bronze Star, Mr. Butler?"

"The Bronze Star is awarded to a member of the armed forces for meritorious service in a combat zone," said E.M. softly and as if reading from a cue card.

"And heroism in combat," added Bradford gently.

"Yes," replied his cousin.

"Mr. Butler," Bradford continued. "Your Bronze Star has a particular addition to it, does it not?"

"Yes," replied E.M. "Mine comes with the "V" Device."

"And what is a "V" Device?"

"It's a tiny metal letter "V" that adheres to the ribbon," E.M. answered.

Bradford Sinclair smiled warmly. "You are being very modest, Mr. Butler," he stated. "Let the record show that my cousin is authorized to wear the "V" Device on his Bronze Star medal because he committed an act of valor in combat when he single-handedly saved the lives of half a dozen wounded people trapped with him in the basement of a collapsed building that had just been hit by a bomb in the middle of the London blitz." And then Bradford turned to face Mr. Martin and added, "for which his entire family is extremely proud of him. So we tend to overlook the shaking hands."

And with that, E.M. Butler's first cousin calmly strolled back over to the defense table and sat down.

CHAPTER 14
KATIE FIGURES IT OUT

"Gosh Gran," declared Katie as she entered the library to have cocktails with her grandmother. "What a day!"

"Pour us both a glass of sherry and tell me all about it," Gran replied, smiling up at Katie. She closed the book she had been reading and placed it on the side table next to her.

"Well, now that I've been re-employed at the *Fairfield Gazette*," Katie began, picking up the decanter and pouring a generous amount of sherry in each glass. "Mr. Connor insisted that I finish writing the article on the Little Miss Daisy Beauty Pageant. Fortunately, it will be printed in the entertainment section this time and I could make it much shorter."

"I know you had some difficulty finding a suitable angle to the story," replied Gran. "What did you finally come up with?"

"Well, it was E.M. who gave me a new perspective on the whole thing," responded Katie, plopping down on the couch next to Nugget. She took a sip of her sherry and then set it on the coffee table in front of her. "He pointed out that valuable lessons can be learned through competition. Things like winning and losing gracefully, being respectful of others, and always doing your best. So I used those lessons as a backdrop as I focused my article around three amazing little girls. The kind and gentle Eleanor Sullivan, who won the pageant, Elizabeth Whitting who showed brilliant independence and I'm sure will be a force to be reckoned with, and Amelia Chishelm, who substituted a debilitating affliction with an amazing talent."

"With the help of Jim Fielding," interjected Gran.

"Well, yes, I did include that in the article," Katie admitted, smiling demurely. "For accuracy."

"Of course. Does he know?" Gran asked.

"No, I thought I'd wait and let him read it in tomorrow morning's edition," replied Katie, chuckling.

"How was the trial?" Gran asked, switching topics. "I understand Judge White recessed it at noon today to resume tomorrow at 9:00."

"Which was fortunate. It gave me time to write my pageant article," replied Katie. "But more importantly, it gave all of us a chance to catch our breaths. The testimony was quite stressful today, especially for E.M. There were several times that I thought he might pass out!"

"That sounds terrible!" exclaimed Gran.

"Indeed it was," Katie replied. "You see, Bradford is presenting the theory that Midge was temporarily out of her mind, due to her experiences during the war, and killed her husband. He used E.M. to strengthen that idea except E.M. didn't know that's what his cousin was up to. But even if he had, he wouldn't have gone along with it."

Gran shook her head and took a sip of her sherry.

"Bradford Sinclair treated his cousin brutally on the stand, which caused E.M.'s hand to shake. One would have thought that E.M. was testifying for the prosecution! Then things became very topsy-turvy because Mr. Martin tried to prove that Midge was in her right mind all along and that E.M. was the crazy one! In the end, Bradford paid homage to his cousin on re-direct."

"Sounds exhausting," Gran replied and then asked, "But surely you don't believe that Midge is guilty, do you?"

"No, I do not," replied Katie, shaking her head. "And that's the most frustrating thing about it. No one is trying to prove her innocence anymore, just whether it was premeditated. Every time I find something new, it only seems to strengthen the prosecution's case."

"Well, it happened a very long time ago, granddaughter," remarked Gran.

"There is one extremely interesting thing, though," said Katie, reaching for her sherry glass. "The autopsy results were submitted to the court today and Poppy read them into the record. The pathologist at the hospital found that Major Pennington didn't bleed to death. He actually died of methanol poisoning."

"Now that is interesting," replied Gran, her eyebrows raising. "So she could have poisoned him. Wives have been known to do that."

"Gran!" exclaimed Katie, but she was smiling. "Now you're sounding like Ruthie and Jim!" She took a sip of her sherry and then reached over to place her glass on the table, accidently tipping it over. "Oh, darn! Now look what I've done!" The spilled sherry started to creep across the table, surrounding a pen that had been left there and over to a flower vase.

"Here, use my handkerchief," said Gran, reaching into the pocket of her sweater.

"I've got it!" replied Katie, jumping to her feet and picking up the glass. She reached inside her skirt pocket and, bringing out her own handkerchief, began dabbing up the spilt liquid. She picked up the pen from the table and placed it in her pocket and then removed the flower vase and handed it to Gran. Turning back to the coffee table, Katie noticed that the sherry had spread around the two objects, now missing, leaving an outline with a void in the middle of each. She bent down and was about to wipe over them when she suddenly gasped.

"What wrong, Katie?" exclaimed Gran. "What's the matter?"

"Oh Gran!" she declared, turning excitedly to her grandmother. "I think I've just solved it! I think I know exactly how Major Pennington died!

* * *

"Are you absolutely sure about this, honey?" asked Bradford, looking doubtfully into the deep blue eyes of Katie Porter. "The prosecutor could destroy her."

Katie had called him early that morning to request that he meet her in the lobby of the courthouse where they now stood in the far corner next to the newspaper stand. She quickly filled him in on her theory and, although he wasn't entirely convinced, he was willing to try anything at this point. After all, things were currently looking pretty bleak for Midge Pennington.

"Yes, I'm sure," replied Katie. "I think Midge can handle it. Besides, it's about time she told everyone the truth. She'll have no other choice when she's under oath."

"OK. And how about the chemist?" asked the attorney.

"I spoke with her over the phone last night," replied Katie. "She verified my conclusions and has agreed to testify. She should be arriving any minute. And I'll round up our last witness when we break for lunch."

"Well, if you're right, then Midge should be on her way home by this evening," said Bradford. "But if you're wrong, she can blame you for sending her to jail."

"Since you have already managed to put her there and now all that's left is to lock the door," Katie countered as she turned to enter the courtroom. "I don't think she has much to lose, do you?"

Midge was already seated at the defense table at the front of the room when Katie entered and made her way over to Ruth and E.M. Jim would be arriving shortly so Katie placed her coat in the chair next to her to reserve it for him.

"Good morning," Katie greeted her two friends, leaning over and kissing each of them on the cheek. "How are you?"

"I'm fine but will be glad when all of this is over and Midge is safely back home," replied E.M. "I feel as though I let her down with my testimony yesterday."

"You could not have known what Bradford was up to. Or Mr. Martin, for that matter," Ruthie said, patting his hand.

"I agree," replied Katie, plopping down in her chair. "The whole thing was terrible! Frankly, I wanted to run up and strangle your cousin!"

"And she would have, too, had Ruthie and I not grabbed her," said a voice coming up behind them. "Hello darling!" added Jim Fielding, leaning over to give Katie a quick kiss before dropping down in the seat she had reserved next to her."

"Hello Jim," replied Katie. "Looks like you got here just in time. Here comes Poppy!"

"All rise!" shouted the bailiff. "The court is now in session, The Honorable Judge White presiding."

"You may be seated," said Poppy, settling down behind the bench. He glanced at a note on his desk and then asked," Mr. Sinclair, are you ready to proceed?"

"Yes, Your Honor," replied Bradford. "The defense calls Mrs. Margaret Pennington to the stand."

"What on earth?" exclaimed E.M. straightening in his chair. "That's not…"

"No, wait," said Katie. "I suspect Midge will actually help her case with her testimony."

"Mrs. Pennington," said Poppy, as Midge moved toward the witness stand. "You are aware that you do not have to testify at your own trial and that your decision not to testify cannot be held against you."

"I understand, Your Honor," Midge replied softly. She took the stand and was sworn in.

"Now Mrs. Pennington," Bradford began. "Please tell us in your own words what happened on the night of Sunday, November 8, 1942 at your residence at 1033 Second Street here in Fairfield."

"I had been in the process of cooking and listening to the Sunday news on the radio," Midge began.

"Would that be the CBS World News Today?" interrupted Bradford.

"Yes," nodded Midge. "You see, our troops had just invaded French North Africa and I felt rather guilty that I was not there covering the story. I also knew several of the officers who would have been involved with Operation Torch and, naturally, I was concerned about them."

"Of course," Bradford agreed.

"It was around 5:50 pm or so when my neighbor, Rosemary Elliott knocked on my door asking to borrow some milk. I let her in and while I was filling her pitcher, she remarked that she, herself, had just been listening to the broadcast so when the sponsor message was over, we stood and listened to the remainder of it together."

"Did you have a conversation about a smear of blood on your dress?"

"Yes," replied Midge. "I had cut my finger while slicing an onion and had gotten a small amount of blood on my dress. It concerned Rosemary quite a bit and she gave me several suggestions as to how to get out the stain."

"What time did Mrs. Elliott leave your home?" Bradford asked.

"Six o'clock," said Midge. "I'm certain of that because she left as the broadcast was ending. We said goodbye and I went back into the kitchen and took the roast out of the oven. I then went to the connecting door leading to the garage with the intention of peeking my head in to tell Bill that dinner was ready. When I didn't see him, I stepped in and walked around the old Packard that we had been working on. It was there that I found him. He was lying right next to the running board face down on the concrete floor of the garage and there was blood everywhere."

"You've originally stated that you only knelt down to assess your husband's condition by taking his pulse," said Bradford. "But that wasn't true was it, Mrs. Pennington?"

"No," replied Midge softly. "It wasn't. I'm afraid I rather panicked. I dropped down to a seated position and rolled Bill onto my lap. His face was covered in blood and I remember trying to wipe it away with the hem of my dress. He was alive and seemed to be gasping for air, although I can't be exactly sure about that."

"Did he say anything? Did he try and speak to you?" Bradford asked, leaning a little in Midge's direction.

"No. I think I called his name several times, but I really can't be sure about that either," said Midge, somewhat embarrassed. "I lost track of time somehow. I can't really explain it other than to say that one minute my husband was looking up at me with a sick expression on his face and the next minute he was dead. I remember feeling suddenly very cold and glancing over my shoulder to see if there was a draft coming from someplace. That's when I noticed that our shelf had broken again and a bottle of rum was spilling its contents all over the worktable and garage floor. I leaned closer to Bill's face and smelled the alcohol on his breath. He had been drinking again and must have fallen over and cut his head."

"Did you report this to the police?"

"No," replied Midge. "But I believe the coroner smelled it when he examined Bill's body because I remember him looking over at the police detective and giving him a wink and a nod in the direction of the coffee mug."

"Then what happened, Mrs. Pennington?" asked Bradford.

"It felt as though I was in a dream but I believe I made my way back into the house and called the Fairfield police," Midge described. "I have no idea how much time had passed by that time."

"You state that your husband had been drinking again. Why were you so hesitant to tell anyone?" Bradford prodded. "Was there a problem with him having a little drink before dinner?"

"Yes," replied Midge. "You see, Bill had become an alcoholic and he was getting into trouble with the Army. When he took part in destroying that hotel, that was the last straw. They sent him home on leave pending a decision as to whether to bust him down to the rank of Captain or boot him out completely with a dishonorable discharge. There were several officers back at the post in LA that were trying to help him, but he was supposed to stay off the bottle. I had found out that he had been sneaking drinks the entire time he was home and that's why we argued in the supermarket and I threw the tomato at him."

"So when you said, 'if you keep doing it, I swear I'll kill you', you were referring to his drinking," Bradford asked.

"Yes," Midge replied, nodding sadly. "But he was in too deep. He just couldn't quit without help. Besides, he was so afraid of the possibility of being sent over to combat in Europe that the drinking helped him cope." She looked over at E.M. in the spectator section. "I suppose my being so enthusiastic about being at the front lines didn't help matters, either. Bill Pennington had a future in banking. He was on his way up when the war broke out. I didn't want folks here in Fairfield to know he was drinking so much. It would have ruined his reputation and his career," she added wearily.

"So that's why you went along with Detective Cunningham's theory that your husband slipped, hit his head, and bled to death. You didn't want anyone knowing the truth about his drinking problem."

"Yes," Midge nodded. "I didn't think it mattered whether he slipped on grease or tripped because he was drunk. I still don't know why it matters," she added, looking down at her hands.

"So, when did you find out the Army's decision concerning Major Pennington?"

"The next morning," replied Midge. "The official letter came in the mail. Bill had lost his commission and had been dishonorably discharged."

"Which is why you couldn't give him a military funeral," Bradford stated, an expression of realization crossing his face. He turned briefly and looked at Katie who gave him a slight nod.

"Yes," said Midge. "I told everyone that Bill did not want any fuss, although I believe that it would have meant a lot to him. I also lost any right to survivor benefits, not that I really cared about that."

"Do you have any idea how methanol may have gotten into your husband's system?" asked Bradford.

"No."

"Could he have taken it himself?" Bradford asked. "Perhaps from a sense of shame for losing his commission?"

"Suicide?" replied Midge, shaking her head. "No. First off, my husband wasn't the type to feel that kind of remorse. He would have blamed his drinking problem on the Army. Secondly, he was pretty certain that he would just lose the rank but remain in the military. The letter about his discharge didn't arrive until after he had died."

Bradford studied his client for a few seconds before asking, "How long had you and Major Pennington been married?"

"Ten years," replied Midge.

"And would you say that you loved your husband?" asked Bradford.

"Yes," Midge replied. "Very much so."

"Thank you, Mrs. Pennington," said Bradford, moving back to the defense table. "I have no further questions."

"Mr. Martin," said Poppy. "Your witness."

"Mrs. Pennington," began the prosecutor. "Did Major Pennington show any signs of having been poisoned when he lay in your lap."

"No," replied Midge.

"Other than the rum bottle being tipped over on the worktable, was there any indication that your husband was drinking?"

"I smelled alcohol on his breath," replied Midge.

"Was there any in his cup?"

"I don't know," Midge replied. "His coffee mug was broken and lying on its side. There was nothing in it when the police picked it up."

"I see," nodded Mr. Martin. "Mrs. Pennington, are you aware that methanol has a sweet smell to it?"

"No, I am not aware of that," replied Midge, shaking her head.

"Interesting," remarked Mr. Martin. "I have no further questions, Your Honor."

"You may step down, Mrs. Pennington," instructed Poppy. "Mr. Sinclair, you may call your next witness."

"Well, that didn't go too badly," whispered E.M. "I thought she did quite well, don't you?"

"Yes," replied Katie, looking across Ruth to smile at E.M. "Quite well, indeed."

"Your Honor," said Bradford. "The defense re-calls Detective Harrell Cunningham."

The police detective had been sitting in the front row of the spectator section and he reluctantly stood up and walked to the witness stand.

"Detective Cunningham," smiled Bradford. "I don't think this will take long as I only have a few questions to ask you. Mostly for clarification, mind you."

"Yes, sir," replied the detective, although it was obvious that he didn't believe it.

Bradford walked over and placed the enlarged photograph of the wide angle shot of the garage that he had shown before.

"Now then," he said. "Would you please identify for the court, once again, the three objects seen in the picture near the body of Major Pennington."

"Well sir," said Detective Cunningham. "That's a hammer and screwdriver near the victim's right shoulder. And that's the coffee mug with the broken handle in the forefront."

"Thank you," replied Bradford. He now lifted a second enlarged photograph and placed it over the first. It was the one that showed the garage after the items and Major Pennington's body had been removed. "Would you please tell the court what items are missing in this photograph?"

"The major's body, of course, and the hammer, screwdriver, and coffee mug," replied the police detective, somewhat puzzled by this line of questioning.

"How do you know?" asked Bradford.

"Because they're not there," replied the detective.

This caused a slight murmur and a few chuckles among the spectators.

"Yes, of course not," smiled Bradford. "What I mean to ask is how would one know that? In other words, if I were a police officer just arriving on the scene, what indication would I have that a hammer, screwdriver, and coffee mug were missing?"

"Because you'd be able to determine that by the outline of the shape of the objects," replied Detective Cunningham. "See there. You can tell where the mug was lying by the outline void left behind in the blood."

"Yes, exactly," nodded Bradford. "These outlines are very distinct. In your expert opinion, how would such a distinct outline be made?"

"By the blood flowing around each object causing a void, which would be seen once they were removed," replied the detective. He started to smile as if he now realized what Bradford was getting at.

"So, the hammer, screwdriver, and coffee mug would have had to been on the floor already in order for the blood to surround them instead of being underneath."

"Yes sir," Detective Cunningham replied. "If the blood was already there, the items would have been dropped into it and no void space would have been created."

"Making it somewhat difficult for someone to hit the major over the head, watch him fall, wait for him to die, and still have time to drop the hammer right next to the victim's head before the blood could flow around it," remarked Bradford. "Not impossible but not probable, given the distinct void shown."

"Yes, indeed," replied Detective Cunningham. "Which was another reason why we never considered that Major Pennington had been hit by the hammer. With all that blood around, it was easy to assume that the cut on his forehead killed him."

"Thank you, sir," said Bradford. "No further questions."

Mr. Martin sat up in his chair and glared at the Fairfield Police Detective. "Why didn't you tell me this earlier, Harrell?" asked the prosecutor still seated behind the table.

"You never asked me," smiled Police Detective Cunningham. "Nor gave me the chance to tell you."

"Do you wish to ask him anything now, Counselor?" prompted Poppy, smiling slightly at the flustered prosecutor.

"No, Your Honor," replied Mr. Martin, after hesitating for a moment. "No questions."

"The defense now calls Dr. Patricia Whitting," announced Bradford Sinclair, and then grinned with admiration as Dr. Whitting entered the courtroom. She seemed even more attractive than when Katie had spoken to her at the auditorium. She had given careful attention to her wardrobe for her courtroom appearance and wore a professional looking suit with matching pumps and gloves. She chose not to wear a hat, highlighting her beautiful auburn hair which hung loose around her shoulders.

"Now Miss…," Bradford began, leaning in toward the witness.

"Doctor," Patricia Whitting corrected him.

"Er, yes, of course," replied Bradford. "My apologies. Dr. Whitting, you are here as an expert witness in the field of Chemistry. Where did you get your education?"

"I got my undergraduate degree from Cal State. I earned my Ph.D from Cornell."

"My, my! You must have been a child prodigy," remarked Bradford flirtatiously.

Dr. Whitting did not respond other than to remove her gloves and casually rest her left hand on the edge of the witness stand revealing her wedding band.

"Get on with it, Counselor," warned Poppy under his breath.

Heeding the warning, Bradford cleared his throat and asked, "Where are you currently employed as a chemist, Doctor?"

"Haldor Topsoe," replied Patricia Whitting. "I'm the chief chemist there."

"I see," remarked Bradford. "What type of work does Haldor Topsoe do?"

"We work with natural gas," she replied. "We find ways to turn it into useful household products through the extraction of compounds like ammonia, hydrogen, and methanol."

"You mention methanol, Dr. Whitting," said Bradford. "In what types of household products would we find methanol?" Once again, he turned slightly to cast a glance at Katie. She was leaning forward in rapt attention, her eyebrows raised.

"Methanol is used in quite a lot of products," the chemist replied. "Paints, varnishes, adhesives, and windshield washer fluid."

Katie grinned and let out the breath she hadn't known she'd been holding. "Katie?" Jim whispered. "You've figured this out, haven't you?"

"Yes," she nodded, giving him a quick wink. "And I'll need your help during lunch. Are you up for a little adventure?"

"With you, always," he chuckled, reaching over and taking her hand.

"Dr. Whitting," continued Bradford. "If someone were to ingest methanol, what would likely happen?"

"The individual would most likely drop dead," she replied evenly. "Methanol is highly dangerous. Toxicity and death can occur even after drinking a small amount."

"What would be the symptoms of methanol poisoning, Doctor?"

"Poor coordination and abdominal pain," Dr. Whitting explained. "Vomiting and, if they've ingested a large amount, loss of consciousness."

"Is it possible to accidently drink methanol?" asked Bradford. "Say, if it was accidently mixed with rum or bourbon?"

"Unfortunately yes. Methanol has a sweet smell and taste, making it tempting, especially to children and animals. It can also be mistaken for alcohol."

"I see," replied Bradford, taking one last long look at his witness. "I have no further questions for this witness, Your Honor."

"I have no questions for Dr. Whitting," added Mr. Martin, quickly standing.

"You may step down, Dr. Whitting," said Poppy. He glanced up at the clock. "Court is recessed until 2:00 pm."

* * *

"So where are we off to, Sherlock?" Jim asked, as he and Katie left their friends back at the courthouse and jumped in Katie's roadster.

"First to the deli to pick up three sandwiches," replied Katie. "And then on to Midge's house."

"Three sandwiches?" Jim asked. "But there are only two of us. Am I to assume we're going to have company?"

"Gosh, I hope so," Katie chuckled.

It only took them a matter of minutes to pick up the sandwiches and soon they were pulling up in front of Midge's house. Katie jumped out quickly but instead of walking towards the house, she turned and made her way over to the neighboring Willow home.

"Hello Thomas," she said, walking up to the young man bent over the engine of a car. "Remember me?"

"Yes, Miss," replied Thomas. "You're Midge's friends. Have you come from the trial? Is it over?"

"No, not yet," Katie said, looking intently at him. "There is still one more witness who needs to be heard."

"Oh yes?" remarked Thomas, wiping his hands on a rag. "Who?"

"You, Thomas," replied Katie solemnly. "Midge needs your help."

CHAPTER 15
THE FINAL WITNESS

"Please state your name and address for the court," Bradford asked the shy young man sitting in the witness stand.

"Thomas Willow," he replied. "1035 Second Street, Fairfield."

"Thank you," said Bradford. "You are the next-door neighbor to Mrs. Margaret Pennington?"

"Yes, sir," replied Thomas.

"How long have you lived next door to the Penningtons?"

"As long as I can remember, sir," said Thomas. "Since I was little."

"Did you know Major Pennington well?"

"No, not as much as I know Midge...er, Mrs. Pennington," replied Thomas. "Mr. Pennington worked a lot before the war and then was mostly gone after he enlisted."

"Did you see much of the major when he was home on leave that week in November of 1942?" asked Bradford.

"I saw him," replied Thomas. "But I only spoke to him maybe once or twice. He was kind of different when he was home on leave."

"Different?" asked Bradford. "What do you mean by different?"

"I saw him sitting on his back porch drinking rum when Midge wasn't home," Thomas replied. "Even though she was also home on leave, the paper had her working on something, so she would be out of the house sometimes. That's when the major would be drinking. He never did that before the war."

"Did you ever speak to him while he was drinking?" Bradford prodded the witness.

"Only once," replied Thomas. "Midge let me borrow tools sometimes when I was trying to fix Ma's car. I saw someone working inside Midge's garage, so I walked over to the window and tapped on it.

That's how I signaled Midge and the Major to open the garage door to let me in."

"You tapped on the window to let them know you where there?" repeated Bradford.

"Yes," said Thomas, nodding his head. "Midge didn't like people coming to the front door with dirty shoes and then tracking stuff through her house. All I usually needed were tools so we set it up that all I had to do was tap on the garage window and either she or Mr. Pennington would open up the garage door for me."

"I see," nodded Bradford, smiling at the young man. "Now, please tell us what happened on the evening of Sunday, November 8, around 6:00 pm. And remember, Thomas, you must tell the truth and nothing but the truth. You're under oath. Do you understand?"

"Yes, sir," replied Thomas solemnly. "I understand." He paused and took a deep breath. "I was working on Ma's car and couldn't remove one of the sparkplugs so I looked over at the Pennington's house and noticed the light was on inside their garage." He looked up at Bradford.

"Go on," nodded the defense counsel.

"Well, I knew that Midge has a wrench that would do the trick, so I walked over and tapped on the garage window. I heard the radio on and thought that maybe she was back inside the house and had forgotten to shut off the garage light so I held up my hands against the glass and peeked in. The major was there and he was pouring some rum from a bottle in a coffee mug." Here Thomas paused and looked down at his feet.

"Yes?" urged Bradford. "Go on, Thomas."

"Well, sir," continued Thomas. "He took a big swallow from his mug while he placed the bottle up on the shelf. He must have noticed that the cap was off it because he put the mug down and reached up to screw it back on the bottle when the shelf broke. It did that a lot if you weren't careful."

"The shelf had broken before?"

"Yes, sir," replied Thomas. "Midge was always saying that she was going to fix it but I don't think she's ever gotten around to it." He looked fondly over at Midge Pennington sitting at the defense table. She gave him a warm smile in return.

"And then what happened?" Bradford asked.

"Major Pennington grabbed a rag and started to wipe up the rum. He kept looking toward the door to the kitchen like he was afraid Midge would come in. He took a step away from the worktable to look underneath and that's when I saw that the jaw of screws had also fallen and the container of windshield washer fluid." Thomas choked for a moment and Katie could see tears begin to run down his cheeks. "I saw some of it spill into his coffee mug. I didn't know it was poison, honest I didn't! I remember saying to myself "that will fix him" because I thought it would taste bad and put him off drinking. I didn't know that would kill him. Honest!"

"No, of course not," replied Bradford soothingly. "You would have only been 12 years old at the time. You would not be expected to know about methanol. What happened then?"

"Major Pennington must have realized he needed another rag because he picked up the coffee mug and turned away from the worktable. He guzzled down everything that was left in it and started walking toward the Packard. I could tell because he held on to the mug but kind of had it dangling from his hand and it was empty. He took about three steps and suddenly stumbled against the car, holding his stomach. He dropped the mug and when it landed on the floor, the handle broke off. He looked like he was going to throw-up or was having a heart attack or something, because he bent over and leaned against the car."

"Did you happen to notice a hammer and screwdriver close by?" asked Bradford.

"Yes, they weren't on the car, though," Thomas replied. "They were on the floor near the front tire. He stepped over them, though. I don't think he even saw them."

"And then what happened, Thomas?" Bradford gently urged.

"I didn't know what to do," said Thomas. "I guess I got scared and just froze. All I know is that Major Pennington got about halfway down the side of the car and started to turn back. I thought that maybe he might call for Midge but he collapsed onto the floor and didn't move."

"Did he land face down on the floor?"

"Yes, sir," replied Thomas. "And then blood started pouring out from under his head. Lots of it. I was really scared but I couldn't just leave him lying there so I decided I'd better get Midge. But before I could move, the door to the kitchen opened and Midge stepped into the garage calling the Major's name."

"Did you speak to her to let her know what happened?"

"No, sir," Thomas replied, dropping his head down. "That's when my Ma called out to me and nearly scared me out of my wits! She had come up behind me without me knowing it and told me to get along home. I tried to tell her what had happened but she said "never mind" and that she would take care of it."

"And did she?" asked Bradford.

"I don't know," replied the young man. "I think so because as I headed back across our yard, I looked back and Ma was looking in the garage window at the Penningtons."

"Did your mother say anything when she returned home?"

"She said everything was taken care of and that the police were there," replied Thomas. "Later Midge told me that her husband had slipped and cut his head and bled to death. So I thought that maybe I should keep quiet about the windshield washer fluid since that's not what the police thought killed him. No use telling Midge that her husband had been drinking again."

"Did you ever tell your mother what you had witnessed?" Bradford asked.

"Yes, later on," he replied. "But I'm not sure she wanted to believe me. I didn't know anything about the letter she sent to Mrs. Percy or what Ma thought she saw when she was looking in the window. Ma always liked Mr. Pennington a lot and I think she was a little jealous of Midge."

"So why did you decide to come forward now with what you saw?"

"Because Miss Porter asked me to come and testify," replied Thomas, pointing to Katie in the spectator section. "She had figured out that I must have seen something and believed my story. She told me that Midge was in trouble and that it was my duty to come and tell the court what really happened."

"Well we are very pleased that you listened to Miss Porter," said Bradford, turning to look at Katie. "And came and did your duty." He then turned back and addressed Poppy. "Your Honor, I have no further questions for this witness."

"Mr. Martin?" asked Poppy, addressing the prosecutor.

"No, Your Honor," replied Mr. Martin softly. "I have no questions for this witness."

"You are excused, young man," said Poppy gently. "You may step down."

"Your Honor," declared Bradford Sinclair as Thomas Willow stepped down from the witness stand. "The defense rests!"

* * *

"Once the autopsy report came back, it confirmed my belief that we'd been barking up the wrong tree since the very beginning," explained Katie.

She was sitting with Jim, Ruth, E.M. and Gran who had just arrived with a thermos of coffee and a basket full of muffins freshly baked by Gertie. They had decided to wait for the verdict under a large oak tree a few yards from the courthouse and Gran thought that they could use some refreshments while they waited. So she had Andrews drive her over with the goodies.

"But what put you onto the idea the Pennington might have drank the methanol in the first place?" asked E.M.

"Well, I suppose it started with the photographs taken by the *Middleton Times*. They told the whole story, but we weren't seeing it," replied Katie thoughtfully. "For instance, the clear void pattern showing the hammer, screwdriver, and cup. That meant that the items had to be there before the blood started flowing, allowing the blood to travel around them. If Midge had hit him with the hammer, she would have held onto it for a moment, anticipating having to strike him again, and then would have dropped the weapon into the blood."

"Which is why you were so excited when you spilled your sherry on the coffee table," said Gran, handing Ruthie a muffin.

"Yes," replied Katie. "The sherry flowed around a pen on the table, leaving the void pattern when I picked it up. Then there was the messy worktable and broken shelf. It always seemed significant but, again, I couldn't figure out why. We were still hung up in the hammer and blood and missed the bench and possible poisoning all together. Then I remember my meeting with Dr. Whitting who spoke of her work with ammonia, hydrogen, and methanol and how these

The Murder of Major Pennington

are used in household solvents and cleaning products. She mentioned that much research was done to make sure these products were safe to use. The photographs showed the spilled wiper fluid. Windshield wiper fluid is a cleaning agent. I called Patricia Whitting and found that it is, indeed, made up of methanol.

"But how on earth did that make you deduce that Major Pennington drank it?" asked Jim, biting into a muffin. "And why assume it was an accident and not suicide?"

"Midge gave the first clue when she told us of her husband's drinking problem," Katie replied, reaching over and brushing a crumb from his cheek. "Remember, there were three items tipped over when the shelf broke. A can of screws, the wiper fluid, and…"

"A bottle of rum!" exclaimed E.M., nodding his head. "Yes, of course! But that explains the alcohol, Katie, but not how he ended up with methanol in his coffee mug. Surely, even drunk, he would have noticed the difference between the rum bottle and the container of wiper fluid."

"You are correct there, E.M." replied Katie. "And I thought about that myself. Midge said in her testimony that she believed it unlikely that her husband would take his own life, so I ruled that out. So the only thing that made sense was in the placement of the coffee mug. It must have been in a position to have accidently received the spilled wiper fluid."

"And Dr. Whitting testified that methanol, due to its sweet smell and taste, can be confused with alcohol," added Ruth. "Poor man!"

"Exactly," replied Katie. "Bill Pennington was so focused on cleaning up the rum before Midge caught him that he didn't notice that wiper fluid had spilled into his mug. But it was Thomas Willow who really saved Midge. He was the one who could confirm my theory."

"Yes, about that, Katie Porter," asked Jim, smiling fondly at her. "How did you figure out he witnessed the whole thing? When we first spoke to him, he insisted that he wasn't even around the day that the major died."

"Ah, but he was," smiled Katie. "He actually gave us several important clues. The first was when he said that Major Pennington wasn't the same when he was home on leave and couldn't remember if he had tools. That meant the man had possibly lost his mind or was under the influence of something. Then there was the fact that

Thomas often borrowed tools from the Penningtons, mostly from Midge. That was contrary to what Midge had told us earlier about her dislike of having other people use her things. Remember, the big fight at the supermarket was supposedly because her husband loaned them out. It's possible, of course, but it just didn't ring true."

"Certainly not enough to sling a tomato," remarked Gran dryly.

"But she told us that to hide his drinking problem," said Ruth.

"She didn't tell us until she was on the witness stand," Katie corrected. "We had spoken with Thomas before then. It was another contradiction in her story."

"Yes, that's right," nodded Ruth.

"The most important thing, though, is that Thomas must have been looking through the window on the night of November 8, 1942. How else would he have known about the broken shelf?" explained Katie. "There is no mention of it in any of the newspaper articles or the police report. The only reason we know about it is because we saw the pictures. No, he had to have seen it through the window on the night Major Pennington died!"

"But how did you know that he had actually witnessed the accident?" asked Jim.

"Well, I couldn't be totally sure, of course, but the timing indicates that he must have," Katie replied. "You see, Midge found her husband at 6:00 pm. He was still alive, although barely. Dr. Whitting testified that a significant amount of methanol kills quickly."

"The victim would drop dead, I believe was her exact phrase," Ruth added grimly.

"Exactly," Katie nodded. "Thomas was at the window when Midge appeared, just in time to be chased away by his mother who then peered into the window herself. That means that Bill Pennington had to have swallowed the methanol just before Midge's arrival. That puts Thomas at the window during that time. I figured he must have at least seen the Major fall and, given his practice of tapping on the window and waiting for a response before looking in, I hoped that he had witnessed the accident, as well."

"Hey!" they suddenly heard a voice yell. They looked up to see Bradford waving at them from the steps of the courthouse. "The jury is coming back. They've made a decision!"

"Good gracious, that was fast!" exclaimed Ruth, getting to her feet along with the others. "The jury's been out less than an hour!"

"I hope that's a good sign," murmured Katie, as Jim took Gran's arm and they joined the group walking quickly back to the courthouse. They arrived at their seats just as the jury was filing silently into the jury box. Poppy was already seated behind the bench and his expression was grim.

A hush fell upon those in the courtroom as Poppy turned to the jury and asked, "Foreman, has the jury made its decision?"

"Yes, Your Honor," replied the foreman, standing with a document in his hand.

"Please hand your decision to the bailiff," instructed Poppy and Officer Kennedy approached the man and retrieved the document. He then turned and handed it up to Poppy.

"Mrs. Pennington, please stand," Poppy said to Midge and Bradford behind the defense table. He quickly glanced over the document before handing it back to the bailiff who returned it to the foreman, still standing.

Gran, who was seated on the aisle, grasped Katie's hand. She, in turn, reached out her other hand and grasped Jim's. Jim, seated next to Ruthie, took hold of her hand as she held E.M.'s with the other. They all held their breaths.

"Mr. Foreman, was the jury's decision unanimous?" Poppy asked.

"Yes Your Honor," replied the jurist.

"Good. Please read the verdict to the court," said Poppy.

"We, the jury, find Mrs. Margaret Pennington not guilty of the charge of murder in the first degree," read the foreman.

"Thank god!" whispered E.M. as Ruth leaned over and hugged him.

Katie received a hug from both Gran and Jim. The relief in the courtroom was palpable as Midge turned and gave her friends a weary smile.

"Mrs. Pennington," continued Poppy. "You have been found not guilty. I hereby release you. You are free to go." He pounded his gavel and added, "this court is adjourned."

"All rise!" shouted the bailiff, as Poppy stepped down from the bench and left the courtroom.

"I think I've aged a hundred years!" exclaimed E.M. as he made his way up to the front of the courtroom to greet his friend.

"I think I've doubled that, E.M. Butler!" countered Midge, but she threw her arms around him and gave him a tight hug.

"See, Katie Porter," Bradford remarked as he collected his brief case and hat. "I told you I'd get her off. Bradford Sinclair never loses a case!"

"My apologies for ever doubting you," replied Katie, looking up at him demurely. Jim had seen that look before and he turned to look at Gran to hide the fact that he was smiling. He knew that Katie Porter was up to something. "We're all going back to Rosegate for a celebration. Won't you please join us?"

"I would but I've got to catch tonight's train to Chicago," Bradford replied, smiling down at her. "I don't wish to spend another day here in this pitiful berg."

"Well, how about you check out of your hotel and come for just a few drinks. E.M. and I will drive you to the station in time to catch the 9:00 train," suggested Katie sweetly. "It's the least we can do to thank you for all you've done for our friend Midge.

"OK, honey," he replied, glancing quickly over at Jim and seeing that his back was turned. "I don't mind if I do."

They were halfway to their cars when Midge stopped Katie and quietly asked, "Did the package arrive?"

"Yes, this morning," Katie replied, grinning. "And Gertie has wrapped it in some very nice paper and ribbon."

"Perfect," smiled Midge, and suddenly she leaned over and gave Katie a hug. "And thanks for saving my neck, Katie Porter," she whispered in Katie's ear. "I owe you one," and then she turned and walked quickly to join E.M. in his car.

The party at Rosegate included plenty of wine, food, music, dancing, and some funny tall tales from the war.

"And you should have seen the expression on the Colonel's face when E.M. pulled that little pig out of the hat box," Midge was saying as everyone in the room laughed.

"That wasn't the half of it, Midge Pennington," added E.M. pointing his wine glass at her. "I would have gotten away with it if you hadn't convinced him that if he rubbed the poor pig's belly it would sing the Marines' Hymn."

Katie chuckled and glanced around the room. It was wonderful to have everything, and everyone, back to normal.

Later that evening, as promised, E.M., Jim, Katie, and Midge drove Bradford Sinclair to the train station in time for him to catch the 9:00 to Chicago. They took Gran's sedan, it being the only vehicle large enough to fit the five of them.

"Remember to send me your bill," Katie said to Bradford, reaching out to shake his hand, leaving a safe distance between them.

"No need, Katie," replied Bradford. "The *Fairfield Gazette* has already paid for my services. Apparently, they really like Midge."

"Goodbye, terrible man," said Midge, smiling as she shook his hand. "I hope never to set eyes upon you again."

"Likewise, I'm sure," smiled Bradford.

"Goodbye Cousin," said E.M., handing Bradford his suitcase. "Please give Aunt Rosemary my love."

"Will do, Dapper," said Bradford, giving E.M. a punch to the shoulder. "See you in the funny papers!" He turned and walked to the train, stepping into the first compartment with the help of the conductor.

"Bradford!" E.M. called after him.

"Yes?" said the attorney, poking his head out of the compartment window.

"I almost forgot," E.M. shouted. "We got together and bought you a gift."

"What?" Bradford shouted back, putting a hand up to his ear.

"A gift. We bought you a gift," shouted E.M. "I put it in your suitcase!"

"Oh, OK!" grinned Bradford, giving them a wave as the train pulled away.

"What was that all about?" asked Jim, wrapping his arm around Katie as they stood on the platform.

"Midge, E.M. and I bought Bradford a little gift," she replied with mock innocence. "From Connecticut. in your honor, actually."

"In my honor?" replied Jim suspiciously. He looked around at them. "What have you all been up too?"

"We bought Bradford a trout from the Connecticut River and had it shipped to Rosegate in time for his departure," explained E.M. "It came from one of the fish markets near your hometown of East Haddam. We thought it very appropriate since the two of you seemed to get on so well."

"Let me get this straight," Jim responded. "You had a frozen trout sent from East Haddam to Rosegate as a gift for Bradford?"

"Who said anything about it being frozen?" chuckled Katie, waving goodbye to the departing train.

That night, just before going to bed, Katie took out her journal to write her daily entry. As always, she addressed it to her mother, a habit she had begun as a small child.

Dear Mother,

In the last few weeks, I learned several lessons I thought I already knew.

To start with, I learned that Midge Pennington loved her husband. This should not have been surprising except I realize that I had never fully appreciated the fact that she was even married. I was judging a book by its cover and that was wrong. Shame on me.

I learned about trauma and perseverance. I had experienced trauma when holding a bleeding Jim in my lap. Midge suffered the same with her husband, except it was far worse for her. She was already suffering from battle fatigue because of the war. Besides, she had been married to Bill Pennington for ten years while my relationship with Jim has just started. And even after her husband was killed, Midge went back to the front lines to continue her important work.

I learned the lesson of true friendship. When others, including myself, wavered in our loyalty to Midge, E.M.'s was steadfast. And I know he would be the same with me should I ever find myself in a similar predicament. He is a loyal and loving friend to the bitter end and I am fortunate to have him in my life.

And then there's Jim. He says that Ruddy will always be my first love, but as I reflect on this, I wonder. I was only 18 when I loved Ruddy. Jim has the love of an adult woman who is old enough to know her own heart. I think that maybe it's Jim who is truly my first love. The one that was always meant to be.

I think, though, the biggest lesson was one I already knew but needed to see again. And that is the strength and determination of women. So many showed these traits these last few weeks. Midge, Lillian Chishelm, Patricia Whitting and, most impressively, the young girls of the Little Miss Daisy Beauty Pageant. Each, in their own way, has made me proud to be a member of their tribe.

Katie

~ THE END ~

ABOUT THE AUTHOR

K.T. McGivens is best known as a poet and her poems have been published in newspapers, community publications, and anthologies. She has written six books of poetry and recently published an anthology of her best works.

She has now ventured into the world of mystery novels and has begun writing a series of short mystery books featuring her character Katie Porter. The novels are geared toward young adults and focus on strong female characters, problem solving, trusted friendships, and tenacity; a formula she learned from growing up reading the Nancy Drew Mysteries.

Ms. McGivens grew up in Maryland and earned both a Bachelor's Degree and a Master's Degree from the University of Maryland. She now lives in the panhandle of Florida.

Made in the USA
Columbia, SC
09 June 2020